CYANIDE WITH CHRISTIE

CYANIDE WITH CHRISTIE

Katherine Bolger Hyde

severn House

This first world edition published 2018
in Great Britain and 2019 in the USA by
SEVERN HOUSE PUBLISHERS LTD of
Eardley House, 4 Uxbridge Street, London W8 7SY.
Trade paperback edition first published
in Great Britain and the USA 2019 by
SEVERN HOUSE PUBLISHERS LTD.

British Library Cataloguing in Publication Data
A CIP catalogue record for this title is available from the British Library.

ISBN-13: 978-0-7278-8844-0 (cased)
ISBN-13: 978-1-84751-968-9 (trade paper)
ISBN-13: 978-1-4483-0178-2 (e-book)

Typeset by Palimpsest Book Production Ltd.,
Falkirk, Stirlingshire, Scotland.

ONE

Emily watched from the entrance hall of Windy Corner, holding a squirming Lizzie, as Katie draped the last gold-ribboned garland around the stair railing. More garlands hung from the arched doorways into the parlor, library, and dining room, while displays of Victorian Christmas cards adorned the walls. Through the parlor door Emily could glimpse the nine-foot noble fir that dominated the room, sparkling with red and gold baubles and white twinkle lights. Every room of the mansion was festooned, bedecked, and bedizened in the spirit of a true Victorian Christmas.

'There.' Katie twisted the last tie and stood back to admire the effect. 'The Windy Corner Writers' Retreat Center is ready for business.'

'Business' was only a manner of speaking; the retreat center had not been conceived as a money-making proposition, but as a way for Emily to share the wealth she'd inherited from her great-aunt, Beatrice. She would accept voluntary donations, proportionate to each guest's means, to cover the cost of food and maintenance, but she would never charge her guests for their stay here.

The retreat center had been the joint brainchild of Emily and Katie back in June, shortly after Emily had taken possession of Beatrice's large Victorian home and hired Katie as her housekeeper. They had worked through the fall to remodel the building and decorate it appropriately, with each of the six guest rooms themed around a different classic author, and Katie had been promoted to co-manager. Now, a week before Christmas, they were ready to receive their first guests. This experiment would help to determine how often Emily would want to open her home in this way in the future.

Emily caught Lizzie as she lunged for one of the baubles dangling above her head. 'Are you sure we have everything? Clean sheets on all the beds?'

'Check,' Katie said cheerfully, taking her daughter from Emily's arms.

'Clean towels laid out in each room?'

'Check.'

'Flowers and welcome basket in the Forster room?' The first guest – an adjunct lit prof from Reed College in Portland, the school from which Emily herself was on sabbatical – would arrive today, Monday; the other guests were not due till Friday. Emily's friend Marguerite from the Reed French department had lined up all the guests, though they did not all have a connection to Reed. Emily had assigned this first guest the Forster room – coincidentally the best room – since he was finishing up his PhD thesis on that author.

'Check. Relax, Mrs C, we've got it covered.'

Emily squeezed Katie's hand. 'I know. You always do. I'm nervous, that's all. It's almost like a blind date. I want to make a good first impression.'

'And we will. Trust me. Everything will go fine.'

Emily prayed that was true. In the few months since she'd inherited the place, Windy Corner had seen more than its share of disaster; surely a little triumph could be allowed.

The doorbell rang. 'Oh my goodness, he's here!' Emily's heart raced as she turned to the hall mirror to check her appearance. 'Do I look all right?'

'You look great, Mrs C. And it's really not a date, after all.'

Emily tucked a stray auburn curl into her loose, high bun, adjusted her hand-knitted shawl over the lace collar of her blouse, and smoothed her mid-calf-length flared tweed skirt. Her retro outfit did coordinate with the Victorian ambiance of the place, but it had been her usual style for years before she came here. 'All right. Here we go.'

She opened the door herself, although normally that was Katie's job. Emily was the official face of Windy Corner, and she wanted to be the first to greet her guests.

A slight young man – everyone under forty was young to Emily now – stood shivering on the porch, warming his hands under his armpits. A battered suitcase stood beside him. The cold had drained all color from his fair skin, and his reddish goatee stood out against it in stark relief.

He extracted his right hand from its heavy leather glove and held it out to her. 'I'm Oscar Lansing,' he said in a pleasant, if somewhat shivery, tenor voice.

Emily took his hand. 'Emily Cavanaugh. Welcome to Windy Corner. Come in before you freeze.' She stood back, and he grabbed his suitcase and darted in.

'You can leave your things here and come into the library. We've got a tremendous fire going in there.' Aunt Beatrice had installed central heating, but Emily kept the thermostat low because she enjoyed having fires in all the fireplaces.

'Thanks.' He pulled off his hand-knitted hat and hung it on a peg of the hall tree, then smoothed his ruffled, longish light brown hair in front of the mirror. Emily noted the hat's clumsily executed cable pattern and deduced Oscar had some woman in his life whose affection for him exceeded her knitting skill. Marguerite had told Emily when she recommended him that he wasn't married. Girlfriend? Sister? Mother? There was something endearing about the care with which Oscar removed the hat and hung it up. Whoever the knitter was, her affection was clearly returned.

He added a coordinating hand-knitted scarf to the rack, then sat on the bench to remove his galoshes. Yes, actual old-fashioned galoshes, covering brown leather wingtips that looked far from new but were polished to a sheen. 'I'll keep my coat on for now, if you don't mind.' He smiled apologetically.

Emily led Oscar to the library and took one of the wing chairs before the fire, waving him to the other one. 'Did you have a good trip?'

He sat on the edge of his chair, chafing his hands in the warmth from the flames. 'Not too bad. Except the heater in my car doesn't work very well.' He glanced toward the semicircular bay window that looked out on the ocean. 'I'm glad I got here when I did. I don't like the look of that sky.'

The sky was a leaden gray, the clouds merging with the frothing sea at the horizon and hanging ominously low over the lawn. 'Me neither. They say it might actually snow.' Winter storms were a near-weekly occurrence on the Oregon coast, but snow here at the beach was rare. However, the temperature had been dropping steadily all day and would surely be well below freezing tonight.

Kitty, the female half of Emily's matched pair of gray cats, rose from her nap on the hearthrug to sniff at Oscar's outstretched hands. 'Well, hello, there,' he said with a smile. He waited a moment for Kitty to get his scent, then moved his hand to scratch her head. 'Aren't you a beauty?'

She arched and purred under his hand, basking in the praise that was only her due. Her identical brother Levin came up to Oscar's left hand looking for a piece of the action. However, Bustopher Jones – the aging, portly tuxedo cat Emily had inherited from her aunt along with the house – merely raised his head, blinked once in dismissal, and went back to sleep.

Emily introduced the cats to Oscar. Bustopher Jones' name elicited an appreciative chuckle. At last, someone who got the reference to T.S. Eliot's *Old Possum's Book of Practical Cats*. 'I guess Bustopher doesn't like strangers,' he said.

'Only if they feed him. Actually, it's more that he's lazy. He must be at least eighteen years old. He doesn't do much these days except eat and sleep.'

Oscar sat back in his chair, and Kitty leapt into his lap. Levin sulked for a nanosecond, then took possession of Emily's lap.

Time to make some real conversation. 'So Marguerite tells me you're an adjunct lit prof.'

Oscar nodded.

'What classes are you teaching?'

'I have a Hum One Ten section, of course.' Humanities 110 was Reed College's unique class, required of all freshmen, which examined the classical period and the Renaissance from an interdisciplinary perspective. Emily remembered her own Hum 110 teaching time with fondness.

'Then I have the early twentieth-century novel, which of course is my specialty.'

'Oh, yes, Marguerite said you were doing your thesis on Forster. He's one of my favorites. What's your focus?'

'I'm looking at his view of the individual in society, across all the novels.'

Emily nodded. 'Lots to work with there.' That focus was one of the things she loved about Forster – that and his sly humor.

Oscar grimaced. 'Too much, I'm afraid. I'm having a really hard time narrowing it down.'

'Well, if talking it out would do any good, feel free. I know Forster pretty well. And not only from the movies.' Emily shot Oscar a grin, which he returned. The films of *A Room with a View*, *Where Angels Fear to Tread*, *A Passage to India*, and *Howards End* were excellent and quite faithful, but a film was never a substitute for a novel – only a way of bringing it to multisensory life.

Katie came in carrying a tea tray laden with little cakes, scones, and sandwiches. Oscar's face brightened at the sight like the sun coming through clouds. 'High tea! How marvelous! I have landed on my feet and no mistake.' His smile told Emily the obscure Narnia reference was deliberate. This guest was going to be fun to have around.

'How do you like your tea?' Emily asked as she poured the first cup.

'Milk and one sugar, thanks,' Oscar replied.

'I have some delicious local blackberry honey – much better for you than sugar.' Or so Beanie, proprietor of the local yarn shop, had assured Emily when she gave it to her. Beanie's health kicks turned over faster than her seasonally alternating stock of yarn. 'Would you like to try it?'

Oscar started visibly. 'Oh, no, thank you. I'm allergic to honey.'

'Oh, I'm sorry. I'll be sure to let Katie know.' Emily twizzled the amber liquid from the small jar with its rather garish homemade label and drizzled a little into her cup. She'd been accustomed to taking her tea with no sweetener, but she had to try the honey for Beanie's sake, and it had proved to be quite delicious.

As they sipped and nibbled, their talk ranged over other favorite authors, revealing they not only liked most of the same ones but liked them for the same reasons: Jane Austen for her strict morality, wicked wit, and incisive grasp of human nature; Charlotte Brontë for her indomitable faith and her pioneering treatment of an independent female mind; L.M. Montgomery for her incomparable descriptions of natural beauty and her inveterate cheerfulness; Dickens for his outrageous characters and the arrow-perfect language in which he brought them to life; and Dostoevsky for his wrestling with the deepest spiritual questions of life, death, and afterlife.

'I'm hoping to write about Dostoevsky myself someday,' Emily confessed, surprised at herself for revealing this closely guarded secret to a virtual stranger. But she felt intuitively she could trust this man – he seemed almost like a male reflection of herself.

'I admire you for that. He's so complex, writing about him sounds quite daunting. Have you made a start?'

'Not yet. I thought I might have time this year, being on sabbatical, but so far I've been so focused on getting the retreat center ready, I haven't had a minute to think about it.' Well, that and helping to solve several murders that had taken place right here on her property. But there was no need to mention that to a guest.

'Marguerite told me you inherited this place recently. Did it need a lot of work?'

'Not *need*, per se. My aunt had kept it in excellent condition. But I did some alterations to make it work better as a retreat center – an expanded bathroom on the guest floor and a private suite of rooms for me on the third floor. And all the bedrooms have been redecorated.'

Oscar set down his empty cup and brushed a few crumbs from his trousers. 'Would you be willing to give me a tour? What I've seen of the house so far is beautiful. I'd love to see the rest.'

'Certainly.' In fact, she inwardly reveled in this opportunity to show off the fruits of her own and Katie's months of planning and labor.

She took him first to the Dickens room, at the back of the main floor, then peeked into the kitchen, where Katie was busy with dinner preparations. They visited the dining room and the parlor, then mounted the U-shaped staircase with its intricately carved balusters and paneled walls to the second floor. Oscar seemed amused, but hardly surprised, to find the five bedrooms named after the very authors they had just been discussing.

Emily preened a bit as she showed him the bathroom

arrangements. She'd taken out the back stairs in order to add a bathroom next to the existing one, but instead of simply creating two separate, complete rooms, she'd planned five small cubicles – two with a toilet and sink each, two with shower stalls, and one with a clawfoot tub. That way, even with all the bedrooms occupied, the wait for any of the facilities should be minimal. Each cubicle had a hand-lettered sign indicating its purpose, with a slider below to show whether or not it was occupied.

Oscar was properly appreciative. 'And I'm so glad you have a bathtub,' he said. 'I think a good soak is the only thing that will completely thaw me out.'

She smiled and turned to the last remaining door. 'And here's where I've put you, in the Forster room.' She opened the door to the spacious, airy room that lay directly above the library and shared its semicircular ocean-view bay.

Oscar caught his breath. 'Oh, but this is marvelous!' He circled the room, stroking the delicate maple furniture and examining the pictures on the walls. One showed an old English manor house that might have been Howards End; others were landscapes of northern Italy.

He stopped in front of one print that depicted a view of the Arno in Florence. Shooting a quizzical look toward Emily, who attempted vainly to keep a neutral face, he lifted the frame from its hook and turned it over. On the paper that covered the back was scribbled a huge question mark.

Oscar burst out laughing. 'I knew it! Emily Cavanaugh, you are a woman after my own heart.'

The feeling was definitely mutual.

TWO

E mily had invited Luke to dinner that evening to fill any gaps in conversation that might arise, since she so often found herself ill qualified to recommend herself to strangers. By dinnertime, though, she felt as if she'd known Oscar for years. Luke's presence as a facilitator was superfluous.

But Luke himself could never be superfluous. They had met as teenagers on one of Emily's annual summer visits to Windy Corner, and she had thought their intense romance would prove to be lasting as well. But circumstances had separated them, and she had not seen Luke again until she returned to Stony Beach as a widow last summer to claim her inheritance. It was thirty-five years since she'd fallen in love with him, and Emily still felt a little thrill every time he caught her eye. Now that her life seemed to be settling down a bit, she'd begun to think she might have to accept his oft-repeated marriage proposal sometime soon. Though they still had a few wrinkles to iron out, such as where they would live.

Luke arrived right on time but still wearing his sheriff's uniform. 'Sorry, got a last-minute call out and didn't have time to change. Figured with a guest you'd rather have me on time in uniform than late in civvies.'

She kissed him lightly. 'You guessed right. Dinner smells heavenly, and I'm starved. And poor Oscar is still thawing out – he needs to get a good meal in him and get under a nice thick down comforter as soon as he can.'

'Oscar?' Luke raised an eyebrow at her. 'First-name basis already, huh?'

'Of course. He's a dear. Come and meet him.' She led the way into the library.

Oscar rose to greet them. He came up to about Luke's shoulder, and Luke could have spanned his upper arm with one hand. Oscar swallowed and gave a nervous smile. Surely he didn't have anything to fear from the law? No, he couldn't.

It was understandable he'd find Luke a trifle intimidating, uniform or no.

'Oscar Lansing, I'd like you to meet Luke Richards. Luke is our local lawman, as you can see, and also my . . .' Here Emily paused, at a loss as to how to describe their relationship. It was obvious to all their local acquaintances, so a formal designation was rarely necessary.

'Boyfriend' sounded ridiculously juvenile for a couple in their fifties; 'gentleman friend' suggested a professional arrangement. 'Lover' would have been accurate in the Victorian sense – one who loves – but not in the modern one; 'partner' didn't convey the right impression either. 'Significant other' was just silly. She might have to accept Luke's proposal simply so she could introduce him as her fiancé. Oh well, the insipid 'very dear friend' would have to do for now, accompanied by a possessive hand on Luke's arm.

Luke stuck out his right hand with a genial smile, and Oscar relaxed and shook it. 'Pleased to meet you. What should I call you? Sheriff?'

'The title's Lieutenant, but Luke will do when I'm off-duty. Which I most certainly am, uniform notwithstanding.' Luke turned his nose toward the kitchen and inhaled deeply. 'Can't wait to see what Katie's cooked up for us this time.'

The gong in the hall – a recent acquisition – sounded its long deep note, and Emily led the way into the dining room. Katie, looking her part in a fresh white blouse and black skirt, whisked the covers off the dishes to reveal a roast duck in some sort of red sauce, surrounded by tiny roasted red potatoes, grated and sautéed Brussels sprouts, and a salad of spinach, beets, and walnuts.

'Good heavens, Katie!' Emily exclaimed. 'You do realize it isn't Christmas yet?'

Katie laughed. 'I've been wanting to do roast duck, but it won't work for the crowd we'll have for Christmas. Don't you worry, Mrs C, I'll do you proud for Christmas dinner. I thought the first guest at the retreat center was worth a little fuss.'

'Right you are.' To Emily – for whom planning food was even more daunting than cooking it – it was a relief to know she could count on Katie always to produce an appropriate meal for any occasion. And she knew Katie was thrilled to have an almost unlimited budget with which to expand her culinary repertoire.

Oscar gazed at his plate with all the wonder of a man who'd been living off college cafeteria food for months. 'This is incredible. It's like something out of Edith Wharton. Remember the canvasbacks?'

Luke looked up with a bite of duck halfway to his mouth. 'Who's that, some chef on TV?'

Emily looked at him, momentarily speechless. She glanced across the table and saw Oscar dumbfounded as well. She took a sip of wine and recovered herself. After all, Luke hadn't been a lit major – had never even made it to college, in fact – and Wharton was comparatively obscure.

'Edith Wharton was an American novelist,' she said, keeping her tone neutral. 'She wrote about upper-class New York society in the late nineteenth century. Canvasback duck was all the rage at that time, apparently.'

'Oh.' Luke gave an unconvincing chuckle. 'Well, would've been a compliment to Katie either way, right?'

'Of course.' Emily gave Katie the smile that meant she could go back to the kitchen now.

She tried a change of subject. 'What was the call that kept you late?' she asked Luke.

'Fender bender. This town goes to extremes, crime-wise,' he explained to Oscar. 'Most of the time my job consists of citing traffic offenders and rescuing cats for little old ladies. Bit of shoplifting, maybe, in tourist season. But then once in a while we get a murder. Hardly ever anything in between.'

'Murder!' Oscar's fork clattered to his plate. 'In a peaceful little town like this?'

Luke opened his mouth to reply, but Emily quelled him with a look. If murder in Stony Beach made her guest that nervous, she certainly didn't want him to know that all the recent murders had happened right here at Windy Corner. 'Just a fluke, I'm sure,' she said cheerfully. 'No reason to think anything like that might happen again.'

'Well, that's a relief.' Oscar composed himself and took a bite of duck. His eyes closed in sheer ecstasy. 'This is going to be the best Christmas break of my entire career. Gorgeous house, great food, congenial company – what more could a poor adjunct professor ask?'

He beamed at Emily and she beamed back. But as she turned her eyes back to her plate, she caught a look on Luke's face that was halfway to a glower. Good heavens, he couldn't be jealous, could he? Oscar might share her love of literature, but one had only to look at him and Luke side by side to know which was the better man. At least the manlier man, and that was the quality in Luke that made her pulse speed up. She'd have to butter him up later, when they were alone.

Meanwhile, she searched for a topic of mutual interest to center the conversation on, but it was like taking a snail for a run. She and Luke usually talked about happenings in the town, mutual acquaintances, and so forth, but none of that had any meaning for Oscar. Oscar knew her Reed colleagues, could fill her in on what had been happening there, but that topic made Luke's eyes glaze over. Discussions of literature and the Portland cultural scene were even worse. What had she been thinking, inviting Luke here tonight? She and Oscar would have been much better off on their own.

They got through dinner somehow, and after a brief interlude for coffee in the library, Oscar excused himself. He said, quite convincingly, that he was exhausted and longed only for a hot bath and a soft bed. But Emily thought perhaps a measure of tact was also involved in his retreat. He seemed like a man who would be sensitive to others' feelings – who would understand that Luke and Emily needed a little time alone.

Emily stood to give Oscar a goodnight handshake, then moved to the loveseat and snuggled up next to Luke. He put his arm around her with a lift of the eyebrows. 'To what do I owe this pleasure?' he asked, planting a kiss on her forehead.

'Do I need an excuse to cuddle with you?' She turned her face up to his for a real kiss.

'No, but lately seems like I've had to work a little harder for my cuddles.'

'I guess I've been distracted with all the preparations. Nervous about how the retreat center would go. Now that things are off to a good start, I can relax.'

'No complaints on my end.'

They didn't speak for several minutes, their mouths being otherwise occupied. Then Emily felt something soft and furry brush her cheek – something that had nothing to do with clean-shaven Luke.

'Levin, you insidious cat, have you no decency?' She pushed his head down, but he bobbed right back up, inserting his face between them as he touched his nose to Emily's in a kitty kiss.

'I think he's jealous,' Luke said. 'He wants you all to himself.'

'Tough kibbles, Levin. This is Luke's time.' She shoved the heavy tom off her lap, stood, and took Luke's hand. 'Let's go upstairs. You haven't seen my sitting room since I got it all gussied up.' He had helped her move in some of the furniture, but she and her antique-dealer friend Veronica Lacey had spent several pleasant afternoons since then adding all the finishing touches. The result was as perfect as Emily had imagined it would be.

They climbed the two flights of stairs to the third floor, Emily puffing a bit by the time they reached the top. She had contemplated installing an elevator, but so far the thought of its incongruity in this elegant old house had deterred her. If she could have had one of the old-fashioned kind with the metal folding gate across the front, it wouldn't have been so bad, but modern building codes would never allow that. She'd cope with the stairs until either her knees or her wind gave out. The exercise was good for her anyway.

She stopped inside the doorway to the sitting room, moving aside so Luke could get the full view. Emily had found an old loveseat in the attic, which she'd had her friend Devon repair and reupholster in a bright gold-and-green chintz with splashes of brick red. This sat in front of the window and set the color scheme for the room. The low-armed wing chair with ottoman in a subdued yellow stripe was perfect for knitting in; her knitting basket stood beside it. Opposite she'd placed a brand-new, cushy club chair covered in deep brick velveteen.

'That's your chair,' she said to Luke. 'Try it.'

He raised his eyebrows and lowered himself into the chair.

Then he sighed in sheer bliss. 'This has got to be the most comfortable chair I have ever sat in.'

'I thought you'd like it.' She followed his eyes around the room, trying to see it as he would. The built-in bookcase that stretched the length of the north wall was filled with some of her own books brought from Portland. They were a hodgepodge of new and old, hardcover and paperback, making for a friendlier appearance than the nearly uniform leather bindings in the library downstairs. She had chosen the pictures, lamps, rugs, and a few knick-knacks because she loved each one, not because she thought they would harmonize. But somehow, miraculously, they all fit together like grown siblings come back to the family home. The result was a room that seemed alive with her own presence.

Luke nodded. 'Yep. You've done a real nice job here.' He turned to her with that look in his eye. 'Almost as pretty as you.'

She sat on the loveseat and patted the space beside her. 'This loveseat is quite comfortable too.'

He took the hint, and they passed a very pleasant quarter-hour. But when things threatened to get too interesting, Emily pulled back. 'We've both got busy days tomorrow.'

Luke sighed. 'Yeah, I guess.' He detached himself and stood. 'Not sure how I feel about leaving you alone with a strange man in the house, though. You gonna be OK?'

'You can't seriously think Oscar's any sort of threat – do you?'

Luke pouched his lips and furrowed his brow. 'Probably not to your virtue, I'll grant you that. Fact, I wouldn't be surprised if he were – well, more Devon's type, y'know?'

Emily considered, remembering Oscar's speech and mannerisms. 'I don't really think so. An ivory-tower type, I'd say.'

Luke's frown deepened. 'You're not reassuring me here.'

She gave a little laugh. 'Don't be ridiculous, Luke. It's perfectly clear to me there's not a scrap of harm in the man. And he did come recommended by Marguerite, remember. She'd know if he were a closet psychopath – she's quite a good judge of character.'

'Well, all right. But will you at least lock your door?'

She stood on tiptoe to kiss his nose. 'For you, yes, I will lock my door.'

She walked him downstairs and waited as he got bundled up. 'See you tomorrow?' he asked. 'Or do you have to entertain your guest all day?'

'Heavens, no. He's come here to write, not to socialize. I should probably show up for meals, though.'

'Does that mean our lunches at the Crab Pot are a thing of the past?'

'No, not permanently. When there are more people here I should be able to come and go as I like. I just don't want to leave Oscar to eat alone. You could come here for lunch.'

He snorted. 'Yeah, and make a fool of myself again like I did tonight? No thanks. You two will get along fine without me.'

He spoke lightly, but Emily could see the tightness around his eyes. 'I'll drop by the office and drag you off for coffee then. Deal?'

'Deal.' His face relaxed into a genuine smile.

Somehow, in all her plans for the writers' retreat center, Emily had never fully considered how Luke would fit into this new phase of her life. It seemed she would need to get proficient at juggling.

THREE

The next morning dawned with skies more leaden than those of the day before, but still withholding whatever form of precipitation they were waiting to unleash. Emily was glad for that, as she had to drive to the south end of town to open one of her rental cottages for a new tenant. Normally her property manager would handle such things, but the entire firm had closed down for the holidays; business was usually nonexistent at this time of year.

Emily arrived fifteen minutes early, just in case, but the tenant was not yet there. She went in and turned on the heat – the cottage seemed even colder than outdoors, having stood empty for months. A quick tour revealed everything was in order. The property managers knew their job.

The knock came on the front door as she descended the stairs. She opened the door to a short, overthin woman who at first glance looked to be in her mid-forties. But when Emily looked more closely, she could see gray roots in the dead-black hair and fine lines beneath the liberally applied makeup. She noted the sagging jawline and stringy neck and revised her estimate up about fifteen years. The woman was further aged by the look she was wearing – skin-tight jeans tucked into knee-high stiletto-heeled boots, topped by a fake-fur jacket.

Emily put on a smile and extended her hand. 'I'm Emily Cavanaugh. And you must be . . .' She consulted the card the manager had given her, but the other woman spoke first.

'Wanda Wilkins.' She touched Emily's fingertips with her own still gloved, her pale blue eyes boring into Emily's like icicles. 'So you came yourself, did you? I figured you'd have minions to do things like that.'

Emily was taken aback. She'd never met this woman – why the attitude? Perhaps she was simply making a poor attempt at a joke.

Going on that assumption, Emily gave a little laugh. 'Usually the property managers would handle it, but they're all on Christmas break right now. It's a rare treat for me to actually get to meet one of my tenants.'

Ms Wilkins set down the cosmetics case she was carrying and directed a pointed look toward the luggage remaining in the open trunk of her battered sports car. Emily could see two good-sized suitcases, a carry-on briefcase/overnight bag, and a garment bag – a lot of luggage for a brief vacation. 'Let me help you take these things to the bedroom.'

Her tenant gave a curt nod and picked up the cosmetics case, but made no move to retrieve a second bag. Emily took the briefcase and the garment bag and headed up the stairs. If Ms Wilkins expected her to make a second trip for those heavy suitcases, she would be disappointed. Emily wasn't about to become a bellboy in middle age.

She pointed out the fully stocked bathroom and linen closet, then led the way downstairs, where she showed her tenant how to work the thermostat and the controls for the generator. Power loss was a not infrequent occurrence in Stony Beach's winter storms.

'There are plenty of logs for the fire, and the kitchen should have all the basics, including a few staples like coffee and spices. I'd suggest you lay in whatever groceries you'll need right away, though – the weather looks like getting pretty bad, and the roads may be blocked soon.'

Wanda ran her still-gloved finger along the top of a door frame and studied it with a frown. Emily knew the house was clean – could Wanda be disappointed to find it so? 'I stopped in Tillamook on the way down. I didn't expect a Podunk town like this to have a decent grocery store.' She spoke with such scorn that Emily wondered why she had even deigned to grace such a backwater with her sophisticated presence. Stony Beach was hardly a prime winter vacation spot. Wanda would meet no aging billionaires here.

Emily contented herself with asking, 'How long do you plan to stay, Ms Wilkins?'

'Through the holidays. My mother's in a nursing home in Seaside.' She named the same facility where Luke's grandmother lived. As if talking were an effort Emily was forcing her to make against her will, she added, 'She's fading fast. But I have to be back at work after New Year's.'

'I'd think you'd want to stay right in Seaside then, to be closer to her.' And to a decent grocery store.

'I would, but Seaside's too expensive on a teacher's salary. Stony Beach is quieter and cheaper.'

That was certainly true, and Emily made sure her rates stayed on the low side of competitive; she felt vacations by the sea should not be the privilege only of the wealthy. But the hilly drive to Seaside was likely to get treacherous if the weather turned to a full freeze. And this woman, a teacher? Emily felt sorry for her students.

'In that case, I'll need the deposit of one week's rent up front, and the rest when you leave.'

'I expected as much.' Her tone implied only the greediest money-grubbing tycoon of a landlord would ask such a thing, although it was standard practice. She produced a check, already filled out, from her handbag, then opened the front door and stood aside for Emily to pass.

'Here's your hat, where's your hurry?' Emily mumbled to herself as she got in her car. She drove the few blocks to Luke's office, feeling quite ready for that coffee they'd arranged – and for a good dose of Luke's warm and straight-forward company.

Luke busied himself with paperwork in the office during the morning, waiting for Emily to come by. Kinda silly for him, a grown man in an established relationship, to get so antsy when she didn't show up by ten o'clock. They hadn't even set a time, for Pete's sake. But Emily did that to him. Her refusal to give a straight answer to his repeated marriage proposals kept him guessing, though her behavior to him in every other way said she cared as much for him as he did for her. If only she'd make up her mind.

And now that new guy, Lansing, looked like he might be trying to muscle in. Well, not *muscle* in, exactly; muscle was obviously not his strong point. Worm his way in, more like. And the pen was supposed to be mightier than the sword, so

Luke couldn't count on his own brawn carrying the day over Oscar Lansing's brains and education. Not for the first time since reconnecting with Emily, Luke wished he'd made time for college after he got back from his stint in the army. He'd never be as intellectual as she was – though he was confident of being smart enough in his own down-to-earth way – but at least with more education he'd have known the difference between a famous novelist and a TV chef. His cheeks burned remembering that blunder.

At eleven minutes past ten he heard her PT Cruiser pull up outside. He had his hat and coat on and was out the door before she could get halfway up the walk. Then it occurred to him, maybe he shouldn't seem so eager – under the circumstances, playing a little hard to get might not be a bad strategy. But he doubted he could pull it off, and it was late for that, anyway. She had to know by now how crazy he was about her.

She stopped for a kiss before turning back to the car. He'd given up on being discreet in front of his subordinates; the whole town knew how matters stood between him and Emily. Probably thought they knew more than there really was to know. But that didn't bother Luke one bit.

'Friendly Fluke?' Emily said, unnecessarily. Only one coffee shop and one regular restaurant in Stony Beach stayed open through the winter. He went around and got in the passenger door – Emily never let anyone else drive her Cruiser – and noted the car's nose was pointing north, toward Windy Corner.

'Where'd you come from?' he asked.

'I had to meet a new tenant down on Cedar. That's why I'm a little late – had to show her around and all that.'

Luke felt a tiny surge of relief at the pronoun 'her'. 'So what's she like?'

'To be perfectly frank, she seems like sixty-year-old mutton dressed as lamb, as the Brits say. But I'm trying to withhold judgment until I know her better. *If* I get to know her better – the prospect isn't that tempting. She's hostile and condescending at the same time, and I have no idea why.' Emily frowned as if blaming herself for the woman's bad behavior.

'Well, it obviously isn't your fault. You've never met the woman before, and anyway, nobody could have a reason to be hostile to you. You're too sweet.'

Emily rewarded him with a smile but still looked troubled. Luke diverted the conversation slightly. 'Wonder why she wants to stay in Stony Beach in the winter. 'Specially with the weather we're having.'

'She said she wanted to be near her mother. She's in Seaside Rest, like your granny.'

'Oh yeah? Come to think of it, I haven't been to see Granny in a donkey's age. I need to get up there, take her something for Christmas. Want to come with me?'

'Sure. I love visiting your granny.' Luke knew, though Emily wouldn't admit it, what she really loved was hearing all the embarrassing stories Granny told her about Luke's childhood. But what the hey, at least she was interested.

At the Fluke, Luke ordered a plain coffee while Emily asked for a triple mocha with whipped cream. He'd never understand what people saw in these fancy coffee drinks, but Emily did look cute with an accidental dot of whipped cream on her nose. He waited a minute, looked around to make sure no one was watching, then leaned across the table and licked it off.

'Whipped cream,' he said in response to her baffled look.

She giggled. 'I'm always doing that. My brother Geoff used to call me Spot because I could never drink hot chocolate without getting whipped cream on my nose.'

She teared up all of a sudden.

'What's wrong?'

She shook her head. 'Just had a flash of missing Geoff. He's been dead for five years, and to be honest we weren't all that close for some time before. But I have no family at all now. It's kind of a lonely feeling.'

Luke knew lonely – the lonely of coming home to an empty house night after night – but he'd never been without family, never been without the knowledge that if push came to shove, somebody would have his back. His parents were gone, but he still had his granny, his sister with her whole brood, his brother with a few more kids, and a passel of uncles, aunts, and who-knows-how-many degrees of cousins, none further away than Tillamook. He'd brought Emily to his aunt's to meet them all at Thanksgiving. They'd taken her to their collective heart, but he knew that wasn't the same as having family of her own.

He reached across the table and squeezed her hand. Then the words tumbled out before he could stop them. 'You could marry me. Then at least I'd be family.'

She gave him a sad smile, obviously not taking that as one of his serious proposals. 'Thanks, but it wouldn't be the same. Blood family comes with a shared history, a whole set of attitudes and presumptions and inside jokes. You and I could build some of that together, but it wouldn't come ready-made. And we'd never have anyone to pass it down to.'

He drew his hand back. She'd gone to a place where he had no comfort to offer – to her or to himself. He had a grown son from a previous marriage, but he and Emily had lost the only chance they ever had for a child together – after they separated as teens, she'd miscarried the baby he hadn't even known she'd conceived. That was a loss he could never make up to her. They both looked on Katie as a sort of adopted daughter, but it wasn't the same, and they all three knew it.

He couldn't take much more of this – not on such a gray, gloomy day. Time to change the subject. 'So tell me about the other guests you're expecting. When do they all get here?'

She blinked and shook her head briefly as if shaking off unwelcome thoughts. 'Most of them are coming Friday night. Let's see – there's Ian MacDonald. He's the star turn.'

'Yeah, even I've heard of him.' MacDonald had been a well-known writer of highbrow mysteries for years – Luke had tried to wade through one of his books but found it too depressing. 'Haven't seen anything from him lately, though.'

'No. I understand his career's in a bit of a slump. He's coming to Windy Corner to recharge.' She squinted at the ceiling. 'Oh, and there's a young memoirist, Dustin Weaver, sort of the golden boy right now. And a cozy writer, Olivia Mountjoy.'

Luke scratched the back of his neck. 'Hold on a sec. I've heard of cozy rooms, cozy fires, but how can a writer be cozy?'

Emily laughed. 'That's mystery jargon. She writes what are called cozy mysteries – the kind with an amateur sleuth, where the blood and gore are neatly tidied away out of sight. You know, like Agatha Christie. Or *Murder, She Wrote*.'

'I get it. So have you read her stuff?'

'I read one after Marguerite proposed her. It was pretty good, definitely above average. Oh, Marguerite's coming too. And she's bringing a student of hers who's trying to write a novel.'

'Is Marguerite responsible for your whole guest list?'

'Pretty much. She doesn't know them all personally, but she has a lot of connections. She put the word out, and this crop is what turned up.'

Luke frowned. 'So essentially, you're going to have a houseful of complete strangers you know nothing about, except they happen to be writers.'

'Well . . .' She bit her lip, then shrugged. 'I guess so. But honestly, writers tend to be pretty decent people. At least the ones I've met. And Marguerite will be there – she's rather brilliant at smoothing over any social awkwardness.'

'I wasn't thinking of awkwardness.' He was thinking of his beloved Emily being murdered in her bed, but he wouldn't say that out loud.

She reached over and took his hand. 'I know you weren't. But you can come Friday night and meet them all and vet them for yourself. You can even do background checks if you want.'

He was already planning to do background checks. He'd filed all those names in his mental notebook. But that wasn't good enough. 'I'd feel better if you'd let me stay over.' He looked at her sideways to see if she'd take his meaning.

'Full house, I'm afraid.' As he expected, she was being deliberately obtuse. He swallowed a sigh. 'If anything really bad happens, I guess you could sleep on the sitting room couch.'

'What, that little loveseat? My knees'd hang over the armrest.'

'It folds out into a bed. I tested it – it's actually fairly comfortable.'

'Hmph.' It could be the best mattress in the world and he wouldn't be comfortable – not ten feet from Emily's bedroom door. He was beginning to wonder if that door would ever open for him, with or without a wedding ring.

FOUR

E mily did some shopping in town before heading back to Windy Corner and got there just in time for lunch. Oscar didn't appear for several minutes after Katie rang the gong. When he finally came into the dining room, he looked a little bewildered.

'I was exploring the house – I hope you don't mind – and believe it or not, I actually got a little lost. I'm starting to feel like I'm staying in Downton Abbey or something.'

Emily laughed. 'Hardly. I've heard that place has a hundred bedrooms. But I'm surprised an adjunct prof working on a PhD has time to watch TV.'

'That show is my guilty pleasure. But I wasn't sure you'd be familiar – I haven't seen a television here. Unless you have it hidden behind the paneling.'

'No. I go to Luke's house when I want to watch TV. My aunt didn't have one, and when I moved in it seemed like a television would violate the spirit of the house. I do keep up with *Downton Abbey*, though. Who's your favorite character?'

'The Dowager Countess, hands down. No one can compete with Maggie Smith.'

Emily reached across the table for a high-five. 'I knew your head was screwed on straight.'

They spent a pleasant lunch trading *Downton* trivia, then ranging into other favorite shows – most of which, for both of them, were British mysteries or productions based on classic literature. Their tastes were so nearly identical that Emily began to wonder if Oscar could be real. If she'd created a congenial companion out of her own imagination, he would have been exactly like Oscar.

And the more she looked at him, the more she had the feeling he reminded her of someone, though she could never put her finger on who it was. Yet more evidence she had made him up. Oh well, if she was going crazy, it was a pleasant way to go.

They eventually got around to the Forster films, of course, and when they'd exhausted that topic, Emily asked him how his writing was going.

Oscar flushed. 'To be perfectly honest, I haven't done much of anything yet. I got all my things arranged on that lovely desk upstairs, but then Katie came up to tell me there were coffee and pastries in here, and of course I had to sample them, and then I had to look over the books in your wonderful library, and then I accidentally discovered your hidden staircase . . .'

He paused, no doubt noticing the suddenly frozen expression on Emily's face. She hadn't visited that staircase in almost two months – not since it had been polluted by bloodshed.

'I'm sorry, is that staircase out of bounds? I didn't mean to snoop, I just happened to try to pull out *Arabian Nights* and the door opened.' The volume of *Arabian Nights* was fake; it disguised the lever that made a section of bookcase swing out to reveal the hidden passage.

Emily shook herself. 'No, it's all right. I don't use it myself because of . . . bad associations. I would prefer you keep it closed from now on.'

'No problem.' Oscar's flood of words dried up after that, and they finished their meal in silence.

He laid his napkin on the table and pushed back his chair. 'I came here to write. Guess I'd better get to work.'

Emily gave him her best smile by way of apology. 'Tea at four in the library.'

'I'll look forward to it.'

After lunch, Emily returned to a task she'd begun before the big push to get the house ready for Christmas and guests: going through some boxes of papers she'd found in the attic when rearranging the storage up there. She didn't expect to find anything of real interest, as the top layers had consisted of outdated business documents, but the slight possibility of encountering some meaningful family history kept her digging. In the absence of living relatives, family history was the only thing she felt could ground her and give context to her life.

The boxes now stood stacked in a corner of her sitting room, where she could peruse them in comfort. She made it all the way through the first box without finding anything of interest. But the second box looked more promising. It contained a stack of photo albums, cracked and yellowing with age.

Her heart racing, Emily lifted out the first album and gingerly eased it open. This must be the oldest of the set: men and women in nineteen-twenties garb romped on the beach or posed in groups at garden parties and balls. The photos were neatly captioned, but none of the names meant anything to Emily until she came to a studio shot of a youngish couple, dressed as if for church, holding a baby whose tiny face was nearly lost in a sea of ruffles and lace that stretched halfway to her mother's feet. A boy who looked about twelve stood by his mother's side. The caption read, *Beatrice Jane Worthing on the day of her christening. June 30, 1929. With her parents, Edward and Maude Worthing, and her brother Eugene.*

Emily smiled at the picture, slightly teary-eyed. To think that boy, looking so serious and protective of his baby sister, was her grandfather, who had died before Emily was born. And that sweet, helpless baby girl had grown up into the ultra-competent, no-nonsense Aunt Beatrice of Emily's childhood. Aunt Beatrice, the anchor that had kept Emily and Geoff from drifting far out to sea when their mother died and their father's rootlessness and alcoholism escalated beyond endurance. Aunt Beatrice, whose common sense and business acumen had built her already substantial inheritance from her husband, Horace Runcible, into the fortune that made Emily's life so comfortable today.

A comfortable life – and no family to share it with. Aunt Beatrice was gone, Geoff was gone, Philip – Emily's husband of almost thirty years – was gone. The tiny life that had once fluttered in her womb, the life that would have carried the best of herself and Luke into posterity – that was long, long gone. Emily had always imagined that baby as a sweet red-haired girl, like Lizzie. Her premature passing had carried with it all chance of any successor.

Emily shut the photo album and had a good cry. Then she

dried her tears and went down to tea, leaving the rest of the papers for another day.

Luke wangled himself a dinner invitation to Windy Corner again mid-week. He didn't trust that Lansing fellow alone with Emily for five whole days.

But once the conversation got going, he was torn between feeling sorry he'd come and thinking it was a damn good thing he had. Oscar and Emily talked like they'd known each other for years, trading references and inside jokes that mostly passed straight over his head. Emily laughed more than he'd known her laugh since they were kids. When had he lost the ability to amuse her like that?

And she sparkled as well. Exactly like a woman basking in the flattering attention of an attractive man. That sparkle was supposed to be for Luke himself – had been, not so very long ago.

He narrowed his eyes at Lansing over dessert. Was he flirting with Emily – deliberately calling out that sparkle? Emily was an attractive woman, but she had to be a good ten to fifteen years older than this fellow. Could he really be interested in her?

Not impossible; there were men who preferred older women, and this guy looked like he might not be super successful with women his own age. And then, of course, Emily had other attractions besides her looks and charm. She was a wealthy woman. A poor adjunct professor – old enough that he was unlikely ever to be more than that – could easily be tempted by Emily's bank account.

When they moved to the library for coffee, Lansing excused himself and made for the restroom. Luke took the opportunity to drop a word in Emily's ear.

'Listen, Em,' he said, closing the door and pitching his voice low. 'I think you need to be careful with this guy. I know you like him, and he seems OK, but you might want to think about what his intentions could be.'

Emily made a disbelieving face. 'Intentions? What on earth do you mean? He's not exactly courting me.'

'Are you sure about that? I'm not.'

She turned toward the coffee tray, hiding her face from him. 'Honestly, Luke, I'm practically old enough to be his mother.'

'That would be a stretch, and anyway it doesn't make any difference. He could be after your money.'

'Oh, so I'm too old and ugly for him to like me for myself? Is that what you're saying?' Her voice was light, playful, but with a little quiver that told Luke he was on dangerous ground.

'You yourself just said—'

'It's one thing for me to say it. I certainly don't want to hear it from *you*.'

He'd dug himself in this time. 'Emily, you ought to know by now that in my eyes you are the most beautiful woman on earth and you always will be. Of course it's possible Lansing is attracted to you for yourself alone. But it'd be a rare fellow who could look at you and see *only* you, and not your money. 'Specially somebody as poor as Lansing appears to be.'

She kept her eyes on his shoes. 'I think I'm capable of judging a man's intentions for myself. And I don't see anything inappropriate in Oscar's behavior toward me. We have a lot in common, and we're becoming friends – that's all.'

He tipped her chin up so she'd have to look him in the eye. He saw defiance there, and behind it something sad and vulnerable. Not what he wanted to see.

'Just be careful, OK? For my sake if not for your own. Will you do that for me?'

She hesitated, then nodded. Behind him he heard the door open. He dropped his hands and stepped back. Emily quickly rearranged her face and handed him a cup of coffee.

Not quickly enough, apparently. 'Did I interrupt something?' Oscar asked. 'I'm sorry, I should have knocked.'

'No, don't be silly, Oscar. If we wanted privacy we'd go upstairs. Come in and have some coffee.' Emily gave Oscar her brightest smile.

Luke was pretty sure going upstairs was not going to be on the agenda for tonight.

As the week passed, Emily and Oscar's friendship deepened day by day. The unpleasantness with Luke was allowed to fade into the background by unspoken mutual consent. Emily found herself being even friendlier to Oscar as if to make up to him for Luke's accusation of fortune-hunting, although Oscar knew nothing about it.

Oscar reported good progress on his book. Emily finished her personal Christmas preparations – which consisted of wrapping the gifts she'd purchased in Portland earlier in the month – and then found herself with time on her hands. Katie was so efficient, there was nothing for Emily to do in the house. The recreational reading and knitting that usually occupied her seemed frivolous now, aware as she acutely was of a genuine scholar doing genuine work right above her head.

After all, Emily herself had been a scholar until quite recently. She'd felt ready to give it up until Oscar appeared, bringing with him the rarefied air of Academe that had been her native environment for so long. Breathing that air again was like emerging from clinging cloud cover onto an Alpine peak – bracing, invigorating. All other concerns looked as trivial from here, as safe and unadventurous, as would the toylike village nestling in the valley below.

Emily got out all the books and papers relating to her long-planned book on Dostoevsky. She wanted to write about his conflicted relationship with his Orthodox faith as it played out in his fiction. She spread the materials out on the library table and read through the notes she'd made over the course of years. That bracing air turned gradually stale and stifling. Her notes were a labyrinth, as Dostoevsky himself was a labyrinth of conflicting ideas, reckless passions, and a spirit that desperately longed to soar above it all and kiss the face of God.

And the cats, who normally had a reliable sense of what was lap time (book in hand) and what was not (knitting or food in hand), were confused by this new activity that was neither. Levin prowled over the table, disturbing the slight semblance of order Emily had achieved with her papers and turning the pages of her open books. Kitty jumped into her lap and pushed her nose into Emily's face, refusing to settle down.

Whatever magic for scholars and writers Marguerite had perceived in this library on her previous visit was clearly not working for Emily.

On Thursday afternoon, she reached her breaking point. Just as she had grasped a fleeting wisp of an idea that might make sense of it all, Levin jumped off a stack of papers, scattering them to the floor and startling Kitty so that she launched herself from Emily's lap by digging in all her claws. The elusive idea dissipated instantly. Emily almost thought she could hear its taunting laughter as it retreated, never to return.

But no, that was the doorbell. She glanced at her watch – ten minutes to four. Katie would be busy preparing tea, and further work was hopeless now. Emily hastily gathered the spilled papers and answered the door herself.

Wanda Wilkins stood on the porch, dressed in the same fake-fur coat and jeans she'd worn on Tuesday. But she'd changed her black boots for a brown pair with even more treacherous heels.

'Oh, hello,' Emily said, unable to keep the surprise from her voice. 'Do come in.' Whatever Wanda's business might be, the day was too cold to stand with the door open. 'Is there a problem with the cottage?'

Wanda stepped inside. 'No problem. You gave me two keys by mistake. I came to return the spare.' She held out a key attached to a plastic tag.

Emily glanced at the key. 'That wasn't a mistake. Those cottages usually have at least two people staying, so I always give two keys. It wasn't necessary to return it.' Wanda stood stubbornly holding out the key, so Emily took it. 'But thank you for taking the trouble.'

Wanda gazed around the foyer with obvious interest. She put out her hand and stroked the wooden paneling. 'Nice place you've got here.'

'Thank you. How did you find me, by the way?' Emily had left a phone number with her but not an address.

'Asked at the Crab Pot. Everybody in town knows where you live.'

Wanda was clearly not ready to leave – odd, since she hadn't seemed particularly friendly when they first met. Emily swallowed her confusion and remembered her manners. 'Would you like to join us for tea? I expect Katie will have it ready shortly.'

'Katie?'

'My housekeeper. Well, really the co-manager of the retreat center now. We're opening up Windy Corner as a writers' retreat.'

'Oh, right, I think I heard something about that. Sure, thanks. I've never had tea made by a *housekeeper* before.' Her voice held a sneer that belied the surface courtesy of her words.

Emily led the way into the library, where the fire presented a cheery glow. Leaving Wanda to warm her hands, she poked her head into the kitchen to warn Katie they had an extra person for tea.

'No problem,' Katie said. 'We've got plenty.'

Emily returned to the library to see Wanda examining the ornaments on the mantelpiece as if appraising them for auction. She had replaced the genuine bronze Tang Dynasty horse and picked up the silver cow creamer when she saw Emily and hastily set the creamer down. 'Really nice place you've got here,' she repeated. 'Nice things.'

'It's only modern Dutch,' Emily said, as a test. The creamer was actually an eighteenth-century English one that Bertie Wooster's Uncle Tom would have drooled over.

But Wanda gave her a look that proved, unsurprisingly, she didn't get the joke. 'Still worth a packet, I bet.'

Emily suppressed a sigh and moved to her favorite chair, gesturing her guest to the chair opposite. 'Katie will be right in with the tea.'

Wanda sat back in the wing chair and, to Emily's dismay, put her wet-booted feet up on the ottoman. 'This is the life. I could get used to this.'

'I've been very fortunate, and I'm grateful. That's why I decided to share this house as a writers' retreat.'

'Guess I'll have to write a book then.'

Emily heard Oscar's voice in the hall and Katie's in reply. 'Come on in, Oscar,' Emily called. Perhaps he could turn this odd exchange into a conversation.

Emily's chair half-faced the door, while Wanda's was turned away from it. Oscar held the door open for Katie with her tray and followed her in, smiling. He bent to help himself to a scone, then jumped at the sight of Wanda's feet on the ottoman, dropping the scone back on to the plate. Sweeping up the stray crumbs into his hand, he said to Emily, 'I'm so sorry. I didn't realize you had company.'

'No problem. Oscar Lansing, I'd like you to meet Wanda Wilkins. She's renting one of my cottages for the holidays.'

Wanda extended her hand to Oscar without getting up. 'Pleased to meet you.'

'Likewise.' Oscar shook her hand, then sat on one of the hearth cushions facing the two wing chairs. His hands still shook slightly. He must have a nervous disposition.

Emily poured tea for Wanda, who declined her offer of local honey in favor of three cubes of sugar. Oscar took his with milk and one sugar, as usual. Emily drizzled a bit of honey into her own tea and sipped it slowly, grateful for the excuse not to talk for a minute.

Wanda seemed completely at ease. She appraised Beatrice's fine bone china with narrowed eyes and pursed lips, but Katie's delectable pastries she barely sampled. 'Got to watch the carbs if I want to fit into these jeans,' she said by way of apology. Emily bit her tongue to avoid commenting that 'fit' was hardly the word.

Oscar said little, finished his tea quickly, and excused himself. 'Better get back to my writing. Nice to have met you, Ms Wilkins.'

Wanda flashed him a smile that seemed warmer than such a brief acquaintance would justify. Surely she wasn't coming on to him? She had to be a full generation older despite her attempts to dress like a twenty-year-old. And Oscar was a nice-enough-looking young man, but hardly what Emily would have considered cougar bait.

She stood to see Oscar out of the room, and to her relief Wanda stood as well. 'Best get going if I want to get to the rest home before dinner. Thanks for the tea. I'll see myself out.'

Emily wasn't completely comfortable with that, but she let it pass. 'Thanks for coming by.' She stayed put until Wanda was out of the room, then softly moved to the door and watched her down the hall, ashamed to admit to herself that she wanted to make sure none of the ornaments in the hall found their way into Wanda's furry pockets. But she was astonished to see instead her guest stopping Oscar at the foot of the stairs and whispering something to him. Oscar turned red and headed on up.

Emily shook her head and turned back into the library. Indeed there were all kinds of people in the world, and it was beginning to look as if most of them would turn up at one time or another in Stony Beach.

FIVE

On Friday morning, Emily made another attempt to address her Dostoevsky notes and felt as if she'd made a tiny increment of progress – traversing perhaps a single verst of the immense vastness that was the Russian Empire. She was in equal parts sorry and relieved that her other guests were expected to arrive in the late afternoon and evening. She would have to tidy her things away to make room for them to work in the library if they wished.

Looking at the weather from her front porch, though, she wondered if they would all be able to get there safely. The solid cloud cover had been growing lower and darker all week, with only a few showers to show for it. She was certain some extremely nasty weather was on the way, and the strength of the icy wind suggested it would probably hit today.

Luke called after breakfast and confirmed her suspicions. He was her source for weather reports since she had neither TV, radio, smartphone, nor computer in the house and didn't take a newspaper except, willy-nilly, the free local weekly, *The Wave*. 'Storm's gonna hit tonight, they say. Lots of freezing rain, maybe even snow. If you have any errands to do, better do them now.'

Emily crossed herself with a silent prayer. 'I think we're good. Katie's laid in enough food for an army, and I've got plenty of yarn stashed away – those are the essentials, right?' She kept her voice light, although in fact she was apprehensive. Power outages were not uncommon in winter storms, and she'd read too many mysteries in which terrible things happened when the lights went out.

'Candles and batteries?'

'Oodles. Beatrice stocked this place like a fortress.'

'What about your guests coming in?'

'I am rather concerned about them. Perhaps I should call and warn them to come early.'

'Might be a good idea. They all coming from Portland?'

'Through Portland, anyway. A couple are flying in.'

Luke whistled. 'You are in the big time. Got people flying in from out of state to come to your retreat center. You still gonna talk to me after you get your head swelled by hobnobbing with the rich and famous?'

'Are you kidding? If they really do act like the rich and famous, I'll need a good, healthy dose of the down-to-earth in the form of you by way of antidote.' He laughed, and she went on, 'You are coming to dinner, right? So you can vet everybody face to face?' Luke had done his background checks and found no red flags, but as he'd said when he gave her the news, 'There's always a first time for a wrong 'un to go wrong.'

'You bet. Got Pete and Heather on duty for emergency calls. I'll be there come hell or high water. Hoping for neither, of course.'

When they finished talking, Emily called Marguerite and gave her the weather report.

'*Dommage. Moi*, I will be there by teatime with Alex.' Alex was her student novelist. 'Also I bring Monsieur MacDonald and Mademoiselle Mountjoy from the airport. Teatime should be early enough to beat the storm, *non*?'

'I certainly hope so.'

'That will leave only young Monsieur Weaver. I will let him know to come as early as he can.'

'Great. Thanks, Marguerite.' That got Emily off the hook with regard to making phone calls to strangers – something she'd never gotten comfortable with in thirty years of professional life. Fortunately she'd surrounded herself with extroverts, to whom talking to strangers came as naturally as holing up alone with a book did to Emily.

By teatime, a light rain had begun to fall, but the temperature was still above freezing. Marguerite and her passengers arrived cold and damp but safe. However, only three people extracted themselves from her Peugeot instead of the expected four.

'Where's Alex?' Emily whispered to Marguerite as the other two struggled out of their wraps in the hall.

Marguerite frowned in disgust. 'He begged off at the last minute, the young fool. Said his father had insisted he come home for Christmas break. But I have never heard before that his father cared to have him around, at Christmas or any other time.' She shrugged. '*Moi*, I think he is afraid to confront the naked page. His loss.'

Marguerite's more illustrious passengers were now divested of their outer garments and waiting to be introduced. 'Emily Cavanaugh, may I present Olivia Mountjoy and Ian MacDonald.'

Emily shook their hands in turn, thinking Luke's quip about hobnobbing with the rich and famous might turn out to have some foundation in reality. Both her guests gave the impression of being strong personalities, seeming to fill more space than their mere physical presence could account for.

Ian MacDonald was tall – about Luke's height, she guessed – with thick salt-and-pepper hair swept back from a noble-looking forehead. His handsome face and well-formed body both showed signs of encroaching age, but he carried his years with distinction and grace. He reminded Emily a bit of Sean Connery. But where the lines in Connery's face seemed etched by good humor, the lines of Ian MacDonald's face suggested worry and discouragement. Nevertheless, he spoke with perfect ease and charm as he brought her hand to his lips.

'Delighted to make your acquaintance.' His slight Scottish burr accentuated the Connery connection – no doubt deliberately. 'And I am so very grateful you have chosen to open your most gracious home.'

'And I that you have consented to honor it with your presence,' Emily replied, feeling herself blush. If Luke was jealous of Oscar, how would he react to the presence of this charmer in her home?

She turned to the woman next to him, noting that she stood deliberately apart. The space between her and Ian crackled with energy, and Emily wondered what history they had together; it seemed unlikely they had met for the first time in Marguerite's car.

Of the two, Olivia Mountjoy was actually the more striking, now that Emily got a good look at her. Tall and willowy with slightly drooping posture, she had the perfect body for the clothes she wore, which were reminiscent of a thirties movie – a well-tailored suit in a soft dove gray, with a fitted jacket and mid-calf-length skirt that flared gently at the hem. A white lace jabot peeked out from between her lapels, and a neat gray hat sat jauntily on her jet-black hair – jet black, that is, except for a streak of pure white shooting back from her left temple. Any internal comparison to the Bride of Frankenstein, however, was immediately forestalled by the regal beauty of her features. Olivia Mountjoy put Marguerite in the shade, and that was saying something.

'Ms Mountjoy. So happy to have you here. I've just read your *Death in the Doorway* and found it quite delightful.'

Olivia had the kind of opaque white skin that does not blush easily, but she lowered her eyes in what looked like embarrassed modesty. Emily was taken aback. Surely such a well-known writer – and one who looked so self-assured – was well accustomed to receiving the praise of fans?

Olivia murmured vague thanks and immediately added, 'Thank you for having me. Marguerite has told me a great deal about Windy Corner, and none of her praise was exaggerated, I assure you.'

Emily smiled at the subtle *Pride and Prejudice* allusion. She was going to like this woman. 'Let's go into the library, shall we? I'll show you your rooms after tea.'

As they led the way, she whispered to Marguerite, 'Any idea when Dustin Weaver might arrive?'

'*Non*. I only got his voicemail.'

Oscar was waiting by the fire, and Emily introduced the newcomers. When he heard Ian MacDonald's name, Oscar flushed and his eyes shone. 'Mr MacDonald, this is indeed an honor. I've admired your work for years. *Congregation of Vapours* was absolutely brilliant.'

Ian inclined his head graciously. He, at least, was clearly accustomed to praise.

'But I must have missed your latest books – I haven't seen a new one for some time.'

Oscar's observation was made in obvious innocence, but it visibly flustered Ian. 'I – ah – I've been working on a major new book, a clear departure from anything I've done before. Needs a lot of research, careful planning. I'm hoping to make some good progress while I'm here.'

After years of listening to student excuses, Emily knew a writerly evasion when she heard one. She would bet her best bottle of aged tawny port that Ian was simply blocked. Possibly the well of inspiration had run permanently dry.

She poured the tea while Katie handed around the finger sandwiches, cakes, and scones. Ian, Oscar, and Marguerite filled their plates, but Olivia declined everything except tea.

'Olivia, aren't you hungry? It would be a shame to miss Katie's superb baking.'

Olivia looked up from petting Kitty to dart a glance at Marguerite, then spoke to her teacup in a voice Emily had to strain to hear. 'I'm so sorry to be a nuisance – didn't Marguerite tell you? – I'm gluten-intolerant. I can't eat wheat flour or anything with gluten.'

Marguerite struck her forehead in exaggerated remorse. '*Mon dieu*, I completely forgot! *Désolée, chérie.* But I am sure the so capable Katie can come up with something for poor Olivia to eat?' She looked entreatingly at Katie.

'No problem. Fruit and cheese OK?'

'Perfect, thank you.' Olivia gave her an apologetic smile. 'I hope this won't play havoc with your dinner plans?'

'Not at all. Tonight the only gluten is in the rolls. But will it be a problem having food that's cooked in the same kitchen with gluten? One of my sisters is celiac and we had to be super careful with her.'

'No, mine isn't quite that serious. A little cross-contamination won't bother me.'

'Awesome. Then we're cool.' Katie whisked out and returned in a couple of minutes with a beautifully arranged plate containing alternating slices of several cheeses, plus apple, persimmon, and kiwi. In the center sat one plump chocolate truffle. 'A little consolation prize,' Katie said as she handed the plate to Olivia.

Olivia broke into a smile of pure delight that transformed her face. 'How very thoughtful. Thank you so much.'

Ian, having worked his way through his first plateful, launched into fulsome praise of the library – both its architecture and its contents. 'What a treasure you have here! Is one allowed to work in this room during the day, or must we confine ourselves to our bedrooms?'

'The library is a designated quiet zone open to all during the day, from after breakfast until teatime. Any who wish to take a break from writing may congregate in the dining room, where Katie will have coffee and snacks available all day, or in the parlor.'

Ian sighed in contentment. 'I'm feeling inspired already.'

The doorbell rang and Katie went to answer it. A couple of minutes later she ushered in a wet and shivering young man. 'Mr Dustin Weaver,' she announced in true parlormaid style.

Emily rose and extended her hand. 'Welcome, Mr Weaver.'

Granted, the young man couldn't be at his best soaked to the skin and freezing, but Emily did not find Dustin Weaver especially prepossessing at first sight. His medium-sized frame tended toward middle-aged spread, although he looked to be only around thirty. His straw-colored hair was over-long, not in a deliberate way but as if he'd simply neglected to have it cut; his beard similarly showed several days' growth – a style Emily particularly disliked, feeling a beard should be all or nothing. His tweed jacket hung lumpily, with visible fraying at the edges, and his T-shirt and jeans looked as if he'd pulled them from the reject pile at Goodwill.

All this could have been forgiven if mitigated by a pleasant expression and gracious words. But Weaver's petulant scowl seemed to blame Emily personally for the inclement weather. 'Practically got blown off the road,' he grumbled. He ignored her proffered hand and strode directly to the fire, jostling the tea tray and stepping on Bustopher Jones' tail in the process. All three cats rose haughtily and stalked off to the parlor. 'And I swear I drove through two or three lakes. This place sure is the back of beyond.'

Emily was taken aback, but a guest's rudeness never excused answering rudeness in a host. 'We did attempt to warn you to come early because of the storm, but Marguerite wasn't able to get through to you by phone. Did you get her message?'

'Yeah, at three o'clock, when it was already too late to get here for your precious "tea". I don't suppose you saved me any food?'

Emily glanced around for Katie and saw her coming in with a replenished three-tiered tray of pastries. 'Plenty to go around, Mr Weaver,' Katie said cheerfully. 'And I'll freshen up the tea.'

'Not on my account. Can't stand the stuff.' He shoved half a teacake into his mouth and mumbled around it, 'Got anything stronger?'

Emily drew herself up, summoning Aunt Beatrice's shade to help her put this oaf in his place without transgressing the bounds of hospitality. 'Katie, please pour Mr Weaver a glass of sherry. Normally the sherry is reserved for the cocktail hour, but in view of your need for warmth we'll make an exception.'

Katie handed him one of the second-best sherry glasses with a little more than the standard amount of Harveys Bristol Cream. He downed it in one gulp and made a face. 'I'm a whiskey man myself.'

'I'm sorry, we don't have any whiskey in the house.' Emily waited until he'd slowed down his face-stuffing to introduce the others, who all sat in stunned silence. 'Mr Weaver, I believe you've met Marguerite Grenier?'

'Nah. Old McClintock at Reed hooked us up by email, never met in person.' He gave Marguerite the once-over and leered. 'Wish we had, though.'

Marguerite looked as frosty as only a Frenchwoman can. 'I also wish we had met before I recommended you to Emily.' The implication was clear, to Emily at least – if she'd met him, he would never have been asked. His lusty grin faded as that possibility appeared to dawn on him.

Emily hurried to continue her introductions. 'And this is Olivia Mountjoy, whom you may have heard of as the author of the Sadie Jones mysteries.'

'Never read that crap. No offense there, Olivia. I'm sure lots of old ladies think it's great.' He leered at Olivia in turn even as he insulted her writing. She did not answer but passed her cup to Emily for a refill of tea.

'And Ian MacDonald, whose work I'm sure you're familiar with.'

This time Dustin condescended to shake hands, though he

neglected to brush the crumbs off his own first. 'Yeah, read one of yours once. Not bad. Haven't written anything for a while, though, am I right?' Unlike Oscar's, Dustin's question was clearly meant to turn the knife in the wound.

Ian drew himself up and repeated his line about having a major project in the works. Dustin gave a skeptical sneer and moved on to Oscar as Emily said, 'And this is Oscar Lansing, who's working on his PhD thesis. He's an adjunct prof at Reed.'

Dustin's sneer intensified. 'Poor sucker. All that advanced degree stuff is crap. A writer needs to live, experience the world, not just read about it.'

'I believe there is a place in the life of a writer for both study and experience, Mr Weaver,' Ian said repressively. 'I myself have an MFA, and I feel it has greatly benefited my writing.'

Dustin snorted. 'One year of college was enough for me. I'm a self-made man, a whaddayacallit – auto-something or other.'

'"Autodidact" is the word you're searching for, I believe,' Oscar said with commendable composure. Emily reflected that 'didact' was an excellent word for Dustin Weaver, and he was certainly 'auto' as well – no other person's instruction, feelings, or convenience would get any consideration from him. Whether he had actually learned anything from his own instruction was another question altogether.

She glanced at her watch. 'If you've all finished, I'll show you to your rooms so you can get settled and freshen up before dinner. We dine at seven.' She turned to Dustin. 'Mr Weaver, you have the Dickens room here on the ground floor. But you're welcome to come up and see the other rooms if you wish.'

He set down his glass and wiped his hands on his jeans. 'Nah, never could see the charm of these drafty old barns. Just point me to my room. That girl bring my bags in?'

'I'm sure Katie has taken your things to your room.' Emily was perilously close to losing her temper with this man. On top of everything, he'd managed to insult her beloved Windy Corner and her beloved Katie all in one breath. It was a good thing she'd given him the Dickens room, though he hardly deserved it – at least he wouldn't be sharing a bathroom with anyone and he'd be a bit out of the others' way. If it weren't for the weather, she'd have seriously considered sending him back to Portland; but she wouldn't send a dog out in this storm. Not that she'd ever met a dog she didn't like better than Dustin Weaver – and a dog person she was not.

'Katie will show you the way.'

Katie smiled cheerfully at Dustin. Thank God for her intrinsic equanimity; even a boor like Dustin couldn't faze her – at least, as long as he kept his hands to himself. Fortunately, Katie didn't appear to be his type, or else he regarded her as beneath his notice, because he barely glanced at her as he followed her out of the room.

Emily turned to her other guests with the brightest smile she could muster. 'Let's go upstairs, shall we?'

Marguerite was charmed by the Austen room – all light colors and delicate eighteenth-century furniture – which she had seen only in its preliminary stages of transformation from the dark and dreary east room of Emily's childhood. '*C'est presque français*,' she said – the highest compliment she could give.

Ian MacDonald gave an appreciative shiver as Emily led him into the Brontë room. She had given him this room, with its heavy walnut furniture and dark red hangings, because of the dark nature of his writing. 'This is absolutely perfect. I can't fail to be inspired here.'

Olivia emitted a little gasp of delight when Emily opened the door of the Montgomery room, cheery even in the midst of a storm with its white iron bedstead, handmade quilt, and braided rag rug. 'Oh, I love it! I could lie down on that quilt and wake up in Prince Edward Island in 1890. Like in *Somewhere in Time*.' She gave Emily an impulsive kiss on the cheek, then turned away in confusion.

Emily smiled. 'I'm so glad you like it. It's the coziest room in the house.'

That left the Dostoevsky room unoccupied, which was fine with Emily. She was going to have her hands quite full as it was.

SIX

Emily was tempted to pray that Dustin Weaver might have an attack of indigestion – not unlikely, given the way he'd wolfed his tea – and decline dinner. Instead she prayed she would have the patience and the wit to deal with him and keep the evening pleasant for her other guests.

Luke's attendance at dinner might be helpful. He was impossible to intimidate and had a way of repressing inappropriate behavior simply by his authoritative presence. She'd asked him to come at six-thirty so they'd have a chance to reconnoiter before the other guests came down for a pre-dinner sherry.

He was prompt, and this time he'd changed into a neatly pressed dress shirt and jeans. Luke only wore a suit when he had to, but he looked as put-together in his current ensemble as most men would in a coat and tie. Emily clung a few extra seconds when they kissed hello.

He took her hands and looked into her eyes. 'Everything OK?' He could always tell when something was bothering her.

She blew out a long breath. 'One of my guests is going to be troublesome.'

Immediately the lawman came to the fore. 'Do I need to intervene?'

'Not as a sheriff. He's not that kind of troublesome. Just extremely rude. Loud, self-centered, deliberately tactless. What I do need you to do is prevent him from dominating the conversation. Everyone else was horrified into silence at tea.'

'I can do that.' He gave her shoulders a squeeze. 'Don't you worry. Between us we'll put him in his place.'

The other guests drifted in from upstairs, and Emily introduced Ian and Olivia to Luke; Marguerite, of course, he already knew. Emily served sherry, and they all chatted pleasantly about nothing of consequence until Katie sounded the gong for dinner. Then Emily awoke from her pleasant dream and realized Dustin had not joined them.

'These two seem nice enough,' Luke said low in her ear as they walked into the dining room. 'Somebody missing?'

'Yes. Dustin Weaver. He has the Dickens room. Maybe he fell asleep – he had a pretty rough trip, apparently.'

But as they were all sitting down, Dustin appeared in the doorway, catching himself against the jamb as he swayed slightly. 'Starting without me, eh?'

'Katie did ring the gong, Mr Weaver. We thought perhaps you'd fallen asleep.'

He belched loudly. 'Just having my own little cocktail hour.' He moved to the nearest chair, bumping against the table as he fell into it.

Emily stared at him, aghast. The man was drunk. He'd obviously made provision against any potential dearth of his favorite beverage.

She shot a panicked glance at Luke, who answered with a *let me handle this* look. 'Maybe you didn't get a chance to read the house rules. No outside alcohol allowed.'

Dustin swung his head in Luke's direction. 'Who the hell are you?'

Emily said in her best Aunt Beatrice voice, 'This is Lieutenant Sheriff Luke Richards, my very dear friend. Luke, this is Dustin Weaver.'

Dustin bridled. 'So what, it's illegal now to bring a bottle into a hotel?'

'This is not a hotel, Mr Weaver. This is my home, and if you wish to remain in it, you had better keep a civil tongue in your head.'

He put up his palms as if warding off an attack. 'Well, excu-u-use me!' But he shut up after that.

'Katie, you may serve now.'

Katie had outdone herself again, this time with boeuf bour-guignon. After a few delicious bites, the other guests recovered from their shock and made polite conversation again. The main topic was the weather, which had grown even worse – the rain was freezing now, and speculation was rife as to whether it would turn to snow.

As they started on their dessert of chocolate mousse with ladyfingers, the doorbell began to ring insistently, accompanied by energetic pounding. Luke looked at Emily with raised eyebrows. 'You expecting somebody else?'

'No. The student who was supposed to come with Marguerite begged off at the last minute.' She stood and laid her napkin on the table. 'I'd better go see who it is.'

Katie had already admitted the insistent ringer, who now stood on the mat divesting herself of her outdoor garments. Layer after layer of brightly colored clothing peeled off until a short, dumpy, middle-aged figure remained. Emily took in the crimson knit hat shoved down over frizzy bleached hair; the kelly green sweater, through the holes of which gleamed a sparkly violet shirt; and the full, ragged-hemmed gauze skirt, a garish print in which every vibrant color known to the modern chemical imagination vied for prominence. The woman looked like a bag lady who'd lost a game of paintball.

'Can I help you?' Emily said when she'd recovered from the initial sensory shock.

The apparition stuck out a grimy, ill-kept hand. 'Cruella Crime. Heard young Alex Gordon couldn't make it and came along in his place.'

Emily was speechless. This woman's effrontery outdid even Dustin's. 'Did you say . . . Cruella Crime?' The name sounded vaguely familiar, but it certainly couldn't be real. And oddly, black and white seemed to be the only colors missing from her ensemble.

'My pen name. Real one's a closely guarded secret. Only my publisher knows for sure.' She gave an exaggerated wink.

Now the name clicked. Emily had seen it splashed across the lurid covers of airport paperbacks. Cruella wrote the worst sort of sensationalist 'true' crime, although according to Luke the crimes were far too imaginative for the average criminal to have plotted.

'I'm very sorry, Ms . . . Crime . . .' That sounded so ridiculous Emily couldn't go on.

'Call me Cruella. Everybody does.'

'Cruella, then – but attendance at this retreat center is by invitation only. We don't take in just anyone who happens to come by, open room or no.'

Cruella threw back her head in a raucous laugh. 'Well, I'm afraid you're stuck with me for now, honey. Have you looked outside? I slid in here on a two-inch coat of ice. No way are my poor bald little tires getting out till this thaws.'

Emily's head whirled as her visions of a stimulating week of polite intellectual conversation and civilized Christmas celebration came crashing down between her ears. Dear God, send a thaw tomorrow, she begged. Early.

Meanwhile, she was a hostess. She'd better pull herself together and act like one. 'The others are finishing dessert. Have you eaten?'

'Not a bite. I'm ravenous.' Cruella bared pointy teeth in a wolflike grin, and Emily hoped there was plenty of beef left over. Otherwise Cruella might start in on the guests themselves.

'This way, please. We'll see what Katie can come up with.'

Katie, seeing the way the wind blew, had already laid another place at the table and heated up the leftovers, which to Emily's relief seemed adequate to the most voracious appetite. Emily showed Cruella to the one empty chair and returned to her own. Settling her napkin back in her lap and taking up her spoon, she smiled around the table at her other guests.

'Everyone, I'd like you to meet Cruella Crime. She's arrived unexpectedly, but in this weather all travelers must be welcomed.'

She was about to begin introducing the others when she realized three of the faces at the table had turned to stone. While Luke, Marguerite, and Oscar regarded Cruella with varying degrees of wary curiosity, the three newcomers – Ian, Olivia, and Dustin – looked as if their worst nightmares had come to life and sat down at the table with them.

Emily shot a glance at Cruella, whose face was split in a self-satisfied leer. 'But perhaps some of you know her already.'

Olivia quietly rose and laid her napkin on the table. The suppressed tremor of her movements betrayed some powerful emotion barely contained. She drew herself up and walked at a measured pace out of the room.

Ian, with a glare at Cruella that would have reduced most women to jelly, rose and strode out after Olivia. Cruella gave another raucous laugh. 'Those two know me, all right.' She elbowed Dustin, who was seated next to her. 'And so does this one. Don't you, *Billy*?'

Dustin, or perhaps Billy, went green. He toppled his chair in his haste to get out of it and rushed out in the direction of the bathroom.

Emily's detective brain was spinning with curiosity, but she was not about to press Cruella for details. She made short work of introducing the others, then rose. 'We'll retire to the library now and leave you to finish your dinner in peace. Katie will show you to your room when you've finished.'

Cruella, who had begun to stuff food into her face like Augustus Gloop in Willy Wonka's chocolate factory, nodded with a grunt. At least she wasn't going to insist on joining the party.

With only Luke, Marguerite, and Oscar for company – and, of course, the cats – Emily could relax at last. Luke excused himself to check on the conditions outside. But as Katie brought in the coffee tray, Emily heard a commotion in the hall. Luke's voice reached her clearly through the hall door.

'Now just where do you think you're going?'

Dustin's voice, slurred and truculent, replied. 'I'm getting out of here. Not gonna stay in the same house with that bitch.'

'I don't think so, Mr Weaver. One, the ice out there is too dangerous for even a sober man to drive on, and two, you left sober behind about half-a-dozen drinks ago. I'd have to arrest you the minute you got behind the wheel.'

Dustin spluttered and blustered, but even sober he would have been no match for Luke. He clattered his bags back to the Dickens room. With luck, his dread of bumping into Cruella would keep him there for the duration of his stay – which, Emily was determined, would not outlast the ice on the road any more than Cruella's would.

Luke returned to his place by Emily's side on the loveseat and gave her hand a reassuring squeeze. 'He'll be out cold in no time.'

'Thank God for small mercies.' She addressed the group. 'So what do you make of all that?'

Oscar shook his head, baffled, but Marguerite nodded knowingly. 'That woman, Cruella as she calls herself, is the ex of Ian MacDonald. Ex-wife, ex-lover, I do not know, but an ex, *bien sûr*. And Olivia is the one she blames for the breakup – though, if you ask me, Ian merely came to his senses and saw Cruella for what she is.'

Emily stared at Marguerite. 'What, do you read the gossip column in the *Times Book Review*? How do you know all that?'

Marguerite tossed her head. 'I do not need to read. It speaks for itself. What other explanation could there be?'

Emily had to admit her friend's interpretation was the most likely one. 'But what about Dustin? He hardly seems like a candidate for a love triangle. Or quadrangle, in this case.'

'*Non.*' Marguerite pursed her lips. 'That, I think, is something else.'

Oscar leaned forward in his chair. 'She called him Billy, didn't she? Maybe he's not who he pretends to be.'

'Luke? Did your background checks come up with anything suspicious?'

Luke pulled out his pocket notebook, leafed through it, and frowned. 'He checked out OK, but I didn't see anything going back farther than '05. He would've been what, about twenty then? Maybe he changed his name.'

'Or maybe he isn't Dustin Weaver at all.' Emily paled. 'I didn't ask to see his ID or anything. And you hadn't met him, right, Marguerite? Or seen a picture?'

'*Pas du tout.* I do not know him from Adam. He could be anyone.' She waved her arm wide as if to include all the characters in all the novels in the room.

Emily turned a worried face to Luke, who stood. 'He's probably passed out by now. Think I'll go do a little snooping.'

He returned shortly. 'He's out, all right. Left his wallet on the desk. Driver's license says Dustin Weaver, and I'm pretty sure it's not a fake. So that's his legal name, at any rate, though he could've changed it from something else.' He shot Emily a smile. 'I don't think we're dealing with a conman.'

'That's something.' But not enough to make her comfortable, with two explosive personalities in her home. 'Did you notice if Cruella was still in the dining room?'

'She's gone. Katie must've taken her up.'

Emily felt suddenly exhausted. 'I've had it for the day. Will you all forgive me if I turn in?'

Oscar and Marguerite made polite noises. Luke accompanied her into the hall. 'I'm not sure even my chains are gonna be enough to handle this ice.'

Emily mentally chided herself for not having thought of this. 'Oh, of course, you'd better stay. I'll make up the bed in my sitting room.' She linked her arm through his and leaned against him. 'I'll feel better knowing you're here.'

SEVEN

B reakfast was a buffet affair, so the guests didn't all congregate simultaneously, for which Emily was grateful. She herself was up early and managed to avoid both Dustin and Cruella.

By nine in the morning, the ice on her driveway was slushy enough, Luke thought, for him to navigate it in his specially equipped vehicle. He made a foray into town and came back to report.

'Still pretty bad out there. Couple degrees above freezing and not likely to get any warmer. Car like mine can get through town all right, just barely.'

Dustin walked into the library in the middle of this speech.

'I'm getting out of here, then.'

'Not so fast, Mr Weaver. I said *I* could get through town – doesn't mean your little car would make it with no chains or even snow tires. No place else to stay around here, anyway. All the hotels are shut for the winter. And as I was about to say when you barged in, nobody's getting out of the area – One-oh-one and Twenty-six are still frozen solid. So unless you're willing to risk getting stuck at the side of the road and having to sleep in your car in the freezing cold, I recommend you stay put.'

Dustin looked as if he was about to protest, but he was sober and visibly hungover this morning, lacking the alcoholic courage that might have allowed him to stand up to Luke. He slumped and trudged back to his room without a word.

Luke turned to Emily. 'I've got to get back out there and do some damage control. Want me to come back this evening?'

'Please. If you're going to get stuck anywhere, I'd rather it was here.'

He smiled at that, kissed her quickly, and took off into town.

Her other unwelcome guest made no attempt to leave. Cruella came down last, and the late breakfasters in the dining room, Ian and Olivia, evaporated at her approach. After eating she established herself with her laptop in the library, whence the other two fled upstairs.

Emily would have liked to bring out her Dostoevsky work again, but Cruella had managed to take over the whole table, and anyway, Emily couldn't stand to be in the same room with her. The parlor had no desk or sizable table, and she didn't want to set up in the dining room, where she would have to clear away for meals. But she felt it was her responsibility to stay on the ground floor in case any confrontations threatened.

Grumbling to herself but conscious that she would never have been able to concentrate in this atmosphere anyway, Emily took a book and her knitting into the parlor, whither the cats followed her, and closed the communicating door. She used the parlor so rarely, it was like a foreign country to her. Like Goldilocks, she had to try all the seats in turn to find one that was comfortable enough to settle in for the day.

The cats were equally disoriented. Bustopher went straight to the hearth and flopped there; Emily had asked Katie to make a fire in this room, too, since it was open to the guests all day. But Levin and Kitty prowled, yowling discontentedly, until they finally settled, one on each arm of Emily's chair.

Knitting was impossible with no room to move her elbows, so she opened her book – *Hercule Poirot's Christmas*. Hmm, Christmas with a bunch of oddly assorted characters, some unpleasant, in a big country house. That felt slightly familiar. At least her guests weren't all related to her or each other, or she'd be looking over her shoulder for a murderer.

She'd barely begun reading when Cruella stuck her head through the door. 'How do I get on the WiFi?' she demanded.

Emily started. She'd assumed her guests would bring computers, but it had never occurred to her they would also want to access the internet while here. She had a dim idea that Katie might have WiFi in her apartment, but apparently the signal didn't reach the main house. 'I'm sorry, we don't have internet service here. It's meant to be a distraction-free environment conducive to concentrated work.'

'Well, I can't work without doing research, and I can't do research without Google.'

Emily bit her tongue to prevent herself from reminding Cruella that she had not, after all, been invited to this party and hence had no grounds for objecting to anything about it. 'I would send you into town to the Friendly Fluke, but I'm afraid the road is still pretty slick.'

'Hmph.' Cruella strode to the front window and peered out. 'How far is it to this Fluke place?'

'About a mile.'

'I've got boots. I'll walk.'

If any of the others had proposed walking to town, Emily would have done her best to dissuade them; she was fairly sure walking would be nearly as dangerous as driving. But Cruella was not the persuadable type, and anyway, Emily would be glad to have her out of the house for a while.

'I suggest you call first and make sure they're open. In this weather they might not bother.' She crossed the hall to the tiny office next to the stairs and fetched a local phone book. 'Here's the number. I assume you have a cell phone?'

Cruella rooted through her many capacious pockets and finally pulled out a cell phone. She punched in the number and waited, her expression growing darker by the minute. At last she hung up. 'No answer. Stupid hick town.'

'As I said, this is meant to be a quiet retreat from the world.'

'Right.' Cruella snorted. 'Well, I'll find something to keep me busy, never you fear.' She bared her pointy teeth in a grin that reminded Emily of all the vampire movies she'd never seen. Then Cruella returned to the library and shut the door.

Emily comforted the cats, whose hackles had raised in Cruella's presence, then lifted her coffee cup for a restoring sip. It was empty. She went through the hall to the dining room for a refill but paused outside the door when she heard voices from the Dickens room.

The voices were Cruella's and Dustin's – the one raised and threatening, the other a hissing whisper – but she could not make out the words. She wrestled a moment with her conscience, but the side that argued she had a responsibility as hostess to know what was going on in her house won out over her scruples. She edged closer to the door, but just then it opened a crack. As she sprang back into the dining room, she heard Cruella say, 'If you want to flush your career down the toilet, it's no skin off my nose – *Billy*.'

Emily found brain-space around her awakened curiosity to wonder whether Cruella's books were as full of clichés as her speech. But far more urgent was the question of why Dustin's – or Billy's – career was in jeopardy and what Cruella had to do with it. With her head full of Christie, the natural conclusion appeared to be blackmail. Did that happen in real life? Emily made a mental note to ask Luke when he returned.

In the course of the morning, Ian and Olivia came down and made a whispered request to Emily that they be allowed to lunch on trays in their rooms.

'I don't mind for this one meal,' she replied. 'I'm sorry you have to put up with Cruella being here, since she obviously makes you uncomfortable. But you may all be stuck here for several days – I doubt you'll be able to avoid each other all that time. Is there any possibility whatever conflict you have with her could be resolved?'

Ian barked a laugh, then quickly silenced himself. 'I'm afraid not. She has behaved unforgivably toward both of us, and far from repenting her actions, she positively glories in them. I think I can speak for Olivia when I say we'd managed to put all that behind us until she showed up here. But being in the same room with her is intolerable.'

Emily was bursting with curiosity about what had happened between the three of them, but they apparently did not want to say, and it wasn't her business anyway. 'I see. I can't allow an uninvited guest to imprison you both in your rooms. I'll inform Cruella that she will have to keep to her room from now on.'

Ian and Olivia exchanged glances. 'I do devoutly hope you will be successful in that, Emily,' said Ian. A younger, less formal person would have said, *Good luck with that*, meaning it would take a universe full of luck to make it happen. Anyway, it would be worth a try. Emily prayed Luke would be back soon – she needed his authority and sheer brawn to back her up.

Cruella agreed with surprising meekness to lunch in her room, though there was something in her eye that made Emily mistrust her show of submission. Now if only Dustin would behave, they might be able to have a civilized meal.

Dustin was mute throughout lunch and ate hardly anything. The others were subdued as well, though Marguerite's valiant attempts to start a conversation eventually met with success. A lively but friendly debate ensued over the relative merits of various books, shows, and films in the broader crime genre. Dustin left partway through, and the remaining five got along famously. Even reserved Olivia contributed a few quiet but intelligent observations. Emily began to feel the retreat plan might not have been so ill advised after all. If only the weather would clear so she could get rid of Cruella and Dustin.

But the temperature fell in the course of the day. Luke arrived a few minutes before teatime looking frazzled, which was unusual for him. 'Pretty bad out there?' Emily asked as he warmed his hands over the library fire. For the moment they had the library to themselves – so far, Cruella had kept her promise to stay in her room.

'Madhouse. Fender benders every which way. Nearly had one myself at the top of your driveway. I skidded in here on pure luck.'

'Goodness! Thank God you made it back safely. And that there was nothing worse than a fender bender.'

'Most locals have the sense to stay home when it gets like this. I put out a radio call asking everyone to stay off the roads until further notice.'

'Does that include you?'

'Unless I get an urgent call about some idiot who didn't comply. You're stuck with me for the time being.' He gave her a one-sided grin, as if unsure of his welcome.

She slipped her arm through his and snuggled up to him. 'That is fine by me.'

He was on the point of showing his appreciation tangibly when Oscar came in. 'Oh dear,' he said. 'I seem to be making a habit of coming in at the wrong moment.'

'No, no, it's fine. It is four o'clock, after all.' The gong sounded in the hall, then Katie came in with the first of the tea trays. For this crowd several trays would be required – first the tea paraphernalia itself, then the sandwiches, then the cakes and scones, and finally a plate of gluten-free treats for Olivia. By the time everything was in place, all the guests were assembled, with the happy exception of Cruella.

Once again, Dustin was subdued and ate little. He did ask Luke whether there was any chance of leaving town soon, but when he got a negative reply he merely took his meager plate and slunk back to his room.

Luke turned to Emily with raised eyebrows, as if to say, *What happened to him?*

Emily pulled Luke aside and replied *sotto voce*, 'I overheard a conversation between Dustin and Cruella this morning that made me think she might be blackmailing him. Does that kind of thing actually happen outside of mystery stories?'

'Heck, yeah, it happens. Lots of people with guilty secrets, lots of people greedy enough to take advantage. Course, some of the reasons you read about in those Agatha Christie books no longer apply. Nobody gives a hoot anymore about a child born out of wedlock, for instance, and lots of people aren't too squeamish about adultery. But something like fraud, embezzlement, any actual crime – if the wrong person finds out, blackmail is a definite possibility.'

Emily's gorge rose at the thought of something so sordid going on in her beloved home. But then she caught herself with the reminder that the house had seen far worse. 'Is there anything you can do about it?'

'Not unless we can prove it, which'd be tough without one of 'em admitting to it. And how likely is that?'

'True. Oh, well. I have Cruella confined to her room for the time being. I may need you to help enforce that, by the way. Let's hope it will put some kind of damper on her activities.'

'Amen to that.'

EIGHT

The evening had been reasonably quiet, and Emily would have felt comfortable leaving her guests to go to church Sunday morning. But the roads were still icy, and Luke pointed out that Father Stephen might not even hold services under those conditions. Emily had to accept defeat on that point. Not for the first time, she wished Windy Corner were a little grander even than it was – grand enough to have its own private chapel, served by her own private Orthodox priest. She'd been managing a weekend in Portland, where she could attend her own church, every month or so, but it wasn't enough. She needed the sustenance of the familiar music, teaching, fellowship, and, most importantly, the sacraments. The local Episcopal church was a pale substitute.

Since even that substitute was unavailable, Emily spent much of the morning on the phone finalizing plans for her Christmas celebration the next day. The forecast was for a thaw, and she prayed it would prove accurate so her friends from town would be able to reach Windy Corner safely. She was expecting Jamie, her young lawyer and Katie's fiancé; Devon and Hilary, local British expats and partners in both an antique business and life; and Veronica Lacey, her closest local friend and owner of an antique accessories shop. Sam Griffiths, the local doctor, had declined, saying she didn't do holidays. Beanie the yarn-shop owner would be with her family, taking her boyfriend Ben, the book dealer, along for self-defense.

A pang of conscience made Emily extend an invitation to her tenant Wanda Wilkins as well. Wanda would probably not be able to get to Seaside to spend the day with her mother, and no one should be alone on Christmas Day.

Katie, with admirable foresight, had laid in all the necessary supplies before the freeze – except for the Christmas crackers, personally imported from England by Devon and Hilary. Emily was looking forward to a real Old English Christmas.

She was disappointed again in the evening, though, by not being able to get to the Christmas Eve service. Instead she gathered all who were willing – Dustin and Cruella declined – in the parlor around the piano. Olivia, it transpired, was an excellent pianist and accompanied the group in half an hour of traditional carols. Oscar and Ian had passable tenor and bass voices, respectively, while Olivia's clear soprano made Emily's shortcomings as a singer less obvious. Katie and Marguerite carried the alto part, and Luke, who was somewhat musically challenged, plowed manfully through on the melody.

'We don't sound bad,' Emily observed after the first few songs. 'We should go around the neighborhood. Except there is no immediate neighborhood here, and we'd never be able to make it to town.'

'*Dommage*,' said Marguerite. 'But at least we have entertained *les chats*.' All three cats had sat attentively, lined up on the window seat, throughout the performance. When they realized the music was over, they all curled up and went to sleep.

The night was yet young, and Katie served mulled wine and homemade eggnog in the library. 'I know,' Oscar said suddenly. 'Let's read *A Christmas Carol*. We can all take turns.'

'Perfect!' said Emily, and she quickly found the book on the shelf – a beautifully illustrated leather-bound edition, its corners rubbed with much use.

Oscar began, since it was his idea. He read with an actor's expression through Marley's appearance, then handed off to Emily for the Ghost of Christmas Past. They each took a turn, Marguerite's French accent lending a peculiar flavor to the Cratchits' Christmas dinner. By the time the book was finished, everyone was stifling yawns, and soon all except Emily, Luke, and Oscar drifted off to bed.

Oscar seemed too elated to sleep. 'This is so cool,' he said. 'This is the kind of Christmas I always dreamed of but never had.'

'Was your family not into the traditional celebration?' Emily asked, hoping she wasn't being too personal.

His face fell. 'Not really.' Oscar stared into the dregs of his wine. Emily offered him more but he shook his head. 'It was just me and my mother growing up. I never knew my father. We weren't exactly poor, but certainly not well off. My mother worked really hard, and when Christmas came, all she wanted to do was put her feet up and think about nothing at all. Some years we didn't even have a tree.'

Memories flooded Emily's mind, making her heart constrict. 'It was like that for us, too, after my mother died. I was eight. From then on, Christmas only happened if I made it happen. It was all a bit much for me to handle.' She gave Oscar a sympathetic smile. 'But I married a man who made Bob Cratchit look like Scrooge, so from then on we went all out every year. I'd almost forgotten what those Scrooge years were like.'

Oscar grimaced. 'I apologize for reminding you.'

She reached over and squeezed his hand. 'Don't apologize. I'm glad we're able to make up a bit of the deficit.'

Oscar stood and stretched his arms over his head. 'I think I'll head up. I want to be well rested for the real party tomorrow.'

'Good idea.' She glanced at Luke. 'Ready?'

He nodded, a deep crease between his brows. Did Luke have bad Christmas memories as well? They'd never talked much about all the years they'd been apart; the present had always been so engrossing.

When they'd said goodnight to Oscar and climbed to the third floor, Emily asked Luke, 'Is something bothering you? You didn't say much – is Christmas a sore spot for you too?'

He shook his head. 'It's not that.' His frown deepened and he shoved his hands into his pockets. 'It's just – well, I've never heard you talk about your husband like that before. I never thought you were that happy together. And you and Lansing are getting so buddy-buddy these days. Seems like I've got competition from the living and the dead.'

Emily was flabbergasted. Lately Luke had been showing a side of his personality she'd never seen before. He'd always seemed so confident, but apparently it was only a show. He must be insecure deep down for a few chance remarks to make him doubt her love for him.

'Luke, you're blowing things out of proportion. Philip and

I were happy together, in a mild sort of way. I guess "contented" would be a better word. But that has nothing to do with my love for you. And as for Oscar, you're being silly. You can't seriously think I'd prefer him over you.'

He looked up at her with pain in his eyes. 'Can't I? He's brainy like you. You know all the same books, you get each other's jokes while I sit by and scratch my head. Why wouldn't you want a man you can share all that with?'

She came up close to him and slid her arms around his waist. 'Because he isn't you.' She stood on tiptoe and kissed him. 'I love *you*. Oscar's a friend, period. It's true, I do miss the kind of conversations I have with him and the others, but clever, well-educated people were as plentiful as books in a library in my old world. I've never met anyone else who could make me feel the way you do. *You* are my man.' She gave him a teasing smile. 'Whether you like it or not.'

His frown lessened but did not disappear. 'Then prove it.'

She pulled back a bit to look him in the eye. Was this about sex? He'd never pressured her about that before. She had her reasons for holding back – her faith was of the conservative stripe that still disapproved of premarital sex – but they'd never really discussed the issue.

'What do you mean?' she said cautiously.

'Marry me.'

'Oh, Luke . . .'

'If you're so sure I'm the one for you, marry me.'

She turned away and paced a small circle, twisting her hands like a silent-movie heroine. This was not the romantic proposal-acceptance scene she'd envisioned. For one thing, the timing was terrible. Just when she was feeling pulled toward her old life – the hushed, cat-free atmosphere of the Reed library, where she would surely be able to grasp the key ideas that eluded her here; her own church, where she could find regular weekly sustenance for her soul – Luke wanted her to abandon all that, completely and permanently, and settle down in Stony Beach as his wife.

She stopped and faced him. 'I can't, Luke. Not now. I thought I was ready to leave academia behind me, but now I'm not so sure. I've been working on my Dostoevsky book, and I feel like I need to finish that before I abandon that life forever. It'll mean a lot of time at Reed, in the library.'

'We've talked about that, Em. Marrying me doesn't mean you have to be imprisoned in Stony Beach. You can still spend time at Reed when you need to.' His jaw clenched momentarily, and she knew he was envisioning her there with Oscar and others of his ilk. 'And I'd feel a heck of a lot better if you spent your time there as my wife.'

She took a moment to imagine herself at Reed as Mrs Luke Richards. That was a person she did not yet even know. How could that hypothetical person belong to Reed?

'It's a question of focus. When I marry you – notice I did say *when* – I want to be free to focus on *you*. I don't want to bring unfinished business into our marriage.' Her feelings were more complex than that, but she couldn't put words to them. She appealed to him with her eyes to understand what her voice could not articulate.

His mouth twisted. 'I get it. What you're really saying is you don't want me as baggage when you go back to Reed. You want to be a free agent.'

She huffed in exasperation. 'There you go again. This is not about Oscar or any other man. It isn't really about *us* at all. It's about me. When I made the transition from Reed to Stony Beach, it was too rushed, too – well, almost forced on me. I mean, I made the choice, but I didn't make it without a certain amount of external pressure. I don't mean you – I mean the whole situation. And now, I'm starting to see that maybe I didn't take into account everything I should have.'

One look at his face was enough to tell her she was only digging herself in deeper. She went up to him and laid her hands on his chest. 'I will marry you eventually, Luke. I promise. I just need some time.'

His face worked, and she realized he was holding back tears. Never in all their time together had she seen him cry.

'I was going to give you a ring for Christmas,' he said in a strangled voice. 'I guess that's off.'

Tears sprang to her eyes at that, but she couldn't give in. At this point she would be caving to emotional blackmail, and she'd be sure to regret it.

'I'm sorry, Luke,' she whispered. 'I'm so sorry.'

His face hardened into a mask she'd never seen before. 'Some Christmas,' he muttered under his breath as he turned away.

Some Christmas indeed. What would tomorrow be like, with all the difficult people she had to deal with, if she didn't even have Luke on her side?

NINE

First thing Christmas morning, while most of them were still in their bathrobes, Emily invited Marguerite along with Katie and Lizzie up to her sitting room to give them their gifts. She'd prepared small, impersonal gifts for her other guests, but she wanted to exchange the more meaningful ones in private.

Luke was still sullen and withdrawn, though he made an effort to appear like his normal self in front of the others. Emily gave him her gift – a pair of hand-tooled Western boots with his initials worked into the design. He showed due appreciation, but nevertheless she felt her gift had fallen flat. What was a pair of boots when what he wanted was her heart and hand?

For Marguerite she had a bottle of Château Lafite Rothschild, a wine she knew her friend revered but could never afford on a professor's salary. Marguerite, in turn, presented her with a bottle of Disaronno amaretto, a treat Emily allowed herself only rarely because its higher alcohol content made her tipsy more quickly than she liked. But as one of the aunts in *A Child's Christmas in Wales* said to justify her own holiday alcohol consumption, 'it was only once a year.' She thanked Marguerite warmly.

'You know, much as I love the contents, this would be worth having for the bottle alone. Isn't it the coolest thing you ever saw?' She showed Katie and Luke the unusually shaped bottle, rectangular with a broad, square lid topping its tapered neck. 'It looks like one of those men in Renaissance paintings with the weird flat hats.'

Luke gave an affirmative grunt, then went back to admiring his boots. Katie looked up from unwrapping her own gifts to say, 'Cool,' but it was clear this particular enthusiasm was Emily's alone.

Never mind; she was happy the others were enjoying their

own gifts. For Lizzie, Emily had made a lovely soft, lacy crib blanket in butter yellow. Because knitted gifts from her to Lizzie were fairly commonplace, she'd also included a complete boxed set of the little Beatrix Potter books that Ben Johnson, the local bookseller, had found for her. 'She's a bit young to appreciate them now, of course. But I don't think a child is ever too young to be read to.'

'I totally agree.' Katie had moved on to admire her own gift, a beautifully bound and illustrated set of the novels of Jane Austen. 'I only ever had these out of the library – except for one old, dog-eared paperback of *Pride and Prejudice*. This is absolutely perfect, Mrs C.' She jumped up and gave Emily an impulsive kiss on the cheek.

Emily teared up as she hugged her. 'You're very welcome, Katie.'

Katie's gift to her was a scrapbook of photographs of Lizzie from birth to the present, with funny or touching memories written in. 'This is perfect too. Makes me feel like a real grandma.' On cue, Lizzie cooed and reached up her arms, entwined in her new blanket. Emily picked her up and rubbed her face in the baby's halo of red-gold hair.

'Thank you all for being here. The rest of the day may get pretty crazy, but I'm glad you were with me to start it off right.'

The others dispersed, Marguerite to shower and dress and Katie to start breakfast. 'Do you want to shower first?' Emily asked Luke. 'You'll probably be faster than I will.'

'Sure.' He was picking up all the used wrappings and stuffing them into a bag. He wouldn't look at her.

She couldn't bear this distance between them. 'Luke—'

'Yeah?' he said without looking up.

'Can't we be – well, normal with each other? After all, nothing's really changed.' What she meant was that she'd been declining his proposals for months; why should this time make such a difference? But somehow she didn't think saying that would help.

He straightened and met her eyes. 'That what you think?' She quailed under his steely gaze. 'Sure feels different to me.'

'Well, then – can we put this on hold till after Christmas? At least pretend to be normal, just for today?'

His jaw clenched as he drew in a long breath. 'All right. I'll make an effort. For the sake of your guests. You have enough loonies to deal with as it is.'

She sagged in relief. 'Thank you. And I know you won't believe this, but I really do love you. No acting required on my part.'

He gave her a look that said, *Yeah, right*, shoved the bag of wrappings in the trash, and headed for the bathroom.

This was going to be a long, long day.

For Christmas Day, Emily felt she had to let Cruella out of her room, at least for meals. When Emily came down for breakfast, Cruella was already there, walking around the table as if to compare the gifts laid out next to each guest's plate. The gifts were identical as wrapped, though slightly varied beneath – a beautiful leather-bound journal and fountain pen in different colors for each writer.

Predictably, Oscar, Ian, and Olivia were properly appreciative. Oscar in particular stroked his journal and fondled his green-marbled pen with the absorption of a child who's just received something he's always longed for. He looked up at Emily with misty eyes.

'Thank you so much. I've been making do with ballpoints and spiral-bound notebooks all my life. These make me feel like I could write something beautiful.'

Emily beamed at him, then caught Luke's glower and looked away. Dustin opened his gifts, set them aside with a grunted 'Thanks,' and dug into his breakfast. Cruella evaluated her journal and pen (originally meant for the absent Alex) as if assessing what she could get for them on eBay, then set to her meal in silence. Her eyes, however, darted between Dustin, Ian, and Olivia as if to be sure they didn't escape.

No one would be escaping the house today. Luke predicted that by midday the road through town would have thawed enough for him to collect all the local dinner guests in his official SUV. But the highways out of town were still frozen solid.

From the time they came in and seated themselves, Ian and Olivia both were restless in their chairs, twitching their shoulders and scratching discreetly from time to time. Olivia ate little – only a bit of fruit and the small, gluten-free coffee cake Katie had baked especially for her – and excused herself, saying, 'I don't know what's wrong – perhaps I've developed an allergy to the fibers in this outfit. I'm going to shower and change.'

Ian finished his breakfast as quickly as politeness would allow and followed her. 'I seem to have the same problem as Olivia,' he said. 'Perhaps it's the dry air. I itch all over.'

Cruella snickered and ducked her head. Emily frowned at her. Was she simply enjoying her enemies' discomfiture, or could she be in some way responsible for it?

Dustin stopped with a huge bite of cinnamon roll half-chewed in his mouth, shoved his chair back, and bolted from the room. The bathroom door slammed, and some time later he reappeared, looking as green as a piece of rotten meat. 'What are you feeding us, anyway? Something's gone bad. Gave me the worst runs I've ever had.' He stared accusingly at Katie, who was coming in with a fresh pot of coffee.

She faltered in her tracks. 'I'm terribly sorry, Mr Weaver. I don't know what the problem could be. Everything was fresh when I cooked it this morning.' She looked entreatingly at Emily.

'Is everyone else feeling all right?' Emily asked of the company in general. Everyone nodded or said, 'Fine.' She said to Dustin, 'I don't think it was the food, since it hasn't affected anyone else. Perhaps you picked up a bug in town and it's just now showing itself.'

He grunted. 'Maybe.' He gulped down the last of his coffee, then made a face. 'This coffee's bad, anyway. Worst I've ever tasted.'

If there was one thing Katie did superlatively well, it was coffee. Emily shot a glance at Luke, who frowned.

'Let me see that cup.' He reached across Marguerite to take the cup from Dustin, brought it up to his eyes, and examined the inside. He sniffed at it, then touched his finger to the bottom and brought it to his lips. He made a face and spat into his empty juice glass.

'It's not the coffee. There's detergent in this cup.'

Katie went white and shifted from foot to foot. 'I swear, all the dishes were properly rinsed. They all went through the dishwasher together. I don't know how one could have detergent left in it and not the others.'

'Maybe some joker decided to give you a little Christmas gift – the kind that keeps on giving.' Luke peered at Cruella, who was shaking with suppressed laughter. 'Cruella, you wouldn't happen to know anything about this, would you?'

She pulled in her cheeks to stop herself giggling and made a long face. 'Who, me? Why would I do such a thing? I find it entertaining, that's all.' The giggles returned in full force.

'Suppose you show me what you've got in your pockets.'

Cruella stood, still laughing. From two capacious pockets in her skirt she pulled a set of keys, some wadded-up tissues, a paperclip, and a bottle of prescription medication. 'Go to town, Sheriff.'

Luke reached for the prescription bottle. 'Toprol XL. What's that?'

Oscar said, 'Blood pressure medication.' When Luke cocked an eyebrow at him, he added, 'My mother takes it.'

Luke uncapped the bottle and shook the tablets into his hand. They were all identical with the same pharmaceutical stamp. 'Looks legit.' He replaced the tablets and passed the recapped bottle back to Cruella.

She smirked. 'Satisfied?'

Luke nodded grudgingly, still frowning. Emily was certain Cruella's outfit must contain more pockets than the two she'd emptied, but since no actual crime had been committed, Luke could hardly insist on a full-body search.

Dustin blurted, 'Well, somebody's gonna pay—' Then he clutched his gut and bolted for the bathroom again.

After breakfast, Katie went into a flurry of cooking for the mid-afternoon feast. Emily offered to keep Lizzie out of her way, so the four of them – Marguerite, Oscar, Luke, and Emily – played with her by turns in the library while the others chatted. Luke stretched his turn with Lizzie the longest; it saved him from keeping up the pretense of being on good terms with Emily. But by the time he left to pick up the other guests, Emily felt enervated from the tension between them. The cats were restless, having picked up on the atmosphere; even Bustopher Jones couldn't settle to his usual place on the hearth but roamed from chair to window seat and even, at one point, to Marguerite's lap. Bustopher was not a lap cat.

Marguerite had clearly noticed the tension too; not much got past her. When Luke had left and Oscar had excused himself for a moment, she said to Emily, '*Alors, qu'est-ce qui se passe?* What is the matter between you and Luke?'

Emily blew out a long breath. 'I refused his marriage proposal last night.'

'And so? You have refused before, *non?*'

'Several times. Never an outright "no", only a "not now". But last night was different. Not what I said, but the way he took it.' She tried to explain what had happened without betraying Luke's confidence. 'It just doesn't feel like the right time. Or the right reason.'

Marguerite threw up her hands. '*Mais, chérie, qu'est-ce que tu veux?* Luke's emotional range is perhaps more than some, but he is still a man, *non?* To him it is simple: if you loved him, you would marry him. If you will not marry him, then you must not love him. *C'est tout.*'

Emily blanched. Was that what she had done to him? No wonder he was distant. She'd jumped into the soup with both feet this time. And it looked as if the only way she'd be able to extricate herself was to say yes. But it went against her nature to let herself be backed into a corner that way.

And anyway, she'd have no time even to think about it today. Within five minutes Oscar had returned to the room, Ian and Olivia had come down looking much more comfortable, and Luke had returned with a carful of Emily's local friends, plus Wanda. Even Dustin and Cruella appeared and managed to melt into the crowd.

Katie brought in hors d'oeuvres to tide everyone over until the four o'clock dinner hour. Emily decanted a new bottle of sherry and had Marguerite's amaretto in her hand, ready to open and offer it around, when Marguerite said, '*Non, chérie, cela, c'est pour toi seule.* If you offer it to this crowd it will be gone like that.' She snapped her fingers. 'You can celebrate on your own later on.' Her knowing smile included Luke in the proposed celebration.

'All right, if you insist.' Emily pushed the distinctive bottle with its square hat to the back of the bar shelf, then poured a couple of sherries and turned to hand them on.

Cruella and Wanda Wilkins were the closest and received the first two glasses. Wanda was absurdly overdressed (or underdressed, speaking in literal terms of the amount of fabric she was wearing) in spike-heeled silver sandals and a red lamé cocktail dress trimmed with white fur around its décolletage, which only served to accent the leathery quality of the skin on her chest. With a smile worthy of a politician, she said, 'Thank you for inviting me. And especially for offering your second-best sherry to a virtual stranger.'

Emily hardly knew whether to respond to the smile and the thanks or to the snark they so thinly concealed. It was her best sherry, after all. But she was the hostess; it was her job to smooth things over. She gave Wanda the warmest smile she could muster. 'No one should spend Christmas alone. I'm so glad you could come.'

Wanda moved away with a smirk. Cruella downed her sherry in one gulp and held out her glass for more. Emily pretended not to see and proceeded to serve the others. By the time all were served, the carafe was empty. She had more, but she would save it for later, if only to teach Cruella not to guzzle.

Now for the requisite mingling. Emily was never comfortable in a group of more than six or eight people, especially if they were not all close friends, and this group would be particularly challenging. She'd deputed Marguerite to stick with Cruella and quell her more outrageous behavior, while Luke had volunteered to keep an eye on Dustin. That left Wanda for Emily to try to integrate into this ill-assorted group without neglecting her other guests. She resolved that next year she would not open the retreat center until Boxing Day. Christmas Day would be reserved for the people she truly wanted to be with.

She introduced Wanda to the other guests, hoping someone would find her more sympathetic than Emily did herself. Devon and Veronica dutifully made conversation with Wanda, while the more reserved Hilary chatted with Ian and Olivia; at least those three had hit it off. Jamie hovered near Katie, helping her as much as she would let him. The sight of the two young people together invariably made Emily smile; Jamie's devotion to Katie and Katie's blossoming under it were palpable.

Oscar acknowledged his previous introduction to Wanda with a nod but seemed disinclined to converse with her. He mumbled a greeting and turned to talk with the other writers. Emily wondered if Wanda actually had made a pass at him the other day and he had refused her – that would certainly account for his apparent aversion.

'What do you teach?' Veronica asked Wanda.

'High school chemistry. For my sins.'

At least it wasn't grade school. High school chemistry was slightly easier to reconcile with Wanda's personality.

'Do you enjoy it?'

That politician's smile appeared again. 'Oh, loads. I adore lecturing to a roomful of teens who can't tear their eyes off their cell phones long enough to register a word I say. And the lab disasters are even more fun. We had a terrific explosion last week. It's a laugh a minute.'

Veronica and Devon exchanged uncomfortable glances. 'Did you ever consider going into research or something?' Devon put in. 'There must be plenty of other jobs for qualified chemists.'

'For BAs? Sure, employers are falling all over themselves to offer us jobs. They can get away with paying us less than a living wage.' Wanda bared her teeth toward Emily, who expected to see fangs where her canines should be. But light was beginning to dawn. Perhaps Wanda's attitude toward her was simply the natural envy of someone who had always struggled financially toward one who apparently had an easy life.

'I myself taught until quite recently,' Emily said, hoping to defuse that envy. 'College level, which isn't quite as grueling. But the pay isn't much better. It was only last summer I inherited this place and decided to take a sabbatical. Or possibly retire for good.'

'Nice work if you can get it.' Wanda sniffed and turned to

refill her plate with hors d'oeuvres, after which she wandered off to resume the examination of the room's expensive ornaments that she'd begun the other day. Dismissing the thought that Wanda could be either a thief or a spy for an auction house, Emily relaxed into pleasant conversation with her other guests.

'How are they all liking their rooms?' Veronica asked. She and Devon had provided invaluable help in the redecorating of the themed bedrooms.

'They're all quite pleased. At least, those who are capable of being pleased. Dustin and Cruella seem unable to appreciate anything other than their own questionable selves.' She'd given her local guests prior warning over the phone about the two difficult members of the party.

Devon *tsk*ed. 'That is a shame. Which rooms are they in?'

'Dustin in Dickens and Cruella in Dostoevsky. That one was meant for Marguerite's student, but he didn't show.'

'Oh, well. I'm sure the next group will appreciate them properly.'

'I certainly hope so. I intend to screen future guests much more carefully than I did this bunch. Though the other three are quite congenial.'

'Can't you get rid of those two?' Veronica asked. 'It is your home, after all.'

'As soon as the roads clear, I will. But even if we'd had a proper thaw today, I couldn't turn anyone out on Christmas Day.'

'No, of course not,' Devon said. 'But darling, with this peculiar group of people . . . I know you were going for a Dickensian Christmas, but doesn't all this have rather an Agatha Christie feel about it? Perhaps we'll have a nice little murder to top it off.'

Emily grimaced. 'I'd settle for a jewel theft. Windy Corner has had its share of murders and then some.' But she couldn't deny that feelings were running high enough in this crowd that murder would not be an improbable outcome.

TEN

To Emily's intense relief, the party made it through to dinnertime with no untoward demonstrations from Cruella or Dustin, though both were made sulky by what they considered the dearth of alcohol. At the gong they all filed into the dining room, where each place held a Christmas cracker Hilary had brought from England. Popping the crackers, donning the enclosed paper party hats, and trading the trinkets created a modicum of general camaraderie.

The dinner Katie produced was enough to silence the most obstreperous guest: roast goose with chestnut stuffing and all the trimmings appropriate to a proper English Christmas feast. Blissful chewing replaced talking for some time, until at last Katie brought in the pièce de résistance: a flaming plum pudding with hard sauce. For gluten-free Olivia there was a miniature cheesecake with a crushed-pecan crust. Katie – along with Jamie, who had eaten in the kitchen with her and Lizzie – joined the others in the dining room for dessert.

'I didn't have a sixpence, but I did put in a quarter, so be careful how you chew,' Katie said. Seeing the confused looks on several faces, she explained, 'The person who gets the coin is supposed to have good luck for the coming year.'

Three bites in, Luke found the quarter. As the others exclaimed in mock dismay, he laid the coin on his plate with a significant glance at Emily. Good luck in the coming year could mean only one thing to Luke: marriage to Emily. She gave him a noncommittal smile.

An exclamation from Ian broke their eye contact. 'There's something else in here,' he said, fishing a lump out of his mouth. 'I bit down thinking it was safe and nearly broke a tooth.'

Katie turned white. 'I didn't put anything else in there, I swear.'

Emily shot her a reassuring glance and asked Ian, 'What is it?'

Ian used his fork to clear the pudding clinging to the object, wiped it on his napkin, and revealed a gold ring set with diamonds in the shape of a heart.

Stunned silence set in around the table, but Ian's face turned crimson. 'No, really, this is too much.' He stood and threw the ring across the table straight into Cruella's face. 'I cannot put up with this woman a moment longer.' He stalked out of the room. Cruella merely grinned.

Emily gathered her wits and followed him into the hall. 'Ian, wait.'

He turned with obvious reluctance, his foot already on the first stair.

'Ian, I understand how upset you are – though I don't know exactly why – but can you possibly be big enough to ignore it just for this evening? I was so hoping we could all have a nice Christmas together. Of course I could banish Cruella to her room again, but if you could possibly endure her for a couple of hours . . .? I'll have Luke put the fear of God into her so she won't try anything else tonight.'

Ian's struggle contorted his handsome features, but he ultimately closed his eyes with a deep sigh. 'Very well. You have been a most gracious hostess, and the others deserve a pleasant holiday. I will make the effort for your sake.'

Impulsively Emily reached out, took his hand in both of hers and kissed him on the cheek. 'You're a dear. Thank you so much. I promise I'll get rid of her the minute the highways open.'

She heard a cough behind her and turned to see Luke outside the dining room door. 'Not to interrupt anything,' he said caustically, 'but I thought you might need a hand.' He looked pointedly at her hands, still wrapped around Ian's.

Emily dropped Ian's hand rather too quickly, conscious that she was blushing and furious with herself for doing so. 'I do need your help, in fact. Ian has graciously agreed to rejoin the party, but I need you to give Cruella a stern talking-to. I don't want to have to seclude her, but it's imperative she behave herself for the rest of the evening.'

'Right.' Luke gave her a frigid imitation of a smile. 'Happy to be of service.' He turned back into the dining room and reappeared a few seconds later with Cruella in tow. With a firm grasp on her fuchsia-sleeved elbow, he led her into the kitchen and shut the door.

Now Luke was really angry, and Emily would have no opportunity to pacify him. The worst of academic life – even the departmental politics – seemed peaceful compared to this.

Emily ushered the others into the library, racking her brains for an inoffensive activity to propose – nothing too active, as they all had a lot of digesting to do.

Devon came to her rescue. 'How about some carols?'

'Perfect,' Emily said. 'We sang some last night and didn't do too badly. With you and Hilary we'll rival the King's College Choir.'

'Hardly that,' Hilary said dryly, 'but perhaps we'll be tolerable.' He moved into the parlor and sat down at the piano before Olivia could get there. But she didn't appear to mind.

Hilary launched into the British version of 'O Little Town of Bethlehem'. Some of the others were unfamiliar with the tune, but Devon's clear countertenor and Hilary's full baritone made up for any deficiencies. They moved on to 'The First Nowell' and even Cruella and Dustin joined in, though neither added much from a musical point of view. After half-a-dozen carols, Emily felt a reasonable degree of both musical and interpersonal harmony had been restored.

When Hilary declared his out-of-practice hands to be exhausted, Cruella piped up from the back of the group. 'Let's play charades!'

Emily quailed at the thought of all the mischief Cruella might get up to in the course of a game of charades, but before she could object, several of the others had voiced their approval. Devon was particularly enthusiastic.

'Let's do it properly, the English way – with tableaux and costumes.' He turned to Emily. 'Surely, darling, in a house like this there must be a dressing-up trunk.'

Emily recalled finding a trunk of vintage clothes in the attic when she and Katie had rearranged it before the remodeling. She'd never gotten around to going through it, but it was sure to contain some treasures. 'We do have something of the sort,' she said. 'Not costumes per se, but old clothes at any rate.'

'Brilliant. We can arrange chairs in the library and set up the tableaux here in the parlor, then open the doors when we're ready.' He counted people off into teams, tactfully ensuring that Cruella and Dustin were grouped with those best equipped to handle them. 'And remember, in the English rules, the word or phrase can be anything well known – it doesn't have to be a book or movie title. It could be a place, a person, a familiar phrase – anything you can fairly expect people to guess.'

'We'll go first,' Cruella decreed. 'Come on, gang. Where's this famous trunk?'

Emily led the way to the attic. Cruella was right behind her, with Luke, Marguerite, Hilary, and Veronica following and Dustin trailing glumly at the rear. Emily pointed out the trunk, and Luke and Hilary hefted it down from its shelf.

'I'll leave you to it, then,' she said. 'Luke, you know where the intercom is – holler down to the kitchen if you need anything else. And ask Katie to ring the gong when you're ready.' She exchanged looks with Luke, silently imploring him to ensure nothing untoward happened. His crisp nod assured her he would, though it conveyed no warmth.

The end of this evening couldn't come too soon.

Devon's team, consisting of Emily, Wanda, Oscar, Ian, and Olivia, moved straight chairs from the dining room into the library and set them up facing the double doors into the parlor. Jamie declined to participate, saying he'd rather help Katie clean up, but he did agree to be timekeeper during the actual tableaux. In case both teams guessed their respective charades correctly, the winning team would be the one that guessed more quickly.

Once the chairs were in place, the guests dispersed briefly – most of them, being introverts, needed a few minutes to themselves in the midst of all this activity. Emily went to the kitchen to make sure Katie and Jamie were managing all right, trying to clean up after dinner for fourteen with Lizzie underfoot.

Katie, as usual, had everything under control, so Emily moved to the dining room to check on the cats, who had found the library and parlor too busy for their taste. Katie had fed them the scraps from the goose, and they were all dozing in blissful repletion.

The gong sounded, and Emily's team reassembled in the library at the semicircle of chairs. Emily felt a draft and wrapped her shawl tighter, making a mental note to nudge the thermostat up a degree or two when the charade was over.

The double doors were opened by invisible hands, and Emily saw her parlor transformed, with pale blue fabric draping the furniture and tufts of white batting scattered about the floor. Cruella must have raided more than the one trunk of clothes. Among the tufts glided the six members of Cruella's team, all draped in white with rings of gold tinsel on their heads, strumming imaginary harps and casting their eyes solemnly upward.

With difficulty Emily stifled a laugh – the only one who managed to look at all convincing was Hilary. Veronica did her best, but a plump, gray-haired angel was a bit difficult to swallow; Marguerite's attempt to look holy merely brought out the pixie in her. Luke and Dustin were glum and uncomfortable, while Cruella as an angel bordered on sacrilege.

Immediately several of Emily's team called out 'Angels!' but Cruella shook her head. Emily said, 'Heaven?' and Cruella nodded with a smile. Her team erupted in guesses involving the word 'heaven'. *'Heavens to Betsy!' 'Heaven Is for Real!' 'Heaven Can Wait!' 'Heaven in Your Arms!' 'Heaven's Gate!'* and finally, *'The Five People You Meet in Heaven!'*

'No, no,' Devon said. '"Heaven" has to be the first word of the phrase.'

Cruella, still smiling, shook her head and closed the double doors. They would have to wait for the next word.

The others milled about in and out of the library, presumably going to visit the restroom, which Emily did herself at one point. After a few minutes Katie came in with a tray, on which she collected a full bottle of sherry, the amaretto, and a glass from the bar shelf. 'Do you mind?' she asked Emily. 'Cruella said she needs these for the charade.'

Emily shrugged. Presumably Marguerite had OK'd this idea, and she was the guardian of the amaretto. For herself, Emily didn't mind sharing.

A couple of minutes later, as Emily was thinking surely the

gong would sound at any moment, the lights suddenly blinked out. Emily's hands went cold. A power outage would be a natural consequence of the current storm, and she'd been prepared, both mentally and practically, for it to happen. But that it should occur right now, in the midst of what already seemed the perfect setting for a country-house murder, was ominous at best.

She felt her way to the mantel, lit a candle, and took it into the hall, calling out to everyone not to worry, they were well supplied for emergencies. Then a bright flashlight bobbed down the stairs, followed by Luke's voice. 'Likely a general outage, but I'm gonna check the circuit breakers just in case,' he said to her in a low voice as he passed.

Emily followed him to the control panel in the tiny office next to the vestibule. When Luke trained his light on the circuit breakers, every single one of them showed red. 'Somebody's idea of a joke,' he growled as he flipped them back on. 'And I bet I know whose. What the hell is she up to now?'

Her sense of foreboding only intensified by this discovery, Emily turned to the guests, who were milling anxiously about the hall, and put on a reassuring smile. 'Nothing to worry about,' she said. 'These old houses – this kind of thing happens from time to time.' Though it had never happened before. The wiring of Windy Corner was fully up to date.

Cruella's disembodied voice floated down from the upper half of the staircase. 'We're ready for the second scene. Team, you know your places.' Marguerite led their group into the parlor. Luke brought up the rear with a look toward Emily that said, *I don't know what Cruella's up to, but I'll make sure it doesn't get out of hand.*

Emily's group took up their chairs in the library, looking flustered. In a moment the doors opened to show the parlor in its normal state and the team, minus their leader, in their ordinary clothing, milling about. Puzzled, Emily watched as Cruella entered from the hall wearing a flaming red wig arranged in an exaggeration of Emily's own typical high bun. She had on an outfit that must have dated from the earliest days of Windy Corner – a tweed suit cut in Edwardian style with a lace-collared blouse. The jacket strained across Cruella's lumpy form so that Emily was afraid a button would pop off and hit someone in the eye. The suit looked so much like something from Emily's own closet that she started, but the color was wrong – she didn't own anything blue. The bright peacock of the jacket against the scarlet wig dazzled her and made her blink.

Emily looked sideways at her silent teammates, who all, except Wanda, were fidgeting in their chairs and shooting her uncomfortable glances. Clearly, they all thought as she did – Cruella's getup was a nasty, tasteless parody of Emily herself – but no one wanted to say it. Wanda, apparently, either didn't know Emily well enough to perceive the parody or didn't mind seeing her mocked.

'Windy Corner?' Olivia said in a small voice.

'Parlor?' Ian suggested.

'Party?' Devon put in.

Grinning snidely, Cruella moved to the side table that held the drinks tray. With exaggerated movements she twisted the square top off the bottle of amaretto, filled the sherry glass almost to the brim, and brought it to her lips.

She drained the glass in a gulp – a feat possible only for a seasoned drinker – and set it down, smacking her lips. Then she turned to mingle with the other performers, who were pretending to talk among themselves.

Oscar suggested, 'Amaretto? Drinks? Bar?' but Cruella only snorted.

'Guests?' Olivia put in and was met with a sneer.

Finally Emily said, 'Obviously, it's me. Emily.' Cruella bared her teeth in a malicious grin and circled her hands to signify, *Take it further.*

'Emily Brontë?' 'Emily Dickinson?' '*Emily of New Moon?*' the others chimed in.

'No,' said Emily. 'We have to combine it with "heaven", remember?'

All furrowed their brows in concentration. 'I can't think of a single thing with both "heaven" and "Emily",' Ian said at last.

Then Devon sat forward in his chair. 'I know! Emily's our *hostess*, yes? It's "heavenly host"!'

Cruella gave an exaggerated bow. 'Your turn,' she said to Devon in a croaky voice, then coughed several times.

'Serve her right if she's not feeling well,' Oscar whispered, echoing Emily's thoughts, 'the way she guzzled that amaretto.'

Emily nodded, surprised Marguerite would agree to such a demonstration. Perhaps she hadn't been fully informed of the plan.

Since only Cruella needed to change, the others went into the library as Emily's team headed upstairs. They heard Cruella coughing her way up ahead of them. 'I hope she doesn't have anything contagious,' Emily said in a low voice to Oscar. 'I'd hate to have everyone iced in *and* sick.'

Luke threw himself into a chair by the library fire, away from the rest of the group, as they waited for Devon's team to prepare their charade. He was disgusted with himself for having allowed that farce to play out. When Cruella first suggested the phrase 'heavenly host' and how they'd depict it, he'd felt sour enough at Emily to think it would serve her right to be made fun of like that. But when he saw Cruella in that ridiculous wig, saw the way she disrespected the woman who'd been gracious enough to take her in, disruptive as she was, when she had no business at all to be there – well, it made him sick. Emily could never deserve *that*.

He worked himself up to give Cruella a piece of his mind. But when he stood and turned to face the rest of the group, she still wasn't there. She must have had plenty of time to change by now. He frowned, wondering if he ought to go and check on her – she hadn't looked too well when she went up to her room.

The gong sounded and Cruella still did not appear. The game wouldn't be fair if his team lacked its leader. Not that he cared about winning at this point, but it was second nature to him to ensure fair play. He told Katie to ask Emily's team to wait a minute while he fetched Cruella.

He took the stairs two at a time and strode to the back of the house to pound on the door of the Dostoevsky room. 'Cruella? We're ready to start.'

He heard an odd, strangled noise from inside and tried the door. It was locked.

He pounded again. 'Cruella? You OK?'

Again the strangled noise. Something was definitely wrong in there. For a split second he weighed his duty against Emily's anger at having one of her doors broken down. Hell, things could hardly get any worse between them, and doors could be fixed. He kicked at the lock once, twice, a third time, and it finally gave.

The scene that met his eyes and nose brought every sordid story associated with a garret to life. Cruella lay on the floor in a pool of vomit, unconscious and gasping for breath. Her face was heavily flushed.

This was no ordinary tummy bug or reaction to too much rich food and drink. He whipped out his cell phone and called Dr Sam Griffiths. 'Sam? How fast can you get here? I think somebody's been poisoned.'

ELEVEN

'On my way,' Sam said. 'Symptoms?'
    'Unconscious, flushed, gasping for breath. Been vomiting.'
'Pulse?'
Luke knelt, wishing he had a free hand to hold a handkerchief over his nose, and felt for a pulse in Cruella's neck. Her hands were covered in vomit.
'Fast and shallow.'
'Diarrhea?'
'Not as far as I can tell.' Thank God for small favors.
'Could be any number of things. Not much you can do by way of first aid. Better call an ambulance. I'll probably get there faster, though.'
Luke swore. Cruella's breathing grew more labored as they spoke.
'Any idea how the patient was poisoned?' Sam asked. The sounds of doors closing, a car starting up came through the line.
'Only thing she had the rest of us didn't, far as I know, was some amaretto. Full glass of it in one gulp.'
'How long ago?'
He checked his watch, which wasn't helpful since he hadn't noted the time during or after the charade. 'Maybe twenty minutes?'
'Full stomach?'
'Pretty much. Dinner finished about an hour and a half ago. She ate a lot.'
'Should help, but still. Time I get there could be too late. Why the hell didn't you call sooner?'
'Didn't know she was sick. She was up here in her own room away from everybody else.'
Sam's voice went small and quiet. 'Not Emily?'
'No. God, no. One of the writers.' The thought of Emily

lying there in such a state sent ice cubes running through his blood.

At that moment Cruella exhaled one long, raspy breath and then went silent. 'Hang on, might be too late already.' He felt her pulse again. Nothing. 'She's gone.'

'I won't hurry, then.' Sam spoke dryly. 'Still want me to examine the body?'

'Please. No way anybody's getting here from Tillamook tonight.'

'Right. Be there with my ME hat on as soon as I safely can.'

Luke hung up and stood, contemplating the inert form on the floor. He felt a spasm of pity for this woman; no matter how big a nuisance she was, nobody deserved to die like that. But pity gave way to annoyance. She'd been a nuisance in life, and now she'd be a nuisance in death. Nothing like a murder investigation to top off everybody's Christmas.

Emily was going to love this.

With the rest of her team, Emily milled around the parlor, wondering what the holdup was. For the umpteenth time she hiked the shoulder of her makeshift toga back into place. Not really a toga, but none of them knew the proper name for the ancient Greek garments they had attempted to imitate using the same sheets Cruella's angels had worn. All the garments were floor-length except Oscar's, which Devon had chopped off above his knees. Oscar was supposed to represent Hercules. Their charade was 'Hercule Poirot'.

Oscar made a rather ridiculous Hercules, being academically pale and flabby, but the diminutive Devon would have been even worse, and he insisted that Ian, whose build was a bit more appropriate, was too old to be convincing – which Ian had accepted with a remarkably good grace. Perhaps he wasn't eager to exhibit his elderly knees. Emily couldn't help wishing they'd had Luke on their team. He was a bit old for Hercules too, but at least he was strong and fit. And she wouldn't mind seeing what he looked like in a tunic.

As her musings reached that point, the hall door opened and Luke came in. Devon was about to protest when Luke held up his hand with a face that brooked no argument. Emily recognized that look and quailed. What had happened to make Luke turn sheriff all of a sudden?

'Folks, I'm sorry, but the game is off. Cruella was sicker than we thought. As a matter of fact, she's dead.'

Emily's hand flew to her throat. Please God, not another murder. 'Did she have a heart attack?'

A shadow of compassion crossed Luke's stern features as he turned to her. ''Fraid not. Looks like she may have been poisoned.'

Emily groped for a chair and fell into it, conscious of blood rushing away from her head. Devon sprang toward the liquor table as if to pour her a restorative sherry, but Luke stopped him with a hand on his arm. 'Don't touch that table. It could contain evidence. In fact, we'd all better get out of this room until we have a better idea what happened.'

Luke opened the library doors and repeated his announcement to the team assembled there. 'I need everybody to stay in here for the time being.' He took Jamie's arm and positioned him in front of the cabinet Katie had taken the drinks from. 'I'm deputizing you till Pete and Heather can get here. Stand right there and make sure nobody touches any of this.' He strode to the hall door and called, 'Katie? Come in here, would you?'

Katie came in, and Luke closed the door behind her. Then he skimmed his eyes over the group as if doing a quick head count. 'Right. Now. We need to go over everything that's happened from dinner on.' He turned to Katie. 'Far as I noticed, Cruella didn't eat or drink anything at dinner the rest of us didn't. That right?'

'I . . . I think so. I certainly didn't give her anything different.'

Emily gathered her wits. 'Could she have had an allergic reaction to something we all ate?'

'That'll be for Sam to say, but I doubt it. Not the right symptoms.' Luke turned a beetled brow around the room. 'Anybody else feeling ill at all? Even a little bit?'

Dustin muttered, 'Not since breakfast.'

Ian cleared his throat. 'Merely a bit of indigestion. The dinner was delicious, but my doctor would have had ten fits if he'd seen me eat it.'

'We'll have the doc check you out when she gets here. Let me know in the meantime if you feel worse.'

Ian nodded, looking slightly green, and lowered himself into a chair. He took a small amber prescription bottle from his pocket and swallowed a tablet.

'Nobody else?' Heads shook all around. 'Right. Working assumption is it wasn't anything in the dinner, then. Not that you would've been responsible if it had been, Katie. We know Cruella tampered with the pudding, got that ring in there somehow. Somebody could've tampered with something else just as easily.'

'Or added something to her food or wine after they were served,' Emily put in.

Luke glanced at her. 'Right. Who was sitting next to her?'

'I was on her right,' Marguerite said. 'But I did not poison her. Though, in my opinion, she deserved it.'

'Let's stick to the facts, please, Marguerite. Who was on her left?'

'I was,' said Hilary in his typical dry tone. 'But I didn't poison her either.'

'Seeing as how neither of you had met her before the last few days, I can't see what motive you could've had anyway.' To Katie: 'I suppose all the dishes have been washed by now?'

'I'm afraid so. The dishwasher's finishing up, and I did all the crystal by hand. Except I hadn't gotten to the glasses in the parlor yet.'

'Good. Leave them right where they are. Now, did anybody see Cruella eat or drink anything between dinner and the second scene of the charade?'

Head shakes and murmured '*no*'s all around. Luke turned to Marguerite. 'Was she ever out of your sight during that time?'

'She went into the *salle de bain* to change for the second scene. Then she went downstairs before I realized she was ready. I believe she deliberately – how you say? – gave me the slip.'

Luke asked the group, 'How did that tray of drinks get into the parlor?'

Katie answered, 'I took it. Cruella asked me to.'

'When was that?'

'Right before the lights went out. I mean, they went out right after I took the tray in, while I was on my way back to the kitchen.'

Emily caught Luke's eye. Anyone in the house could have snuck into the parlor while the lights were out and poisoned the amaretto – either the bottle or the glass. She'd never get to drink that amaretto now.

Luke asked Katie, 'Did you take a close look at the glass when you put it on the tray?'

'No. It was upside down on the shelf, so I knew it had to be clean.'

That ruled out poison put into the glass before it was taken to the parlor. And that would have been foolish on the poisoner's part, anyway – he or she would have had no way of knowing which glass would be chosen.

'What about the amaretto bottle? Did you see if it had been opened?'

'It looked full, but I didn't notice whether the seal was broken. With that big lid it's kind of hard to tell.'

So it was possible the whole bottle had been poisoned. That is, assuming they were dealing with poison at all.

And that meant it was possible the poison was meant for Emily. But all these people were either friends or virtual strangers – not enemies. Who would want to poison her? No, she was being silly. Cruella must have been the target. That woman was practically begging to be murdered.

Luke must have had the same thoughts, but he didn't voice them. Difficult as it was to believe, one of the thirteen people in this room was most likely guilty of murder. He wouldn't dare give too much away.

He paced in a small circle, one hand at the back of his neck, the other at his belt. He'd taken off the jacket and tie Emily had insisted he wear for dinner. In a white dress shirt and gray slacks, he was neither the casual Luke she was used to in off-hours nor the uniformed on-duty Luke. With his distant, official attitude, he almost seemed like a stranger.

He stopped, facing her. 'Did you all stay here in the library while you were waiting for the charades?'

'No, people were in and out. I think dinner had caught up with most of us.'

'So you couldn't say if anyone was alone in here at any time?'

'Not for sure, no. There were others here when I left and when I came back in, but I can't swear to in between.'

He turned to the others. 'You others on Emily's team – anybody in here alone at any time?' They all shook their heads as he stared at each one in turn. All met his accusing glare without flinching.

'My team. I know we were together most of the time – women in Emily's bedroom, men in the sitting room changing out of our angel robes. But I visited the restroom myself at one point. Anybody go downstairs before the lights went out?'

Another round of responses in the negative. 'Only Cruella,' Marguerite said.

Luke rounded on her. 'Cruella? But she was on the landing when I got the lights back on.'

'*Oui, d'accord*, but she did go down before. To speak to Katie. Probably it was she who turned the lights out.'

Luke snorted in agreement. 'Anybody notice anyone else missing?'

Hilary said, 'Dustin went out immediately after you did. I assumed to the restroom as well.'

Luke rounded on Dustin. 'That right?'

Dustin, who had been relaxed up till this point – almost, Emily would have said, relieved – now bridled. In Cruella's permanent absence, his old truculence seemed to be returning. 'Sure, I used the facilities. So what?'

'So you lied when you said you didn't go downstairs. There's only one toilet on the third floor and I was in it. You must have gone down at least one flight.'

Dustin rolled his eyes. 'Oh, well, if you want to get technical. Yeah, I went down to the second floor. When you said "downstairs" I assumed you meant all the way down here.'

Jamie opened his mouth, then shut it again. Luke didn't seem to notice. He narrowed his eyes at Dustin, then moved on. 'Marguerite? Veronica? You two together the whole time?'

'*Oui*. And after all, as you said before, we had only just met the woman. Why would we poison her?'

Veronica nodded her agreement.

Luke raked both hands over his cropped head and blew out a long breath. 'All right. That's about all we can do with everybody together.'

The doorbell rang. Katie moved to answer it, but Luke stopped her with a raised hand. 'I'll go.'

That must be Sam, along with Luke's deputies and perhaps a crime scene team, though it wasn't likely the team could have gotten there that quickly from Tillamook. Emily withdrew to a private place within herself and prayed for strength. She had hoped never to have to go through all this again.

TWELVE

uke showed Dr Sam and Deputy Pete to the Dostoevsky room, while he had his other deputy, Heather, tackle the parlor and then start searching the guests' bedrooms. Heather would have gamely taken on the Dostoevsky room, but Luke had enough chivalry in him not to wish that on her, tough and capable though he knew her to be. Pete and Heather would have to fill in for the crime scene team – they told him the team couldn't get there from Tillamook until the roads thawed again. The temperature drop at nightfall had frozen the highway back to a solid ribbon of ice.

Luke himself returned to the library. 'I'm gonna need to interview each of you individually,' he told the group. 'I'd like you all to stay in here, and I'll go in the dining room and call for you one by one.' He turned to Jamie. 'You make sure nobody leaves unauthorized or touches that bar shelf, right?'

Jamie nodded, his Adam's apple bobbing in his skinny throat. He probably never figured being a tax and estate lawyer would land him in the position of actually helping to enforce the law. But Katie shot him a *my hero* look, and his chest expanded. 'Yes, sir,' he said, barely short of saluting.

Luke bit off a grin and turned toward Dustin, but his eyes caught Emily's on the way. Hers were sparkling – with the same observation about Jamie, no doubt. Would they sparkle if she realized what he'd already figured out – that the poison could have been meant for her? It all hinged on when and where it had been introduced. His gut clenched at the thought of Emily being in danger, although he had no idea why any of these people would want to hurt her. Certainly not Marguerite, source of the amaretto, who'd been her best friend for over twenty years. And anyway, he was about eighty percent sure the bottle had been sealed when Emily showed it around that morning.

He turned to Dustin. 'You first.'

Dustin scowled. 'That's right, pick on me. Just because I couldn't stand the woman. I'm not the only one, y'know.' His words slurred slightly, and Luke wondered if that suspicious trip to the restroom hadn't maybe included a visit to his whiskey flask as well.

'I'm quite aware of that, and I'm not picking on you. Think of it as getting it over with. Like going to the dentist. You could even say I'm doing you a favor.' He motioned Dustin out the hall door ahead of him. At least the man wasn't swaying on his feet much yet. He might even be precisely the right amount of drunk – deep enough not to be careful with his words but not too far gone to make sense. 'Katie, can we get some coffee in there?' he asked on his way out. Wouldn't hurt to have insurance against the fellow passing out. 'And in here, too, if folks want it.' It was going to be a long night.

In the dining room, Dustin slumped into the first chair he came to. Luke pulled up a chair across from him. Katie brought in the coffee right away; she must have had it brewing already. She poured two cups, set them down, and slid out the door.

Dustin pulled the sugar bowl close and dumped four spoonfuls into his coffee. Luke grimaced and left his black.

'All right. First of all, it's time you told me exactly what was going on between you and Cruella.'

Dustin crossed his arms over his chest. 'Going on? Nothing was going on. What do you think, I was having an affair with that harpy? You must be nuttier than you look.'

'That is not what I meant and you know it. Lots of things can go on between two people besides an affair. So what was it?'

'I told you, nothing. Never met the woman before she came here.'

Luke raised one eyebrow. 'Right. She just waltzed in here and started harassing you for no reason whatsoever.'

'What do you mean, harassing me? She was nasty to everybody.'

Luke ticked off on his fingers. 'When she first got here, she claimed to know you and called you Billy. The next day, Emily heard the two of you arguing in your room. Cruella threatened you with the ruin of your career. And this morning, it was pretty obvious she was the one who put the detergent in your coffee. That adds up to harassment in my book.'

'Well, what about those other two, MacDonald and that chick who writes the cat books? She was harassing them too.'

'I know it, but I'm talking to you right now. I'll talk to them later. Now quit stalling and tell me what was going on.'

Dustin took a testing sip of his coffee, then a long gulp. He put the cup down with shaking hands.

'This doesn't have to leave this room, does it?'

'Depends whether you killed her or not. Anything you tell me that isn't relevant to her death will be kept confidential.'

'Well, I didn't kill her. I swear I didn't.' He shot Luke an imploring look. Frankly, Luke had to wonder if this jellyfish had the guts to kill anybody, but if he did work up the nerve, poison would likely be his method of choice. No direct action required, no risk of a face-to-face confrontation going wrong. And damned hard to trace back to him afterward.

Luke stared at Dustin unblinking until the young man started blabbing, the words spilling out faster than he could edit them. 'All right, she was blackmailing me. We come from the same town, way back. She knew my parents, watched me grow up. She knows me as Billy Williams. But Dustin Weaver is my legal name, I swear. I changed it after I dropped out of college.'

Luke nodded. 'I know. I checked. So she knows your birth name. What of it?'

'Well, I – you know I wrote a memoir, right?'

'Emily mentioned something about it.'

'Well, when you write a memoir, of course things get slanted a little. You tell it the way you saw it, the way you remember it, but other people remember it different.'

'Uh-huh. In other words, you lied, and Cruella knew it.'

'I didn't *lie*. It's possible a few things in that memoir might not be exactly the way they happened. I may have . . . embellished. A bit. Here and there.'

'Or possibly you made the whole thing up out of thin air. You wrote what you wanted to have happened. What you thought would sell books.'

Dustin stared miserably at his coffee cup.

'So Cruella was blackmailing you. Threatening to expose your lies if you didn't pay up.'

'It wasn't money she was after. She'd been dropped by her publisher – wanted me to use my influence to get my editor to take her on.'

'Would that have been so big a price to pay?'

He twisted in his chair. 'Well, I didn't think I could do it, see? My book did pretty well, but they were pressuring me for a follow-up, and – I don't have any more to say. I'm bone dry. That's why I came down here, to try to get inspired. If I went to my editor now and pitched Cruella, he'd laugh in my face. Her stuff isn't up his alley anyway. It was hopeless.'

'So if you did your best and it didn't work – what could she've done? You would've fulfilled your part of the bargain.'

Dustin gave Luke a withering look. 'You obviously didn't know Cruella like I did. That woman didn't have enough honor to fill a shot glass. She would've gone ahead and exposed me out of spite.'

Luke gave Dustin a minute to see the implications. 'So you were trapped. Desperate. She had you right where she wanted you, with no way out.'

The young man nodded glumly, then looked up at Luke with panic in his eyes. 'But I didn't kill her! You can't really think I killed her!'

Luke just looked at him.

Dustin's eyes darted around the room as if looking for an escape route – logical if not physical. 'But – where would I have gotten the poison? If she was even poisoned. Maybe she died naturally. Maybe she had some kind of disease. Did you think of that?'

'Of course that is a possibility. The medical examiner will have to determine the exact cause of death.'

An ugly smile of triumph spread across Dustin's face. 'So you can't pin a murder on me when you don't even know it's a murder. Habeas corpus, right? Or something like that.'

Luke's patience with this sorry excuse for a man was wearing thin. 'I've got enough experience to be pretty darn sure I know poison when I see it. It may take some time to get the medical evidence nailed down, but in the meantime it's my duty to

investigate as if we were sure. So you tell me. Where would
you have gotten the poison?'

'Nowhere. I mean, I didn't. I wouldn't have any idea. Hell,
I didn't even know she was going to be here. I came down
here thinking I could escape her. Why would I bring poison
with me? And you know I haven't been out of this house since
I came. You saw to that.'

Luke had to admit the justice of these words, even though
they were spoken by a desperate, gibbering drunk. But until
he knew what the poison was, no possibility could be ruled
out. It could have been something concocted from ordinary
household ingredients.

'All right, leaving all that aside, let's go over your movements this evening. And I'm warning you, you'd better tell
the whole truth and nothing but the truth, because if you don't,
some other person in this house is going to know.'

Dustin gulped the remainder of his coffee and glanced at
the pot. Luke topped off his cup and waited while he stirred
in four more spoonfuls of sugar and sipped.

'Starting when?'

'Let's start before dinner, when we had sherry in the
library.'

Dustin scrubbed his hands over his face. 'Hell, I don't think
I can remember that far back.'

'Do the best you can.'

'I stayed in the library all through that so-called cocktail
hour. With no cocktails. You should know, you had your eye
on me the whole time.'

'I did lose sight of you when we all went in to dinner.'

'Yeah, I, uh – I nipped into my room for a real cocktail.'
He managed a sheepish half-smile. 'Then you know I was at
the table all through dinner.'

'And after dinner?'

'There again, you know I was in the front room singing
with everybody else.'

'You didn't by any chance nip into your room again after
dinner, did you?'

'Did I?' He looked genuinely puzzled. 'Maybe I did. But in
between singing and charades, I didn't have a chance, did I?'

Luke thought back. He'd had Dustin in view that whole time. 'No, I reckon not.'

'So I was with the rest of you all through the whole "charades" charade.' Dustin chuckled at his own dubious joke.

'Except when you went to the bathroom.'

'Oh, right, except for that.'

'And I suppose you ducked into your room again at that point.'

'Um . . . well, maybe I did.'

Luke leaned toward him. 'Now listen, Dustin. I want you to think real hard. Did you at any time during our team's turn at charades go into the library for any reason at all?'

'The library?' His eyebrows shot up. 'No. Why should I?'

'Where were you when the lights went out?' Those few minutes of darkness were the time Luke favored for the poison to have been added – either to the bottle or the glass. Not only did the darkness give the killer the opportunity to do his work unobserved, but before that time no one could have had any idea Cruella might be drinking amaretto from that particular glass.

Dustin scratched his head. 'Either my room or the bathroom. Oh yeah, I was in the bathroom, 'cause I think I missed the john a little when everything went black.' He snickered. 'Give that girl a chance to earn her keep.'

With an effort, Luke ignored that remark. 'Did you stay there till the lights came back on?'

'Hell no, I hightailed it out of there soon as I finished. I figured it was only that bulb till I got out in the hall.'

'And then what did you do?'

'I milled around with everybody else till the lights came on. Well, I say everybody, but of course I couldn't see who was there and who wasn't. I just heard voices.'

'Whose voices specifically?'

'I don't know. Some male, some female. I wasn't paying attention.'

Luke doubted this pitiful specimen ever paid attention to anything that didn't directly concern himself. 'And when the lights came on?'

'I went into the parlor along with the rest of our team.'

'Were you the first one in?'

'Nah. Probably the last. The rest of you were near the stairs; I was way at the back of the hall.'

Luke sat back and glanced at his notes. They'd pretty much covered everything. At no single point could he be sure Dustin was lying; but if he was telling the whole truth and nothing but, Luke would eat his sheriff's cap, metal insignia and all.

THIRTEEN

L eft in the library with her guests, Emily suddenly realized she and her teammates were still wearing their togas from the charade. In the context the effect was surreal, as if the gods of Olympus had come down to pass judgment on the murderer.

Fortunately they'd all wrapped the sheets over their regular clothing, so she simply tore hers off, and saw her teammates doing the same. Oscar rolled down his pant legs, and normality – in appearance, at least – was restored. But true normality could not be achieved until the murderer was discovered and removed from their midst.

Emily was torn between her relatively new role as hostess and the role she was becoming accustomed to as Luke's assistant sleuth. Should she look for a neutral topic of conversation, try to make everyone comfortable as each awaited his or her turn to be grilled? Or should she discreetly begin to pump them all for information, listen in to the private conversations in the corners of the room? What would Luke want her to do? Was there, in fact, anything she could do at this point that would banish the chill from his eyes when he looked at her?

While she dithered, little knots of talk sprang up about the room. Hilary, Devon, Veronica, and Oscar spoke together in low tones on the window seat in the bay; Katie talked with Jamie as he kept his vigil over the bar; Marguerite crouched on the hearthrug, comforting the undisturbed cats; Wanda sat silent in one of the wing chairs by the fire, drumming her fingers on the chair's upholstered arm. Ian and Olivia huddled together at a small table in the far corner of the room, speaking in earnest whispers. Emily could see that under the table Ian held Olivia's slender hand clasped tenderly in both his own.

If Cruella had indeed been murdered, of all the people in the house, Emily would favor Dustin as the murderer. But as much as she hated to admit it, if Dustin were somehow to be ruled out, Ian and Olivia would be the next strongest contenders. After all, no one but those three had any history with Cruella that Emily knew of, and therefore the others could have no motive for killing her. Granted, the woman was a nuisance, but one didn't murder nuisances. Not if one was sane, which all her guests appeared to be. If there had been an exception, it was Cruella herself.

What could Ian and Olivia's history with Cruella be? Marguerite's theory of an old love triangle had its points, but it needed filling out. Emily found it difficult to believe a man as sophisticated and amiable as Ian could ever have endured Cruella's company, let alone been in love with her. A lesbian triangle? But Olivia having loved Cruella seemed even more improbable.

Without actually deciding to eavesdrop, Emily found herself rising and moving toward the fiction shelf, across the parlor doorway from where Ian and Olivia sat. She'd left *Hercule Poirot's Christmas* in the parlor, which was now off limits as a crime scene, and as long as all the others were either in conversation or deep in their own thoughts, Emily might as well pass her time with a book.

She skimmed the shelves, but nothing seemed to speak to her. Meanwhile, fragments of Ian and Olivia's conversation drifted her way. 'It's all so far in the past . . . no need to mention . . .' 'They must know there's something . . .' 'Let them guess. It's nothing to do with us.' That last was Ian speaking. Emily shot a discreet glance in their direction and caught Olivia gazing into Ian's eyes, her own full of fear and doubt.

Ian started back. 'You don't think . . .? You couldn't think I would do that.'

Olivia blinked twice, then shook her head. 'No, no, of course not. It's just that it's all so terrible. My head's like a blacksmith's shop.' She put her fists to her temples. 'I don't know what to think.'

Ian stole his arm about her and pulled her head down to his shoulder. 'My poor darling. You need to rest. I'll get Richards to talk to you next, and then you can take something and lie down. Shall I?'

Olivia nodded weakly and sagged against him. Emily's conscience assailed her, so she pulled a book off the shelf at random and returned to her chair by the fire. There was definitely at least a love circle binding Ian and Olivia, but whether Cruella had pulled it into a triangle or simply disrupted it somehow remained unclear.

Emily was immersed in her random book pick – which turned out to be another Christie, *A Murder Is Announced* – when Luke came back into the room and addressed the group.

'Before I take the next person, I need to find out about Cruella's next of kin so we can notify them. Dustin admitted knowing her but couldn't remember anything about her family. Ian? Olivia? Either of you help me out?'

Olivia merely shook her head, an effort that caused her to wince. Her head must indeed be pounding.

Ian had stood as soon as Luke entered, and now a ripple passed over his rigid features. He closed his eyes momentarily as his jaw clenched. 'She had no family,' he said in a strangled voice. 'None living.'

'No husband?' Luke asked. 'Even an estranged one would need to be notified.'

Again the clench and release. 'I believe not.'

'All right, then. MacDonald, I'll take you now.'

'Would you mind interviewing Olivia first? She's feeling quite unwell. She needs to get this over with and get to bed.'

Emily watched Luke take in Olivia's pallor, even more pronounced than usual, and the languid way she supported her head in her hands. 'No problem. Katie, would you ask Heather to do Olivia's room first?'

A spasm of alarm crossed several faces at these words. Apparently it hadn't occurred to her guests that their rooms would be searched.

Luke walked across the room, took Olivia gently by the elbow, and guided her to the door. Emily felt a tiny pang of jealousy at seeing him so solicitous, but she forced it down. She could hardly hold Luke's jealousy against him if she gave in to the same emotion herself.

*   *   *

Luke didn't offer Olivia coffee. She needed to get to sleep. He poured her a small brandy instead. She sipped it gratefully, and a bit of color returned to her cheeks.

'We'll keep this short for now. I need to know your movements this evening. Let's say from the beginning of the charades.'

'I was in the library nearly the whole time. I only went out for a minute to use the restroom.'

'This one down here?'

'No, I went upstairs. And I also looked into my room for a moment to get this shawl.' She wrapped the filmy black shawl more closely about her. It looked like something Emily might knit.

'Were you ever alone in the library?'

'No. Not completely alone.'

Luke assumed that meant she'd been alone with Ian – which counted as being alone in his book, as far as opportunity for murder was concerned. But opportunity didn't equal guilt.

'Anybody else alone in there to your knowledge? When you left or when you went back?'

She shook her head, then massaged her forehead with her free hand.

'What about during the blackout? What did you do then?'

'I stayed in the library. I'm not very good in the dark.'

Luke considered. He needed to explore her past connection with Cruella, but he was ninety-nine percent sure that history was linked with Ian's. Given Olivia's state of exhaustion, he'd probably get a better story out of Ian.

'All right, you can go. We'll talk more tomorrow.'

He escorted her to the foot of the stairs, then opened the library door and called for Ian.

Luke closed the dining room door behind the two of them to see Ian still standing, facing him. 'Thank you,' he said with dignity. 'Thank you for letting her go so quickly.'

'No problem,' Luke returned. 'I can talk to her more tomorrow when she's rested. No point trying to get sense from somebody in that state anyway.' He motioned to a chair. 'Have a seat. Coffee?'

'Yes, please.' Ian passed a hand over his eyes. 'This has

been an ordeal for all of us. But Olivia is not physically strong.
Though her strength of character would surprise you.'

Luke let that pass, though he'd already chalked Olivia up as
a strong woman for the way she handled Cruella's persecution.
Strong enough to murder? Hard to say.

'Now then. Let's talk about you. How do you know Cruella?'

'We met many years ago. We moved in the same circle of
writers in New York back in the eighties.'

'And?'

'And what? I hadn't seen her for a number of years before
she turned up here.'

'It's obvious there's some history between you. Something
that involves Olivia, too. Otherwise why the hostility?'

Ian's jaw set, and the color left his face. 'You saw what she
was like. A prankster. Deliberately provocative. She needed
no particular motivation to annoy us beyond the fact that she
knew who we were. And we needed no further reason to avoid
her than knowing her character.'

Luke kept silent a minute, his eyes on Ian's face. 'You know,
I might buy that except for that incident with the ring in the
pudding. That ring meant something to her, and to you. I'd
like to know what that was.'

Ian ran his finger underneath the collar of his dress shirt.
'Can you not simply take my word it has nothing to do with
this investigation?'

'No, sir, I'm afraid I cannot. As it stands, I have three people
with a possible motive for killing Cruella. You are one of them,
and I need to know just how strong your motive was.' He
waited a bit, then added, 'Not telling me is only going to make
me think something even worse than the truth, you know.'

Ian stared at him wide-eyed. 'Lieutenant, I swear to you, I
did not kill Cruella. And neither did Olivia.'

'If that's the case, you have nothing to fear from telling me
the truth.'

Ian buried his head in his hands for a long moment, then
raised it, took a deep drink of his coffee, and set the cup down.
'Cruella and I were married. Briefly. A long time ago.' He
shot a glance at Luke and added, 'You are no doubt wondering
what possessed me to marry her. I can hardly say myself. Back

then she was beautiful, believe it or not. And exciting, unpre-
dictable. Passionate. I came under her spell.' He shuddered.
'It only took a few months for me to see the harpy's pinions
beneath the surface charm. But it took me years to get free
of her.'

'The ring?'

'Our engagement ring. I was . . . well provided for, which
is no doubt why she pursued me in the first place. And very
much infatuated. I bought the showiest ring I could find.'

'So what does Olivia have to do with all this?'

Ian's face froze. 'I'm sorry, Lieutenant, but I refuse to drag
Olivia into this. She is completely innocent – not only of
murder, but of Cruella's suspicions as well. Please take my
word that she cannot possibly be involved.'

Luke gazed at him a long minute until the ice began to
crack. 'I'm sorry, but I can't do that. I'll respect your chivalry
for now, but I'm going to have to find out one way or the
other – from you or from her.'

Ian gave a curt nod. 'You must do your duty, Lieutenant.
But please be gentle with her. She's been through too much
on my account already.'

Luke returned the nod, then took Ian through his movements
in the course of the evening. 'Were you alone in the library
at any time?'

'I don't believe so. Everyone was in and out – it's difficult
to be sure.'

'How about you and Olivia together?'

'No. Never.' He spat that out too fast. Luke envisioned a
stolen kiss or three.

'And when the lights went out? Where were you?'

'I was in the library. I heard voices in the hall and went to
the door, but no farther. Then when the lights came on I went
back to my seat to wait for the charade.'

All very pat. Possibly even true. And it got Luke absolutely
nowhere.

'May I go now, Lieutenant? I have something of a headache
myself.'

'One more thing. Can you tell me Cruella's real name?
Gonna need it for the death certificate.'

Ian grimaced. 'Jane Smith.' Luke's eyebrows shot up, and Ian added, 'I know. Hard to believe, isn't it? But you can see why a woman like that couldn't bear to go through life as plain Jane Smith.'

'Did she change it legally to Cruella Crime?'

'She tried, after she became successful with that pseudonym, but the judge wouldn't do it. He insisted a legal name had to be reasonable. And there was nothing reasonable about Cruella Crime.'

FOURTEEN

an came back in alone and said Luke would like to speak with Veronica. 'He's hoping to let those of you staying elsewhere get home sometime tonight.'

Emily seized the opportunity. 'Give me a minute with Luke, would you, Veronica? I promise I'll be quick.'

She darted into the dining room. 'Luke, can I have a quick word?'

He looked up at her, and she watched the usual pleasure in his eyes at seeing her shut down to blankness. 'OK, but it better be quick. Got a lot of people to get through tonight.'

She swallowed her hurt. 'Yes, I know. It's just – well, you've probably thought of this already, but . . . I was wondering, doesn't it have to be someone on your charades team? Because how could anyone else have known Cruella would drink out of that glass?'

Luke frowned. 'That's a good point.' He drummed his fingers on the table. 'What exactly was said when Katie took the tray out?'

Emily concentrated, trying to remember Katie's exact words. 'Katie said to me, "Do you mind? Cruella said she needs these for the charade."'

'And did you answer?'

'Not with words. I think I nodded or shrugged or something.'

He rubbed the back of his neck. 'Possible somebody could have assumed from that Cruella would be the one drinking it.'

'I suppose so, but that would be a terrible risk to take.'

'I know.' He squinted at the wall. 'Was your whole team there in the library when Katie came for the tray?'

'I think so. We were expecting the gong to go at any time.'

He faced her straight on. 'Look, Em, there's one possibility we have to face, unpleasant as it might be.'

She quailed. 'I know. The poison could have been meant for me.'

'Anything you haven't told me about any of these people? Any connection you have with the new ones? Conflicts with people in town?'

'No. Not a thing. Wanda doesn't seem to like me much – I think she's jealous because I have money. But you don't kill somebody on that basis.'

'No. I'm going to proceed on the assumption Cruella was the target. But we can't rule the other thing out.' He glanced at her sideways. 'You OK with me staying on the premises for now? I don't want to leave you alone, just in case.'

'Fine by me. In fact, I wouldn't have it any other way.' Emily assayed a smile, and it was met by something that at least was not a frown. 'I'll let you get on with your interviews.'

Luke ducked upstairs for a minute to tell Pete and Heather to pay special attention to anything in the bathrooms or kitchen that might conceivably be used to poison someone. Then he returned to the dining room, where Veronica was stirring cream into a cup of coffee.

'Thanks for waiting. I won't keep you too long.'

She smiled wearily. 'No problem.'

'First, I have to ask you formally, did you have any connection at all with Cruella before this afternoon?'

'None whatsoever. Emily had mentioned her to me on the phone – warned me about her, actually – but other than that I'd never even heard of the woman.' Veronica's demeanor was serene, as usual. Luke had known her for years and had no reason to doubt her.

'Good. Now if you would, cast your mind back and tell me if you saw anyone behaving suspiciously at any time. Any little detail that struck you as off? Or anything that might suggest a connection we don't know about?'

'I've been thinking about this while we were waiting. The only thing I've come up with may have no significance at all.'

'Let me be the judge of that.'

'Of course. It's only that when we were all gathered in the

library before dinner, I heard Cruella say she was going to get
her hands on Emily's amaretto, one way or another.'
Luke pricked up his ears at that. 'Now that does sound significant.' Not to mention it was a huge relief – making it much less
likely Emily was the target. 'Who was she talking to?'
'No one in particular. Just making a pronouncement.'
'Anybody else hear her say it?'
'I can't say with certainty what another person heard or
didn't hear, but as I recall, Ian, Oscar, and Dustin were all
close enough to hear. And Devon, but I don't suppose he's
high on your list of suspects.'
Luke gave a slight smile. He'd suspected Devon of murder
once, but in all seriousness he hardly seemed capable of it,
and in this case certainly had no motive. If anyone could
have found Cruella more amusing than infuriating, it
would have been Devon.
'Any of those people seem to react to what she said?'
Veronica pondered. 'Ian studiously ignored Cruella, not only
at that moment but all the time. Dustin was sullen as usual. I
think Oscar frowned – I got the impression he was offended
on Emily's behalf. Devon, of course, simply lapped up the
drama.'
Luke pouched his lips, drumming his pen on his notebook.
'You didn't see any follow-up to this threat from Cruella? I
mean, other than her using the amaretto in the charade.'
'No. I expect the charade was her follow-up.'
'Yeah. All right. Anything else you can tell me?'
'Nothing I've thought of so far. I'll let you know if anything
else occurs to me.'
'Thanks. You've been a big help.' He stood and shook her
hand.
'Is there any chance of us locals getting home tonight?'
'I'll do what I can. I'm going to talk to the others right
now, then I think Pete can manage to get you all home safe
with his chains.'
Luke interviewed Hilary, who had nothing of interest to add
to what he had said previously and raised no red flags. Then
he called Devon.
Devon bounced in as if he had absorbed all the energy

everyone else in the group had lost. 'Here we are again, Lieutenant. Nice little murder on our hands. Personally, I think Emily engineered the whole thing to look like an Agatha Christie novel. Cruella will probably come back to life any minute and tell us it was all an elaborate joke.'

Luke quelled him with a look. 'I saw Cruella die, and I promise you she is not coming back to life. Not unless you believe in zombies. And *you* may have the kind of sick sense of humor that would plan this, but Emily does not.'

Devon cleared his throat and looked at his perfectly polished shoes. 'No, of course not. Sorry. I tend to get facetious under stress. I can't seem to help it.'

'No need for you to feel stressed. You're not under suspicion this time. That is, unless you had some connection with the victim I don't know about?'

'Me? Heavens, no. I didn't know she existed until yesterday, when Emily rang to warn us about her.' He smiled brightly.

Was that smile a little too bright? He let it pass – this was Devon, after all. 'OK. So I need to know from you whether you saw or heard anything suspicious in the course of the evening – anything that seemed off in any way, anything that could shed light on this business.'

'Well, I think Veronica already told you what Cruella said about the amaretto.'

'She did.'

'Other than that . . . I really can't think of anything.'

'How about when your team was waiting around for the charades to start? Anybody go near the bar shelf then?'

'Not that I saw.'

'Anybody alone in the library at any point that you know of?'

'How would I know if I wasn't there with them?'

'You might have gone out and left one person behind, or come back in and seen only one person there.'

'Oh, yes, of course. But no, I didn't. I was in there most of the time myself; I only nipped out for a tick to use the loo. Except for when the lights went out – I went into the hall then, along with practically everyone else, apparently.'

'Who was there when you left for the restroom?'

'Oh dear, let me think.' Devon put his hand to his brow in a theatrical gesture. 'I *believe* Oscar was there. And that unpleasant woman, Wanda – I think she was lurking in one of those wing chairs by the fire. That *might* be all – or was Ian there too? I'm sorry, I really can't remember.'

'And when you came back?'

'Hmm – those three plus Emily, I think. And Olivia came in right after me.'

'So that's the whole gang.' Luke blew out a long breath. 'Looks like no joy on that front. All right, Devon, you can go. I need to talk to Wanda, and then I'll get Pete to drive you all home.'

Luke ushered Devon back to the library and called for Wanda. She didn't answer right away, and Luke couldn't see her. Emily gestured toward the wing chair opposite her, and then Luke noticed the silver high heels propped up on the ottoman. He moved around to face the chair.

Wanda sat motionless with her eyes closed. Was it really possible for anybody to fall asleep in the middle of a murder investigation?

'Wanda?' No response. He touched her arm. 'Ms Wilkins?'

She jerked and her eyelids sprang open. 'What? What's happening?'

'I'd like to talk to you in the dining room, please.'

'What, now?'

'Yes, now. I've talked to all the others who aren't staying here in the house, and I'm hoping to get you all home before too long.'

'Well, that's a relief. This is a good chair, but I wouldn't want to spend the night in it.' She levered herself up, smoothed the back of her hair, and gave him a flirtatious smile that sat appallingly on her aging, overly made-up face. 'At your service, Lieutenant.'

When Luke did not respond to the smile, it vanished in an instant. He waved her ahead of him and watched her hip-swinging walk out with a puzzled frown. Luke considered himself a pretty good judge of character in general, but he couldn't seem to peg this woman. Curt and sarcastic one minute, flirting the next, and seemingly unconcerned about the murder in their midst. Maybe this interview would clear things up.

He eased into it by getting her full name and address and the name of the high school where she taught, in Corvallis. Then he said, 'You're kind of an unknown quantity compared to the other people here. Did you have any kind of connection with Cruella Crime?'

Wanda examined her long, blood-red sparkly nails and picked a stray bit of polish off her cuticle. 'Never met the woman before. Tried to read one of her books once. Not a bad writer, but she got the science all wrong. Couldn't finish it.'

'Science?'

'It was about a poisoning case. She claimed the victim died instantly from ingesting arsenic. That doesn't happen. It's long and extremely messy.'

Luke knew that from personal experience – not of being poisoned himself, but of seeing someone die that way. In fact, it was not impossible arsenic had been the cause of Cruella's death, though it would have taken an impressive amount to finish her off that quickly.

'So you've made a study of these things?'

She gave him a withering look. 'I teach chemistry. It's my job to know how chemicals work. Whether they're poisons, acids, explosives, or completely harmless.'

'Right. So you have no time for people who get science wrong.'

'No.' She smiled her signature sardonic smile – the one she alternated with the flirty version. 'But I don't go so far as to murder them.'

Luke cleared his throat. 'Let's go over your movements this evening, shall we?'

'What's to go over? I was with the group the entire time.'

'You never went off by yourself? Not even to the restroom?'

'Oh, yes, I suppose I did go to the restroom. Right after dinner. And again while we were waiting for your team to prepare the charades.'

'Were you alone in the library at any time?'

'Not that I know of. I holed up in that lovely chair, and I

may have dropped off at some point, so I can't be sure what
the others were doing.'

'And when you went to the restroom – you didn't leave
anybody alone, or find anybody alone when you came back?'

'No. Those two writers – Ian and . . . Lydia? – were there
together when I left and when I came back.' She smirked.
'Very much together when I came back.'

So Luke's instinct about that had been correct. 'And what
about when the lights went out? What did you do then?'

'I stayed put, of course. There was obviously nothing I
could do, and I wasn't about to go barging around in the dark
tripping over things. I might have broken a heel.'

'Right.' Might have broken a heel – never mind an ankle.
Luke still couldn't make this woman out. Without being
deliberately obstructive, she was managing to give him no
help at all.

'I guess that's all then, Ms Wilkins. Unless there's anything
you'd like to tell me? Anything you might have seen or heard
that seemed suspicious at all?'

'I'm afraid I'm lamentably unobservant, Lieutenant. Except
in my laboratory, of course.'

Luke stood. 'That's it for tonight, then. I'll get my deputy
to drive you back to your cottage. But I will have to ask you
not to leave town until I give you permission.'

She cocked an eyebrow. 'Or until the weather gives me
permission. That doesn't seem likely to happen any time soon.'

Luke went back to the library and sent Devon and Hilary,
Veronica, and Wanda off with Pete. 'Jamie, I don't think there's
any way we can get you to Tillamook tonight. Emily, you'll
have to find him a couch or something.'

Jamie colored deeply. 'Actually, Katie said I could sleep at
her place.' Too quickly, he added, 'On the couch, of course.'

'That's covered, then. I can wait till morning to talk to the
two of you. You can go on over there if you want.'

Jamie relaxed his vigilance over the bar shelf with obvious
relief, and he and Katie left the room holding hands. Luke
summoned Marguerite into the dining room.

This was going to be a tricky interview. As a conscientious

lawman, he couldn't ignore the fact that the amaretto had been a gift to Emily from Marguerite. Theoretically, if the poison had been in the bottle, Marguerite would have had the best opportunity of anyone to put it there.

On the other hand, Marguerite was Emily's oldest friend – other than himself – and although she could be peculiar, her affection for Emily seemed genuine. Luke knew she'd inherit something in Emily's will, but Emily had already been generous to her in life; if Marguerite needed money, she'd only have to ask. And he didn't see her being too proud to do that.

On top of all that, if he were to offend Marguerite by even seeming to suspect her, she'd be bound to carry the tale straight back to Emily. And then they'd be right where they'd been in the last case, when Katie's position had been so precarious.

'Damned if you do and damned if you don't,' he muttered to himself as he shut the dining room door behind Marguerite.

He started off with a friendly smile. 'We'll get this over with as quick as possible, Marguerite. I'm mainly interested in anything you may have seen or heard, but for form's sake, I have to ask – can you be one hundred percent certain the amaretto bottle was sealed when you gave it to Emily?'

Marguerite's well-trained eyebrows went up like the McDonald's arches – a comparison she would have disdained. Make that the Arc de Triomphe times two. '*Bien sûr*, it was sealed. I made sure of that when I bought it, and I checked it again when I wrapped it. I would not give my friend a bottle that might have been tampered with.'

'Right. That's what I figured, but I had to ask. You understand.' He cleared his throat. If Marguerite felt like lying, she could probably do it as convincingly as anyone he knew; but everything he'd observed about her said she loved Emily like a sister. He'd take her word on this point.

'OK, then. Did you see anybody touch the bottle at any point? Besides Emily, I mean.'

'*Non*, and I watched it like, how would you say, the hawk. That Cruella, she heard me say to Emily that she should keep it for herself, and several times I saw her go close, trying to sneak a drink. But I was there before her.' She gave a self-satisfied smile.

'That was before dinner?'

'*Oui*, and when we passed through afterwards on the way to the parlor to sing. After that, you know, I was not in the library at all.'

'Right. Now I know when we planned our second scene, Cruella said she was going to have the sherry brought in and drink some, but she didn't mention the amaretto. Did you have any idea she was going to use that too?'

'*Pas du tout.* I would never have allowed it had I known. And Cruella, she knew that. That is why she did it sneakily, behind my back.'

Luke drummed his pencil on his notebook. 'So nobody could have known for sure she was going to drink the amaretto.'

'I do not see how they could. *Non.*'

'Right. That pretty much takes it down to poison in the glass after the tray went into the parlor. While the lights were out.'

'*Oui.* That is, if the poison was really meant for Cruella.'

He glanced up at her sharply. 'You thought of that too, huh?'

'*Mais oui, c'est évident, n'est-ce pas?* Someone could have meant the poison for Emily.'

Surely she wouldn't have pointed that out if she'd been the one who'd so meant it. He breathed an internal sigh of relief. 'Any idea who might want to . . . harm Emily?' He couldn't use the words 'kill' or 'murder' and 'Emily' in the same breath.

She gave an eloquent shrug. 'Who knows? Those who benefit by her will are all her close friends, *non? Moi*, Katie, you yourself. None of us would harm her.' Her pixie mouth curved into a sly smile and she leaned across the table toward him. 'Perhaps the financial aid people at Reed are overanxious for their scholarship fund. Perhaps they sent Oscar down here to hurry it along.'

He gave a wry grin. He couldn't claim to like Oscar, but he wouldn't suspect him on that basis. 'What about personal reasons? Emily ever have any enemies you know of?'

'Emily? Enemies?' Marguerite threw her hands wide.

'*Mais, mon cher, elle est la femme la plus aimable du monde! Non*, she has no enemies. Some are jealous of her good fortune, *oui*, but not so as to kill her. Especially since they would not benefit themselves. Now, if it were *I* who was threatened . . .' She waved an elegant arm as if to suggest her own legions of enemies might be lurking in the walls.

'All right. I'm going on the assumption Cruella was the target, for now. Back to the blackout – did you see anyone go into the parlor at that point?'

'See? One could not see one's hand before one's face!'

'That's not quite true. There was a little light from the fireplaces and my flashlight. But what I meant was were you in any way aware of anyone going in?'

'*Non*. I was not near the parlor door. I was up beyond the bend of the stairs.'

'Right. OK, I think that's it for now. You can go on to bed if you want.'

'I may go to my room. But to sleep when there is such excitement in the house? *Impossible!*'

Excitement. Trust Marguerite to see the presence of a murderer in their midst – possibly even threatening her own best friend – as excitement. He'd save his excitement for when the murderer was found.

FIFTEEN

After the locals were sent home, Emily and Oscar were left alone in the library. Oscar paced in front of the bay window, twisting his hands. 'I wish he'd call me and get it over with. Why did he have to leave me for last?'

'I think he wanted to talk to the obvious suspects first, and then the local people so they could leave.'

'But why take Marguerite ahead of me? She's got to be the least suspect of all. I mean, she's your friend and everything.'

'Probably just the women-and-children-first idea. Calm down, Oscar. You have nothing to worry about. Let me get you some sherry.' She turned to the bar shelf, then remembered. 'Oh, right, we're not supposed to touch that stuff. Sorry. Coffee?'

'Heavens, no, I'm much too wired already.' He plopped on the window seat. 'Wired and exhausted at the same time.'

Emily sat beside him, concerned for his mood. Of all the guests here tonight – with the possible exception of Olivia – he seemed the most affected by the murder, which made no sense to her. 'Oscar, please don't be offended, but I can't help wondering why you're so upset. It's not as if Cruella were a friend of yours.' She remembered his reaction back on his first day here when Luke had mentioned murder in Stony Beach. 'Have you been – somehow involved in a murder before? Do you have bad associations?'

Oscar sat up straight and stared at her. 'Listen to yourself, Emily. Bad associations? How could anyone have good associations with murder?'

'I didn't mean that, it's just—'

'A woman has been killed here tonight. OK, so she was a pretty nasty woman, and the world is probably better off without her. But if she was murdered, that means someone in this house is a murderer. Doesn't that bother you?'

Emily sighed deeply. Of course it bothered her. How could she explain that she'd been through all this before? It had made her – not blasé, exactly, but it had certainly taken the edge off the horror of it all. Especially since this time she'd been spared the sight of the body. 'The thing is, Oscar, it's not as if any of the rest of us had anything to fear. Cruella – not to put too fine a point on it, but she was practically begging to be murdered. Whoever killed her would have no reason to kill anyone else. Unless someone else could implicate the killer, which doesn't appear to be the case.'

She stared at Oscar, seized by a new thought. 'Oscar, did *you* see something? Is that what's bothering you? Do you have some idea who killed her?'

'Me? Of course not. I would have said.' He spoke quickly, nervously, not meeting her eyes.

'If you do know anything, you've got to tell Luke right away. You realize that's your only protection, don't you? Once Luke knows, the killer will have no reason to go after you.'

'I know that. Of course I do. I read mysteries too, you know.' He gave a wry grin. 'There's always some idiot who tries to blackmail the murderer, isn't there? How do they not get that once a person has killed, he's even more likely to kill again?' He dropped his eyes. 'Or she.'

Emily took Oscar's hand and stroked it as she would with a child, to calm him. 'Don't worry, Oscar. Nothing's going to happen to you. Luke's here to make sure of that.'

And right on cue, the hall door opened and Luke came in. His gaze went immediately to Oscar's hand encased in hers, and his ocean-gray eyes turned to black. Lovely. She'd done it again.

Luke had been too preoccupied with the investigation to think about his jealousy until that moment. But seeing Emily sitting there so calmly, holding Lansing's hand, brought it back full-force and then some. Her words said one thing, and her actions said another. In his world, it was actions that counted.

But he was damned if he was going to let her see how much her actions hurt him. He kept his voice plumb-even as he said, 'I'd like to talk to you now, Oscar.'

The man visibly blanched at these words, though he had to be expecting them. What was up with this guy? He was skittish as a thoroughbred, though Luke couldn't see any reason he needed to be. Could be his basic personality, but Luke made a mental note to do a more thorough check on his background.

In the dining room, he waved Lansing to a chair. 'Coffee?'

'No thanks. I wouldn't turn down a brandy, though.' Oscar glanced toward the decanter on the sideboard.

Luke examined him narrowly, noting the tremor of his hands as well as his pallor, and decided a little brandy might do him good. He poured two fingers' worth into a snifter and handed it to him.

Oscar took a long sip, then cradled the snifter in both hands, swirling the brandy and watching its legs drip down the inside of the glass. 'Thanks. That hits the spot.'

Luke did battle with the beast in him that wanted to attack this man who seemed out to steal his woman. He was on the job now, and he had to be objective. In the end he overcompensated a little and took on a fatherly tone.

'Now, Oscar, I want you to know I've got no reason to hold you under suspicion at this point. So you can relax, OK? I need your mind open so you can remember anything that might help me out.'

Oscar nodded. 'I'll try.'

'First of all, to be absolutely clear: did you ever have any kind of contact or connection with Cruella before she came here?'

'No. I'd heard of her, but frankly her books are the kind of thing I wouldn't read if I were alone on a desert island with them.'

'Understandable. So apart from her general unpleasantness, you had no personal animosity toward her?'

'No. I was annoyed with her because she was causing trouble for Emily, but that's all.'

Again, Luke fought down the beast. It was *his* business to protect Emily, damn it, not this pipsqueak's. He won the internal battle and plowed on.

'So let's look back on your movements today. Were you away from the group at any time?'

'Not for long. I went up to my room at one point – I think it was while we were waiting for the second charade. I had to take some medication. But I was only gone for a minute or two.'

'You didn't go to the restroom at any time?'

'Yes, on the same trip. I used the toilet upstairs since I was already there. The downstairs one seemed to be in pretty high demand.'

'Run into anyone else on your way?'

'I saw Dustin. I think he'd just come down from the third floor. He went down the main stairs ahead of me.'

'Right, we know about that. OK. Where were you when the lights went out?'

'Back in the library.'

'Go anywhere while it was dark?'

'No. I stayed put. I . . . I'm not very good in the dark.'

Luke hid a smirk. 'To your knowledge, was anybody alone in the library at any time?'

Oscar sipped his brandy, his hands shaking harder now. 'Not that I know of.'

'Did you see anybody go near the bar?'

His eyes widened like a startled animal's. 'No. Never.'

Luke frowned. Oscar was lying, obviously, and he wasn't used to it. But why? Who among this lot would he be concerned to protect?

Only Emily. But Emily was out of the question.

Maybe it wasn't protection but fear of reprisal. 'Listen to me very carefully, Oscar. If you saw anything suspicious, you have to tell me. For your own sake as much as for the truth. Do you understand that?'

Oscar nodded, not meeting Luke's eyes.

'If you're afraid of somebody, you've got to understand the safest thing you can possibly do is to tell me everything you know. I'm staying right here, and I will protect you. I'll sleep across your doorway if need be.'

Oscar's mouth twitched into a fleeting smile. 'Thank you, Lieutenant. But there's nothing. I'm not afraid of anybody. Honest.'

Luke took a deep breath and steeled himself. 'The same

thing applies if you're protecting somebody. The truth is going to come out, one way or another, whether you tell me what you know or not. And if it turns out you've withheld vital information, it's possible you could be charged as an accessory after the fact. You do understand that?'

Oscar turned even paler, beyond white to gray. But he only shook his head.

Luke fumed in silence. He'd shot his whole arsenal, and this fellow who looked like a pushover had not yielded an inch. What on earth could be going on? Could he have developed a crush on Olivia and be protecting her? She was a looker, no doubt about that, and nearer Oscar's age than Emily was. And though he hadn't fully sussed it out yet, it looked like Olivia could have a motive for murder.

Well, Oscar wasn't going anywhere, and it was clear Luke wasn't getting anywhere with him tonight. Might as well let him stew for a while. Nobody as freaked out as he was could stay silent forever.

Luke sent Oscar to bed but stayed on in the dining room. He couldn't face Emily right now, not after that scene he'd walked in on in the library, and his night's work was not yet done. He had to get reports from Sam, Heather, and Pete, who should be back from his chauffeur service by now.

He scrubbed his face with his hands, poured himself another cup of coffee, and went into the front hall. He called up the stairs to Heather. 'Done up there yet?'

'All finished, boss, be right down.'

The three of them trooped into the dining room a minute later. 'Help yourselves to coffee.' He'd taken the cups and glasses used by the various interviewees and placed each one in a labeled evidence bag for fingerprint purposes. But he didn't honestly expect fingerprints would turn out to be helpful in this case. Everybody's prints would be all over everything after a party like tonight's.

'You first, Sam. What's your analysis of the cause of death?'

'Analysis?' She snorted. 'Funny man. Analysis needs a lab and a slab. Only guesses here.'

'All right, your guesses, then.'

'Right, but don't quote me. Time of death we know. Cause of death, almost certainly some kind of poison. My money's on cyanide, but there are other options.'

'We talking murder, then?'

Sam shrugged. 'Your call. No way to tell how the poison was administered. Accident, suicide, homicide – all possible at this point.'

'Surely nobody would commit suicide like that. She was in agony.'

'Wouldn't think so. Might've thought it'd be quicker – cyanide usually is in the movies. And people do strange things. Want to punish themselves for something. Who knows.'

'Not Cruella. Her name says it all – she was cruel to other people, not to herself.'

'Like I said, your call.'

'So of those other options that might have caused it – any of them ordinary household stuff? Or could be made from?'

'Could be. Drain cleaner, ammonia, rat poison. All look different on the inside, but outside you can't really tell.'

He turned to Pete and Heather. 'You two find any of that stuff?'

'Sure thing,' Pete said. 'All three, in fact. Drain cleaner in the bathroom, ammonia in the kitchen, rat poison in the attic.'

'Any of them look like they'd been tampered with recently?'

'I'd say no on the rat poison; the tin was pretty solidly stuck shut. The drain cleaner and the ammonia were partially used, but I couldn't say how recently. Got them all bagged up for you.'

'Good. I don't know when we'll be able to get all this stuff to the lab. Or the body to the morgue, for that matter. Guess we better stick her in the basement for now, where it's cooler. Pete and Heather, can you rig up some sort of table to put her on?'

'Sure, boss. There's already something down there. Workbench or some such. We'll clean it off.'

'Right. What about the bedrooms? Find anything there?'

'Nothing suspicious,' Heather replied. 'Just normal guest stuff and writer stuff. I collected all their phones and computers in case you want to go through those.'

'Good work. I'll get on that in the morning. Might find some connection we don't know about. Get the key to that little front office from Emily and secure the electronics in there, please, Heather.'

She nodded and left the room.

'I think we're done here for tonight. Sam, you be able to get home OK?'

'Yeah, I've got chains.'

'Pete, I need you and Heather back here first thing. We'll have to search outside the house in daylight.'

Not that he expected to find anything there. He had a feeling this case would have to be solved on psychology rather than physical evidence. And that was where Emily's intuition had proved invaluable in the past. He was going to have to work with her if he was to have any hope of solving this case.

If only she'd agree to work with him. Permanently.

SIXTEEN

Everyone in the house except Luke slept late the next morning; when Emily got up, the loveseat was already folded up with the bedding stacked neatly on top. Where in happier times she might have seen that neatness as loving consideration, in the light of last night's events it looked like an attempt to leave as invisible a footprint on her space as possible. Like Luke pretending he hadn't been there at all.

Emily herself got up reluctantly and groggily. She'd had a terrible time getting to sleep the night before. The immediate shock of a murder in the house might have been slightly lessened by prior experience, and she certainly was not mourning Cruella personally; but nevertheless, the situation caused a severe strain on her nerves. Every time she'd felt herself starting to drift off, she'd been startled awake again by some sinister-sounding noise. She yawned her way through her grooming routine and finally trudged downstairs.

In the dining room she found only Marguerite. 'The others wished to eat in their rooms,' she told Emily. '*Moi*, I came down to keep company with *les chats*.' At Emily's look she added, 'And with you, of course, *chérie*. Now that you are here.'

Emily helped herself from the sideboard, taking only coffee, a spoonful of scrambled eggs, and a half-slice of toast with Katie's homemade blackberry jam; food didn't seem terribly appealing.

'We didn't get a chance to talk last night. What do you make of all this?'

'*C'est évident, n'est-ce pas?* Cruella made some threat to the fair Olivia, and the so devoted, so manly and charming Ian, he has avenged her.'

'You seem awfully sure about that.'

'*Mais oui*, how could it be otherwise? Olivia, she has not the temperament to murder; she is a martyr, that one. And

Dustin – *pfft*! He has no more gumption than a drunken snail. He had something against her, *évidemment*, but to take the decisive action – *non*, that is beyond his power.'

'But if it was Ian, how would he have known Cruella would drink the amaretto? Or drink out of that particular glass? Only her charades team could have known that.'

'*Mais chérie*, did you not know? Veronica told me she heard Cruella boast that she would get her hands on your amaretto, one way or another. And Ian heard her say it.'

Emily sat back in her chair as if pushed by an unseen hand. Luke must have known that and chosen not to tell her. Did he plan to shut her out of the investigation completely?

And then, too: 'Wouldn't Ian have been afraid someone else might drink the amaretto before Cruella got to it? Me, for instance? I can't see him being callous enough to take that chance.'

Marguerite shrugged. 'We do not know the poison was in the bottle. More likely it was in the glass.'

'I suppose, but even so . . . My money's still on Dustin. It's true he's spineless, but poison is a coward's weapon, after all. Ian is no coward.'

Marguerite shook her head sagely. 'He is not a coward, but he is clever. Shrewd. He would know poison would be the way to leave the least evidence behind. No bloodstains, no weapon to conceal, no marks on him at all. And he must not be caught, because that would leave his beloved Olivia unprotected. *Écoute-moi, chérie*. It is Ian. I am certain.'

She took a long drink of her café au lait. 'Not that I blame him, *tu comprends*. That woman was a menace. We are all much better off without her. And Olivia, she is *une femme pour assassiner* – a woman to kill for. *Non*, I do not blame him at all.'

Emily knew there was no point in arguing with Marguerite once her mind was made up. But she couldn't keep her thoughts to herself this morning, and it seemed unlikely Luke would care to hear them. 'I don't think it's that simple. This whole thing feels so much like an Agatha Christie novel, and her plots are never that simple. There's always some weird wrinkle – either the method isn't what it appears to be, or the people aren't who they appear to be, or what looks like murder isn't really murder at all. This feels like that.'

She pondered as she chewed her toast. 'I know – what about this? Cruella obviously had it in for Ian and Olivia; I agree with you that far. What if she committed suicide in such a way as to throw suspicion on Ian in order to punish him and break them up permanently?'

Marguerite actually took a minute to consider this. 'You know, *chérie*, it is possible you have something there. Cruella was that cruel and that devious. But to sacrifice her own life for the sake of her revenge – is it not more likely she would have killed, *par exemple*, Dustin, and then thrown the blame on Ian?'

'Maybe she couldn't figure out a failsafe way to do that. She might be willing to die for her revenge but not to go to prison for it. Or maybe she didn't plan to actually die but miscalculated the dose.'

'Mmm . . .' Marguerite shrugged. '*Peut-être*. But I still prefer my theory.' She turned her attention to her newspaper and calmly finished her breakfast.

Emily gave up on eating and stared absently out the window, coffee cup at her lips. Suddenly a man's blond head popped up over the shrubbery and she started, sloshing coffee into her saucer. Then she recognized Pete and relaxed. A protector, not a threat. They must be searching the outside of the house.

While Pete and Heather searched the perimeter of the house, Luke set to work on the guests' phones and laptops, using his own phone to create a WiFi hotspot, since Emily was still living in the Stone Age with no internet. He started with Dustin, who'd left both phone and laptop turned on and unprotected by passwords.

First Luke searched for any mention of poison or cyanide in Dustin's browsing history, but found nothing. When he could get into the office, he'd have to look at his credit card records. And, for that matter, it might be worth checking out his history as Billy Williams as well. If the connection with Cruella went back that far, there could be more to their story than Dustin was telling him.

Next he searched for any mention of Cruella and found a series of emails and phone messages that confirmed what Dustin had admitted about the blackmail. She'd also been trolling his Facebook author page using a variety of false identities – at least, they all sounded like Cruella. He'd check her laptop, too, to make sure.

He'd been wondering all along how Cruella had found out that Dustin and the others would be at Windy Corner this week. Emily didn't exactly advertise her guest list. But when he looked at Dustin's author page, that question was answered. He'd posted a few days before his arrival, *Heading to the brand-new, super posh Windy Corner Writers' Retreat Center in Stony Beach for some much-needed R&R. Be good little boys and girls while I'm gone.* He'd even listed the names of the other people who would be here. That explained how Cruella knew about Alex Gordon. Maybe she'd even bribed him not to come.

Luke shook his head. It never ceased to amaze him how stupid people could be with social media. Could Dustin seriously not have realized that all those trolls were Cruella, and that she might see the post and decide to follow him? Well, that was one mystery explained, anyhow. And it also brought up the possibility that Dustin had in fact suspected all along that Cruella might follow him – he might even have deliberately lured her here in order to kill her. He could have had the poison with him, after all.

Ian's and Olivia's devices were password-protected, so Luke had to ask their permission to search them. Both agreed with fairly good grace, no doubt realizing how bad it would look to refuse. In both their cases, Luke could find traces of harassment that had been dealt with promptly – email addresses hacked and changed, and (in Olivia's case; Ian had no Facebook page) trolling identities on Facebook recognized and blocked. They'd both managed to keep their phone numbers private, apparently, as he could find no trace of voice or text messages that might have been from Cruella.

Luke couldn't see the content of any of the erased email or Facebook messages, so he still didn't know exactly what Cruella's persecution of Olivia was based on. But it wasn't difficult to guess. She'd probably blamed the breakup of her marriage to Ian on his relationship with Olivia. Whether they'd actually been having an affair at that time or not was pretty much irrelevant; it was Cruella's perception of the situation that mattered.

Luke sat back in his chair, rubbing the back of his neck. How would a woman like Olivia respond to persecution like that? Would it be enough to break her, make her want to fight back? Somehow he didn't think so. She seemed more like the type who might commit suicide to escape the bullying than the type who would resort to murder.

But what about Ian? He obviously loved Olivia and was strongly protective of her. Luke could imagine him murdering Cruella to save Olivia, though he might not go that far on his own account.

Luke searched for any online evidence that Ian might have suspected Cruella would follow him to Windy Corner, but found nothing. Ian didn't even have a Facebook author page or an author website or blog. Probably got tired of fans asking him when his next book was coming out.

Olivia had an active online presence – as a prolific author with a major publisher, she'd be required to – but her posts were discreet and impersonal, focused on her characters and the world of her books along with publishing and speaking news. She certainly hadn't mentioned Windy Corner.

As a formality, Luke did a quick search for 'Cruella' on Marguerite's and Oscar's computers but came up blank. Oscar appeared to have few friends and little social life. All his files were related to his work at Reed or his thesis, and he had no Facebook page. In his personal email account and on his phone, Luke saw message after message from 'mom1026', every single one of them answered.

Luke smirked. Oscar was a mama's boy, all right. That alone might account for his nervousness – he'd never left the nest and learned to fly on his own. He was probably in his room crying for his mommy right now. Maybe Luke should return Oscar's phone so he could call her – he might calm down after that.

A cursory glance at Marguerite's messages revealed nothing

pertinent to the case, but it did hint strongly at an impressively active love life. Luke got out of there fast before he could yield to the temptation to read what didn't concern him.

He saved Cruella's devices for last. Here he found himself blocked from square one – she'd logged out of her user account, and none of the obvious password options he tried worked. He'd have to get this laptop and phone to the tech people in Tillamook to see if they could crack them. And that would have to wait for a thaw.

After breakfast, Emily felt her duty as a hostess nagging at her. Her house was full of guests whom she hadn't seen since a traumatic series of events the night before. She felt the need to check on them, though what she could possibly do to help any of them, she had no idea.

She knocked on Dustin's door – on the principle of 'eat the liver first' – but got no answer. Then she discerned the sound of snoring. He must still be sleeping off his overindulgence of the night before. Upstairs, she crossed the hall to Oscar's door and knocked. He opened it at once, as if he'd been expecting someone, but then his eyes darted past her to the stairs.

'Oh, hi, Emily. I was hoping the sheriff would be returning my phone and computer. Do you have any idea how long he'll be? I can't get anything done without my laptop.' Reasonable as that sounded, Oscar was still so nervous that Emily wondered whether his desire to write was really what was so pressing.

'I'm afraid I have no idea. I didn't even know he had them.' Again, Luke's lack of communication with her about the case bit deep. 'I'll see if I can find him and ask.' She surveyed Oscar's uncharacteristically disheveled appearance – hair lank and unwashed, cheeks unshaven above his goatee, clothes rumpled as if he'd slept in them – and asked, 'Are you all right? Is there anything I can do for you, get for you?'

He shook his head briskly. 'No, no. There's nothing you can do.' Then he seemed to recollect himself and smiled, returning his face to normal. 'I'm fine, really. But thank you.'

'Let me know if you think of anything, OK?' She wanted to lay a reassuring hand on his arm but stopped herself. It would be just her luck for Luke to come up the stairs at that moment and misinterpret the situation, as usual. Everything she did only seemed to dig her in deeper with him.

She moved on to Ian's door and knocked. He answered looking strained and tired, with shadows under his eyes, but as carefully put together as always. He graciously thanked Emily for her concern but insisted he needed nothing from her. 'I found a good book in your library,' he said, holding up a first edition of Christie's *Ten Little Indians*. 'I'll be fine. I am concerned about Olivia, though. If you wouldn't mind looking in on her?' A shadow crossed his handsome features. 'She didn't seem to want my company this morning.'

'Of course.' Emily gave Ian a reassuring smile and moved next door to the Montgomery room.

At her knock a faint voice called, 'Who is it?'

'It's Emily. Just checking whether you need anything.'

She heard the creak of bedsprings and rustle of fabric, then a moment later Olivia opened the door, wearing a negligée worthy of Ginger Rogers. But her hair was unbrushed, her normal pallor had turned translucent, and her eyes looked bruised; the skin was stretched taut over her high cheekbones. 'Come in, please. I need to sit down.'

She sank into the wicker armchair and motioned Emily toward the fabric-covered stool at the dressing table. 'I'm so exhausted I can hardly speak, yet I can't sleep. I keep thinking of—' She broke off with a shudder.

'Let me call Dr Griffiths. I'm sure she could give you something to help you sleep.'

'I don't want to give you any trouble. I'll be all right.'

Emily doubted that. 'At least let Katie make you some chamomile tea. That's always relaxing.'

Olivia gave an enervated nod. 'Yes, all right. Tea sounds good.'

Emily stepped to the intercom and called down to the kitchen. 'Right away, Mrs C,' Katie replied cheerfully. At least there was one person in the house Emily didn't need to worry about. Well, two, counting Marguerite.

Emily returned to her stool and leaned toward her guest. 'Olivia, please don't think me callous or anything, but it seems like Cruella was the one person in the world you had most reason to hate. Don't you feel some – well, relief – that she's out of the way and can't pester you anymore?'

Olivia gave a hoot of dark laughter that startled Emily with its vehemence. 'Pester! Is that what you call it? Emily, that woman ruined my life! And Ian's as well.'

'I'm sorry, I didn't know. I was only speaking of what I could see here in the last few days.' She hesitated, then took the plunge. 'Would you like to talk about it?'

'Maybe that would help . . .'

Olivia trailed off as a knock came at the door. Katie must have had water hot already, because she stood there with fully equipped tea tray in hand. 'I thought a little something to eat might help as well,' she said, indicating a trio of chocolate truffles on a paper doily.

'Thanks, Katie,' Emily said as she took the tray. 'You think of everything.'

She poured a cup and handed it to Olivia, who blew on it to cool it and then sipped. 'That's better.' She nibbled at one of the truffles. 'Much better.' She even managed a pale smile. 'So you want the story of my life?'

'Only if you want to tell it,' Emily put in hastily. 'I don't want to pry.'

'I think I've been waiting for someone like you to tell it to for years. I knew when I first saw you that you were a kindred spirit.' She smiled to reinforce the reference to the writer for whom her room was named.

'It all started quite a few years ago. I met Ian and Cruella together – would you believe he was married to her at one time?'

Emily started. Although Marguerite had floated the idea early on, she'd never been able to absorb it. 'Really?'

'She was actually sort of attractive back then, in a kind of gypsy, tantalizing way, I suppose. Ian said she'd bewitched him, but it didn't take him long to wake up from her spell. By the time I met them he was already miserable with her.'

'And so he naturally fell in love with you.'

'Not right away. At least, he resisted it as long as he could. But we were thrown together a lot – we were both on the board of the Mystery Writers of America, active in the New York chapter, so we couldn't help seeing each other. Eventually we had to admit we were in love.'

Olivia's dreamy expression suggested she was lost in pleasant memories. To recall her, Emily said, 'And Cruella found out?'

'She assumed it before it even happened. And assumed we were having an affair when we weren't. She was terribly jealous where Ian was concerned, always. Every attractive woman he met was a threat.' Olivia raised her cup to her lips and saw what Emily had just noticed herself – a spider crawling on the saucer. Emily cringed away – she couldn't stand spiders – but Olivia calmly set her cup down, carried the saucer to the window, opened it a crack, and tipped the spider gently out on to the sill.

Emily swallowed her discomfiture. 'So Cruella blamed you for their breakup?'

'She did. But I wasn't responsible for their divorce – Ian had already started proceedings before we even met.' She sighed miserably. 'The thing is, if it hadn't been for me, she might not have put up such a fight. I think she was tired of Ian herself by that time – as long as she got a good settlement out of him, she would have been happy. But once I came on the scene, she started fighting for him like a she-tiger. She couldn't stand to see him happy with someone else.'

'He did get the divorce eventually, though?'

'Oh yes, he got it. But at a terrible cost.'

'Financially, you mean?'

Olivia waved a languid hand. 'The money was nothing. She milked him, all right, but Ian had plenty of family money she couldn't touch. No, she took her revenge where it really hurt.' Olivia closed her eyes and took a deep, shuddering breath. 'She killed his writing.'

Emily was shocked and baffled at the same time. 'How could she do that?'

'She stole the best idea he'd ever had and twisted it

beyond recognition. She made it laughable, really pitiably bad.' She looked down and her voice went small. 'And she put me in the book too. That was what Ian ultimately could not forgive.'

Emily winced in empathy. 'I presume the portrait was unflattering.'

'You could say that.' Olivia's voice was dry enough to absorb her entire cup of tea. 'It was the worst kind of caricature, with just enough truth to make it recognizable and the rest as calumnious as even she could imagine. It nearly broke me.' She passed a hand over the streak of white hair at her temple. 'It gave me this.'

'Did you try suing her for libel?'

'That would only have called attention to it – all the world would have recognized the caricature instead of only the people who knew me. And Ian couldn't sue for plagiarism, because he had nothing in writing – the idea was all in his head. Believe me, he rued the day he ever spoke of it to Cruella.'

A moment of silence was called for at that point. But Emily was still curious. 'You say that killed Ian's writing – but you managed to keep on.'

'Eventually, yes. After I recovered from my nervous breakdown. My stiff-upper-lip British side pulled through and made me start over. You see, I couldn't let Cruella's victory be complete.' She gave a one-sided smile. 'But I've always thought I could have been a better writer, a deeper one, if she hadn't made me so gun-shy. I was always afraid of writing anything that might set her off again.'

Not for the first time, Emily marveled at the depth of malice the human soul could contain. If she'd been a pagan who believed in the evil spirits of the dead lingering near the place where they died, she would have had to move out of Windy Corner to escape the evil that was Cruella. 'So did you and Ian . . . get together after that?'

'No. She had poisoned our love. We never could get over it – at least I couldn't. We both moved away from New York and didn't see each other for years.' She looked up at Emily with tears in her eyes. 'Until now.'

Emily reached over and took Olivia's cold hands in her own. 'You still love each other, don't you?'

Olivia nodded. 'More than ever.'

'And he would do anything for you.'

She nodded again, then jerked her head up. 'But not kill. You don't know Ian. He would never kill.'

SEVENTEEN

Luke was closing Cruella's laptop when somebody knocked on the office door. At his 'Yeah?' Emily poked her head in and said, 'Do you have a minute?'

It almost softened him to see how tentative she was, like she was afraid he might bite her head off. But then he remembered her sitting there bold as brass holding Lansing's hand. He wouldn't bite – but it wouldn't hurt her to worry about it.

'Shoot.'

'I was just talking to Olivia.' When his brows shot up, she added hurriedly, 'I didn't mean to trespass on your territory or anything, but she wanted to talk, and I think she needed to talk to another woman. Nothing about the murder – only about their past. Hers and Ian's and Cruella's.'

He got to his feet, crowding her in the tiny space. 'Let's go in the library.'

He stood in front of the hearth while she sat in one of the wing chairs, having picked up Levin and settled him on her lap.

'Ian and Cruella were married a long time ago.'

'Yeah, he told me that much.'

She looked startled. 'Oh! Well, maybe you already know the whole story then.'

'He wouldn't say anything about Olivia. Did she break them up?'

'Don't rush me. She said it wasn't like that – Ian was already trying to get a divorce when they met. They fell in love, but they kept it platonic. But Cruella fought the divorce and blamed Olivia for everything.'

'Pretty much what I figured. Except the platonic part. Not sure I buy that anyway.'

'But you haven't heard the really bizarre bit yet.' She told him about Cruella trying to ruin both Ian's and Olivia's careers.

Luke whistled. 'Now there is a double motive for murder

if I ever heard one. Each of them wanting revenge, both for their own sake and for the other's. That woman was begging to be murdered.'

Emily bit her lip. 'Olivia was adamant Ian didn't do it. Wouldn't do it. And I really can't see Olivia killing anyone.' She shook her head as if in disbelief. 'Do you know, while we were talking, distraught as she was, she put a spider out the window rather than kill it?'

'Hmm. That shows compassion, but it also shows a cool head. I wouldn't rule Olivia out. She might not kill to avenge herself, but to avenge the man she loved . . . She still loves him? That the impression you got?'

'Absolutely. Devoted, I'd say.'

'Me too. Lot of high emotion running there. I'm not ruling either of them out.' He noticed the fire was burning less hot on his legs and turned to poke it up. Another thought was nagging at him, but he hesitated to let it in.

Then Emily spoke it for him. 'You know, Luke, if Cruella trashed Ian and Olivia in one of her books, she might have done the same to someone else. Maybe even someone who was here.'

He straightened and faced her. 'I was just thinking about that. I hate to say it, but it looks like somebody needs to read her books. At least skim them.'

Emily shuddered. 'Perish the thought. Although we are stuck here with not much to do until the weather breaks . . . But how would we even get hold of the books?'

'Yeah, that's a problem. She might have copies on her laptop, but I can't get into that yet.' He scratched the back of his neck. 'Wonder if anybody here's got an e-reader of some sort.'

'I think Katie has one.' Her voice went stiff with disapproval, and Luke smiled. To Emily, a book was made of paper and cardboard – or preferably leather – not of bits and bytes. Half of him wanted to drag her into the twenty-first century, kicking and screaming if need be, but the other half loved her exactly the way she was, with her old-fashioned courtesy, kindness, and respect for other people to match her old-fashioned taste and style.

'Perfect. I'll ask her.' He hesitated, knowing his next

request would stretch her sensibilities to their limits and beyond. 'Would you be willing to do some reading?'

She closed her eyes and took in a long breath. 'I guess so. If . . .'

'If . . .?'

'If you'll let me explain about last night. When you saw me with Oscar, it wasn't what it looked like. He was really upset, and I was trying to comfort him. Like a friend. Or a mother, even. It wasn't romantic at all, I promise you. I really and truly do not have that kind of feelings for him.'

He frowned at her. She seemed sincere, and Emily had never been the kind of woman to fudge the truth – except for that one time, but that was because Katie was involved. Katie brought out the mother tiger in Emily. Maybe it was true, she felt motherly toward Lansing too, despite the age difference being less than a full generation. He did seem like the kind of guy who badly needed a good mom.

'All right. Apology accepted.' She hadn't actually apologized, but he'd ignore that if she would.

Her smile lit up the room. She stood and came up close to him. 'Kiss and make up?'

He wasn't quite ready to go that far. 'Why, I'm surprised at you, ma'am. I'm an officer on duty.' He said it jokingly, but she stepped back, crestfallen. Fine. Let her stay in the doghouse a little longer. Maybe it would make her see reason about marrying him.

She started to leave the room, then turned back. 'Oh, I almost forgot. Oscar wanted me to ask you when he can have his phone and computer back. He can't get any writing done without them.'

Yeah, right. You mean he can't call Mommy and whine. 'I'm done. I'll take all the stuff back right now. It's only Cruella's I need to hang on to. Gotta send that one in to get hacked.'

'Did you find out anything interesting from the others?'

'Only confirming what I already knew. Oh, I did figure out how Cruella knew to come here. Dustin splashed it all over his Facebook page. Idiot. Trying to avoid a blackmailer and he puts his destination up for all the world to see.'

He saw the same realization he'd had dawn in Emily's eyes. 'Do you think he might have done that on purpose? To lure her here so he could kill her?'

'It's a possibility. One I need to check on very carefully.'

Luke went off to return the laptops and borrow Katie's e-reader, leaving Emily in the library, cautiously optimistic. She hadn't been fully restored to his good graces, but at least he'd accepted her explanation. And he wasn't shutting her out of the investigation. They could be partners on that level as before. Perhaps the rest would follow.

She was debating whether or not to make another attempt at Dostoevsky when she heard Dustin stumble out of his room and into the bathroom. A few minutes later he appeared in the doorway. 'Can't a fellow get anything to eat around here?' he grumbled. 'And close those curtains, can't you? That sun is blinding me.'

Emily glanced at the west-facing window, where the morning sun would not have been visible even without the solid gray cloud cover. 'Why don't you go in the dining room and I'll see if Katie can find you some breakfast. Everyone else finished some time ago.'

He shuffled off, still grumbling, and Emily went to the kitchen. 'Katie, can you find some breakfast for Dustin? Don't cook anything special – it's his own fault he missed out. I suspect he has the mother of all hangovers from the way he's acting.'

Katie made a disgusted face. 'I've got just the thing for hangovers. Plenty of practice with my dad.' She reached into the refrigerator and brought out a handful of eggs and a can of tomato juice. 'A Jeeves special, coming right up.'

'That's my girl.' She turned to go, then remembered. 'Did Luke ask you about borrowing your e-reader?'

She nodded. 'I told him where to find it. He can use my WiFi to download the books.'

Of course, Katie had WiFi at her apartment. Emily was always forgetting about that. 'Does your WiFi work here in the house?'

'Kind of. It's weak, but I can usually get a little signal in the rooms on this side of the house. Upstairs is better than down.'

Emily filed that information away for the future, in case a guest had a legitimate pressing need to get on the internet. She supposed such things did happen.

She waited a few minutes to allow the Jeeves special to be prepared, consumed, and take effect. Then she entered the dining room as quietly as she could manage.

'Is everything to your satisfaction?' she asked in her best Jeevesian voice.

'Mmph. Not a bad pick-me-up that girl came up with. Feel better already.'

'I'm so glad to hear it.'

Katie came in with a plateful of scrambled eggs and toast, which she set in front of Dustin. As he began to shovel them in, Emily said, 'I understand from Lieutenant Richards we have you to thank for Cruella descending on us this weekend.'

Dustin spluttered out a mouthful of coffee. 'What the hell do you mean by that? I've been trying to avoid that bitch for months. I sure as hell didn't invite her here.'

'No, but you did post about this retreat on your Facebook page – where she could easily have seen it.'

Dustin stared at her with what she could swear was pure astonishment. He picked up his jaw and mumbled, 'Hell. Never thought about that.'

No, this man did not seem like a clever, foresighted murderer who would lure his victim to an out-of-the-way place in order to do her in. He was a plain, shortsighted, self-absorbed idiot.

Emily returned to the library, and shortly afterward, Luke came in with Katie's e-reader. 'Got the books on here,' he said. 'Lucky for you she's a slow writer – only six of them. Given how long she's been at it, I expected about twenty.'

'Six is bad enough. You'll have to show me how to work this thing. Do you need special glasses or something?'

He laughed. 'Nothing like that.' He gave her a crash course in the device controls and opened the first book, *Quandary on Queer Street*. 'Go to town.'

She poised the reader between her fingertips as if it might

zap her with intelligence-draining rays. 'What am I looking for, exactly?'

'Can't tell you exactly. Anything that sounds like it might have anything to do with anybody who was here last night. You could start out by searching all the names, but chances are she'll have changed them.'

She groaned. 'Lord, give me strength.' This job had better put her firmly back in Luke's good graces, because it was going to be like picking through the cats' litter box by hand looking for the juiciest bits. She felt polluted already.

Luke came out of the library to find Pete in the hall looking for him. 'Hey, boss. We found something outside. Come and look.'

Luke shrugged into his sheepskin jacket and followed Pete outside. His deputy led the way around the west side of the house to the library windows. He pointed into the shrubbery under the small, working window around the corner from the fixed windows of the bay.

Nestled deep in the green needles was a tiny bottle.

Luke turned with his hand held out and, smooth as any OR nurse, Pete handed him a latex glove. Luke snapped it on and reached into the bush.

'There you are, you little beauty,' he murmured to the bottle. It was amber glass, about two inches high and half an inch wide, with a neck threaded for a cap, but the cap was missing. Luke held the bottle up to the light – empty. He brought it close to his nose, not right under, and wafted the vapors toward him with his ungloved left hand. A slight smell of bitter almonds met his nostrils.

Cyanide.

He thought back over Cruella's dying moments. The way her face was flushed, the vomiting and gasping for breath – all consistent with cyanide poisoning.

'I believe we have our murder weapon. Bag this and keep looking for the cap. Lab may have a hard time finding enough in the bottle to test. Oh, and be sure you print it before you send it off.' Chances were the murderer had handled the bottle with gloves on, but you never could tell. Some killers were so arrogant, so sure of not being caught, they didn't bother.

Luke shivered – the temperature was still below freezing, and he hadn't taken time to button up his coat. He walked around the bay window to the French doors and entered the library.

Emily looked up from her reading, startled. 'Luke! Don't scare me like that. We're all prone to seeing monsters in the shadows right now.'

'Sorry.' He moved to the fire, took off his coat, and draped it over a chair. 'Pete's made a discovery.'

'Oh?'

'Little amber vial in the shrubbery right outside that window.' He pointed across the room to where the bar shelf stood beside the window. 'Smells like cyanide.'

Emily stared. 'But that means—'

'Yup. It was planned.'

Her brow furrowed. 'I just talked to Dustin about him posting his plans on Facebook. I would swear in a court of law it had never occurred to him Cruella might see that and follow him.' She looked up at him. 'So where does that leave us?'

Luke frowned, hands on hips. His feeling of triumph at finding the bottle evaporated. 'That leaves us right back at square one.'

Emily wrapped her shawl tighter and shivered. 'There has to be something behind all this that we haven't seen yet. It really is like a Christie novel – layers on layers of connections and motivations.' One corner of her mouth went up in a wry smile. 'Any minute now, we're going to find out that somebody is somebody else's unacknowledged child. Christie used that trope at least a hundred times.'

She screwed up her eyes a minute, facing the bay window, then spun toward him, grinning. 'What do you want to bet it's Dustin and Cruella? She abandoned him as a baby and he's hated her ever since.'

He barked a laugh. 'Gotta admit, there is a family resemblance there. Almost want to say two people that obnoxious in the same part of the world have got to be related.'

'They'd get the Dysfunctional Family of the Year award, for sure.'

They shared a good laugh over that, and Luke reflected he

couldn't remember when they'd last laughed together that way. What kind of crazy relationship did they have that it took a murder investigation to break down the walls between them?

At Luke's request, Emily coaxed all the guests down to the dining room for lunch – even Dustin, who had breakfasted barely an hour before. 'I want to see how they all interact,' Luke said. 'See if I can figure out who Oscar's so afraid of, for one.'

Emily was quite curious about that herself. She lured them all with the promise of a delectable hot lunch that would cool and spoil if carried to their rooms, augmented by the argument that keeping themselves isolated would only add to the tension in the atmosphere. Fears and suspicions might dissipate in the open air of fellowship.

Ian seemed relieved to be asked; Oscar was only a little hesitant, and Olivia demurred merely because she needed time to dress. She said she had managed to get a little sleep after the chamomile tea and her talk with Emily, and she felt almost human again. Dustin was truculent, as always, but put up no serious fight.

Luke had suggested they keep the conversation neutral, so Emily started off by asking what good books each person had read lately. That was a topic guaranteed to be popular among writers – except Dustin, who apparently did not read as much as he watched TV.

'I've started reading Agatha Christie's *Ten Little Indians*,' Ian said cheerfully. 'Quite an extraordinary book, really. Haven't read it since I was a boy. Of course, now the title is *And Then There Were None*. They changed it because the reference to Indians wasn't considered PC.'

'Isn't that the one where ten people are stuck on an island and they all get killed off one by one?' Emily said. Then she heard a fork clatter and glanced across the table to see Oscar white and staring. Oh dear. Not the best topic of conversation.

'Completely unrealistic, of course,' she went on. 'That could never happen in real life. I mean, these days people wouldn't simply accept an invitation to a remote island from a stranger without checking into it first.'

That remark did not improve the situation. Windy Corner might not be on an island, but it was fairly remote, and the weather had cut it off as effectively as the sea could do. And Emily had been a stranger to all of them except Marguerite before they came.

She tried another save. 'My favorite Christie novel is *Orient Express*. Kind of an opposite situation – twelve people killing one man instead of one killing ten.'

Oscar's color began to return. 'An unofficial jury, judge, and executioner, as I recall,' he said, apparently determined to act normally.

'Yes. They claim they're remedying a miscarriage of justice, and Poirot ends up agreeing with them. But it always sounded more like revenge to me.' She turned to Luke. 'What do you think? Is private justice ever allowable? If official justice fails?'

Luke shook his head. 'That's a dangerous precedent. Once you allow something like that, you've got vigilantism, people deciding for themselves what's justice and what isn't. Not everybody's qualified to do that. 'Specially not people who are emotionally involved.'

'Load of crap,' Dustin muttered. 'Justice system's all screwed up. No protection for the average citizen.'

But Olivia, who might have had ample reason to feel the same, said, 'I think I agree with you, Lieutenant. Justice is for the state to administer. The individual must strive for forgiveness.' She looked up, directly into Ian's eyes, with something like an appeal. 'That is the only way to find peace.'

He smiled at her and pressed her hand. 'You speak like a saint, as always, my dear. For some of us, forgiveness is not so easy.' He sighed deeply. 'And yet we must try.'

'Forgiveness is easier when we understand why the person acted as he did,' Emily said. 'At least, that's how it's always been for me.' She had harbored resentment against her father for years, until she began to understand that his grief over her mother's death had undone the last strings of manliness left in him. His spiral into alcoholism, his failure to care properly for his children, even his early death when Emily was twenty, could all be traced to that grief, exacerbated by the guilt of believing he had driven his wife to her grave.

'True,' said Ian. 'But you have to admit that some people's behavior is nearly impossible to understand.'

'It can usually be traced to early influences, I think – sometimes so subtle the person isn't even aware of them and thus cannot enlighten anyone else. It seems to me, when people act badly, it's nearly always because they have never felt truly loved.'

Ian shook his head. 'Maybe. But I can't help thinking certain people are simply and irredeemably bad.'

'People can choose evil, certainly. And in doing so, ultimately put themselves beyond the possibility of redemption.' Emily noticed the other faces around the table were looking either blank or uncomfortable. This conversation was getting awfully deep for the lunch table.

She turned to Luke. 'Do you have any updates for us?'

'Not about the investigation. I have heard a weather report, though – looks like it'll probably thaw tomorrow. Then we'll be able to get stuff off to the lab.'

'Thank God,' Ian said. 'The sooner this whole thing gets resolved, the better.' He reached over and pressed Olivia's hand.

'Amen to that,' she said.

EIGHTEEN

After lunch, Emily reluctantly returned to her perusal of Cruella's oeuvre. Within a couple of hours she hit pay dirt – 'dirt' being the operative word – with that first book of Cruella's, *Quandary on Queer Street*. This one was set in England, and the title was a pun – 'Queer Street' being British slang for a difficult situation, but also 'queer' in the outmoded, politically incorrect sense of 'homosexual'. The purportedly true story – in which, as Luke had predicted, the names had been changed to protect the author from lawsuits – involved the suspicious death of a gay man. The strong implication, though it lacked any sort of proof, was that the man's surviving partner had killed him. And that surviving partner bore an unmistakable resemblance to Hilary.

It seemed an almost incredible coincidence that Hilary's and Cruella's paths could have crossed before, but then everything about this case was incredible. Emily couldn't dismiss the possibility on that basis. She could not believe Hilary capable of murder – either of a partner or of Cruella. But if she was honest with herself, she had to admit the only reason for her disbelief was their friendship. Unlike the timid and flippant Devon, Hilary had a core as hard as diamond – combined with an unusually cool head.

She tracked Luke down in Cruella's room, where he was going through her things one more time, hoping to find something of significance his deputies might have missed.

'I think I've found something.' She explained the book's plot and the possibility of Hilary's involvement.

Luke whistled through his teeth. 'Time to talk to our friend Hilary,' he said. 'Obviously he wasn't convicted of murder in a court of law, but after a slam like this, he could easily have been convicted in the court of popular opinion. Sounds like something that could make a fellow contemplate revenge.'

'If he really was the target,' Emily put in. 'I mean, Hilary stands out in a place like Stony Beach, but within the British gay community he may not be all that distinctive. The resemblance could be accidental. And we know nothing about his history. I've always had the impression he and Devon have been together a long time.'

'Same here, but it's only an impression, right? Neither of them's ever said so straight out, have they?'

'No, I suppose not.'

'Besides, what's the pub date on that book?'

Emily stared at the e-reader in her hand. 'No idea.'

Luke took it from her and made mysterious passes over it with his hand. 'Two thousand and one. So it could be him, and he and Devon could have gotten together after that – that'd still give them fifteen-plus years. That's enough to give the impression of an old married couple.'

Emily quailed internally. 'I really don't want to believe it. But I guess we have to talk to him.'

Luke raised one eyebrow at her. 'We?'

Oh, right, she wasn't an official detective. 'Could I be present, please? I promise I won't do anything to throw things off. He might be more comfortable talking to me.'

'Just one of the girls, huh? All right, we can do that. It'll have to wait for a thaw, though.' He glanced out the window at the ice glinting on the bare branches in the last rays of the setting sun. 'Have to be pretty darn urgent to drag me out on those slick roads tonight. A fifteen-year-old story can keep till tomorrow.'

Emily spent another sleepless night and woke groggy and disoriented. Even several cups of coffee didn't help to clear her brain. This would never do – she needed all her wits about her until this case was solved. She'd have to call Sam Griffiths and ask for a prescription for Ambien, which she'd used in past times of stress without ill effect. In the ordinary way Emily avoided drugs as much as possible, but this was not the ordinary way.

The thaw arrived as promised once the sun was fully up. Emily herself had no desire to stir outside; slush was not her preferred element. But she could sense her guests getting antsy

– especially Dustin. He paced through the downstairs rooms, pausing at every window and jingling the keys in his pocket.

Eventually he confronted Luke head-on in the hall as Emily watched from the dining room, sipping her third cup of coffee. 'I need to get out of here,' he said. 'I've got responsibilities to get back to. You can't keep me here.'

Luke stood before him, unflappable as usual. 'As a matter of fact, I can. And didn't you plan to be down here till New Year's anyway? I think your responsibilities can wait till we get this murder solved.'

Dustin spluttered and blustered, and finally Luke said, 'I'm going to have to ask you to hand over your car keys until I say you can go.'

At that Dustin's face turned so red Emily feared he would burst like an overripe tomato. 'What? No way! You can't do that. I have my rights!'

Luke stood there with his hand out, not saying a word. In the end Dustin ran out of bluster and dropped his keys into Luke's hand. Then he stomped into his room, slammed the door, and did not reappear until lunchtime.

It really was too bad Luke had to detain him. Emily would have been so happy to see him go.

A van arrived mid-morning to carry Cruella's body off to the morgue for a post-mortem. Emily was relieved, both to have the body gone and to be one step closer to knowing for certain what killed her, so the investigation could proceed on solid ground.

'I need to go into the main office for a while,' Luke told Emily when the van was gone. 'I'll leave Pete here to make sure everybody behaves. But I need to take all the evidence to the lab and get it tested for cyanide or whatever. And hand over Cruella's phone and computer to the tech guys and make sure they crack them right away. I'll pick up Hilary on my way back.'

Emily nodded, her heart misgiving her. Her head believed what she had said to Oscar – that whoever had killed Cruella was unlikely to kill again – but the removal of Luke's personal protection, even for a few hours, left her feeling exposed and vulnerable. Pete was a powerful young man – six-four and built like a football player – and he knew his job, but he wasn't Luke.

'Can you do me a favor while you're out? Sam called in a prescription for me. Could you pick it up?'

'Sure thing.' He frowned. 'You not feeling well?'

'Nothing serious. Just having trouble sleeping. She's giving me some Ambien.'

Oscar descended the last stair as she shut the door behind Luke. 'Good morning,' he said, not sounding as if he found it particularly good.

'Didn't you sleep well either?' Emily asked.

Oscar shook his head. 'I heard you tell Luke about that prescription. I may need to borrow some, if you don't mind.'

'No problem.' Emily wasn't in the habit of sharing prescriptions, but Ambien seemed to be doled out like candy these days, so it probably couldn't hurt.

Jamie came in as Oscar moved on to the dining room. 'I have to go into the office,' he said. 'I wanted to thank you for everything.'

'For getting you involved in another murder investigation?' she said wryly. 'You're welcome. Any time.'

He waved a dismissive hand. 'It was a great Christmas up till then. And I hate to leave. I've been taking care of Lizzie while Katie was busy over here, and she's so much more fun than deeds and trusts and wills. But if I don't take care of the deeds and trusts and wills, I'll never be able to afford to get married, so I'd better get back.'

Emily gave him a kiss on the cheek. 'You know you're welcome here any time. And you must absolutely come for Twelfth Night.' Emily was planning an Epiphany celebration at the end of the twelve days of Christmas – all the more reason to pray the investigation would be satisfactorily concluded by that time.

'I wouldn't miss it.' He flashed his shy grin at her and was gone.

All the writers kept to their rooms – even Marguerite, who was writing a paper for an academic journal – and Emily was left to herself in the library with the cats. Ordinarily she would have been perfectly content in that state, but recent events had left her restless. Returning to her Dostoevsky work was hopeless in her current mood; she couldn't even settle to reading or knitting. Thank God she'd found what she was looking for in Cruella's books and didn't need to subject herself to any more of that filth. For another person involved in the case to be a victim of Cruella's 'journalism' as well as Hilary would be more of a coincidence than Emily could swallow.

Then she remembered the task the arrival of most of her guests had interrupted: going through the boxes of old papers she'd found in the attic. She headed up to her sitting room to continue the job.

She paged through the remaining photo albums, skimming quickly over the ones that documented Beatrice's childhood, young womanhood, and marriage to Horace Runcible. At the bottom of the stack she came to an album that began with pictures of her father, Ernest Worthing, as a child and young man.

Her father used to joke about his name, which was taken from Oscar Wilde's hilarious farce, *The Importance of Being Earnest*. The layers of inauthenticity involved in that name – a fictional name adopted by a fictional character for the purpose of getting away with irresponsible behavior and deceiving the woman he loved – made Emily's head spin. But the name fit her father so perfectly, she had to wonder whether her grandparents had been prescient in giving it to him or whether he had spent his life deliberately living up to it. Or down to it, as the case might be.

He had been handsome as a young man, her father; there was no doubt about that. His auburn hair waved dashingly above a noble forehead, and the teasing light in his eye reminded her a bit of the young Luke. No mystery about why her mother would have fallen for him. The weakness of his character must not have been so apparent when they married in their late teens. But her mother, Eleanor – whose photos also began to appear now in the book – had deserved so much better.

Eleanor was a woman of character, sweet-tempered and long-suffering, but Ernest's drinking and inability to hold down a job had worn her down in the end. The album showed her progression, as summer succeeded summer, from a lovely, smiling, innocent young girl to a careworn, faded, hopeless woman grown old before her time. She had died of heart disease – a broken heart, Emily had always believed – when Geoff was ten and Emily only eight.

Emily saw her child self appear in the photos, always cherished by her mother, clinging shyly to her skirts as a little one, then venturing out a bit – but never far from her mother or Geoff – as she grew older. Dear Geoff. He had always watched out for her, protecting her from her father's occasional drunken rages (he was normally the more sentimental sort of drunk) as her father should have protected her from the world. In the end, though, Geoff himself had succumbed to the strain of weakness that seemed to be carried in the family's blood. She had watched with helpless and infinite sadness as, within the space of a few years after his divorce, he killed himself with drink.

Maybe it was a good thing the Worthing bloodline would die out with her. But it was lonely, nevertheless.

Luke delivered the amaretto, the amber vial, and the glass Cruella had drunk from to the lab in Tillamook with a request that they be handled as quickly as possible, testing for cyanide first. 'No prob,' Caitlyn, the pretty young technician, said. 'We're dead right now.' She grimaced. 'In a manner of speaking.'

He had to call in a tech guy specially; most of the support staff of the Tillamook County Sheriff's Office had been given leave for the holidays. The tech guy, Jordan, wasn't too happy about being pulled away from gobbling his turkey leftovers and playing with his brand-new drone.

'This better be important,' he growled as he sat at his desk and pulled Cruella's laptop toward him.

'Murder,' Luke said.

Jordan looked up at him, startled. Tillamook County still didn't see that many murders.

'This the victim's or a suspect's?'

'Victim. I only need you to get me in – pretty sure I can find what I'm looking for from there.'

'Got any hints for me?'

'Not really. I already tried everything I could think of based on what we know about her. She was a "true crime" writer – not that anything she wrote was strictly true – and a blackmailer on the side. Obnoxious as hell. Thoroughly nasty piece of work.'

Jordan fiddled for fifteen minutes while Luke fidgeted. Then he said, 'This one's not going to be easy. You sure you want to wait around? Could be hours.'

Luke huffed. That was not what he wanted to hear. 'Nah, I got things to do. Better leave it with you, I guess. But call me the minute you get in.'

'Will do.'

Luke sent off an email to London's Metropolitan Police asking for anything they had on Hilary Carmichael up through 2001. Then he searched credit card records for Dustin, Ian, and Olivia, looking for any purchase that could have been poison. Ian's and Olivia's records were completely normal; the only remarkable thing about Dustin's was how deeply he was in debt. He used plastic for almost everything – only withdrew twenty dollars a month in cash. But wait. Here, just a few days before he came to Windy Corner, he took out two hundred. For poison? To try to pay off Cruella? Or simply for extra expenses on the trip?

Cursing his lack of a decent break on this case, Luke picked up Emily's prescription at Fred Meyer on the way out of Tillamook and crawled back through the slush to Stony Beach. His gut wanted to hurry, but he knew he'd be likely to land himself in a ditch if he drove anywhere close to normal speed.

After what seemed like days, he pulled up in front of Remembrance of Things Past, where Devon and Hilary lived above their antique shop. The shop was closed, unsurprisingly, so he rang the bell for their apartment.

After a minute, Devon came sprinting down the stairs. 'Oh, hello, Lieutenant,' he said cheerfully. 'Caught any murderers lately?'

'Not yet.' Luke cleared his throat. 'As a matter of fact, I need to talk to Hilary. I'd like him to come with me to Windy Corner.' Whatever Hilary's history was, Luke had no guarantee

Devon was privy to it; Hilary would likely talk more freely with him not around.

Devon's flippant smile wavered as concern crept into his eyes. 'Didn't you talk to Hilary the other night? What could he have to add?'

'Just need to clarify a couple things. Nothing for you to worry about.' He hoped that was true. Luke wasn't as friendly with the couple as Emily was, but they were on good terms, and he'd hate to have to face Devon after arresting his partner for murder.

'Hil's in the office. This way.' Devon opened a door to the right of the staircase and led Luke through the shop to the back rooms, where Hilary perched on a stool in front of a computer. 'Hilary dear, it appears the lieutenant didn't get enough of your company the other night. He's come to carry you off to Windy Corner again.'

Hilary glanced up, frowning. He looked annoyed rather than worried. 'Can't we talk here, Lieutenant? I'm in the middle of an online auction. Damn, there goes that escritoire.'

'Sorry, no. Need to be on the spot to go over some things from your statement.'

'My statement? All twenty words of it?' Apprehension crept into his eyes at that.

'Twenty crucial words. Got to be sure of our facts.' *Don't make me come out with the story in front of Devon*, he said with his eyes.

Hilary appeared to get the message. 'All right, guv, I'll come quietly,' he said in broad Cockney. He gave Devon's shoulder a squeeze in passing. 'Won't be long.'

NINETEEN

To guarantee privacy for their talk, Emily suggested Luke and Hilary accompany her upstairs to her sitting room. Levin and Kitty followed, and Kitty took possession of Emily's lap. Levin jumped on to Hilary's legs, to his obvious chagrin; Emily inferred he was worried about cat hair polluting his immaculate trousers. But Levin was not easily dislodged. With a grimace Hilary resigned himself to his fate.

Luke led off the conversation. 'So as you know, Hilary, we've got no shortage of people with a motive to do Cruella in. She was that kind of gal, apparently. Trouble is, the facts don't quite seem to add up for any of them. So I asked Emily to do a little sleuthing in Cruella's books.'

At this Hilary's jaw clenched. Emily took up the tale.

'I started out with a dreadful piece of pulp called *Quandary on Queer Street*. Have you heard of it?'

Hilary's nostrils flared. 'Oh, yes, I've heard of it.'

'There's a character, Archibald – are there really still people in England called Archibald? – who seemed an awful lot like you. Not that I could believe you'd ever act the way this character supposedly did, but we did wonder if there might be any connection, however tenuous.'

Hilary's long, slender fingers caressed Levin's thick gray fur as if the fate of the world hung on the precise alignment of every hair. 'What sort of connection?'

'Well, to be blunt – was that character in any way based on you?'

Hilary's hand tightened on Levin's neck until the cat yowled and sprang off his lap. 'Sorry, old chap. For a minute I thought I had Cruella's neck in my hands.' He looked up at Emily, his eyes bleak. 'Yes, there was a time I would gladly have strangled that woman if I'd had any idea where to find her. She took the most painful episode of my life and turned it into a tabloid sensation. Oh, she changed the names, all right, but everyone knew exactly who she was talking about. And half-believed all her lies into the bargain.'

Emily wanted to reach for his hand and give it a reassuring squeeze, but Hilary was not one to welcome such contact. 'So what did actually happen? If you can bear to talk about it.'

'It was quite simple, really. No mystery about it at all. My partner at the time – Nigel – contracted HIV. It happened before we were together, but he didn't know until after. I nursed him up to the end. When the doctors said he was weeks, maybe days, from death, he had a bad reaction to a new medication and died.'

Hilary squeezed his linked fingers together until the knuckles stood white. 'There was a post-mortem, and it was perfectly clear what had happened. But Cruella got hold of the story and decided I had given Nigel the medication on purpose, knowing it would kill him. She couldn't make up her mind whether to call it a mercy killing or revenge on him for having given me the disease – which he didn't; we were always safe. All a complete fabrication. The doctors didn't even know the meds would hurt him – how could I have been supposed to know?' He turned appealing eyes from Emily to Luke and back again.

'That must have been awful,' Emily said quietly, genuinely moved. 'On top of your grief, to have to deal with an accusation like that.'

'As I said, it was the most painful episode of my life. I don't know how I would ever have recovered if it hadn't been for Devon.'

'You met soon after that?'

'We already knew each other, in fact. Through the business. I think he'd fancied me for some time.' A tiny smile played around Hilary's mouth. 'He was very kind, very supportive. You wouldn't think to look at him that he'd be a person to lean on, but he saved me. Definitely from a breakdown. Probably from suicide.'

Luke gave him a minute, then said, 'You mentioned that other people believed Cruella's lies.'

Hilary's smile transformed into a sneer. 'Oh, yes. All my so-called friends, except for Devon. Oh, they were kind about it – they could all understand why I'd want to put Nigel out of his misery, it must have been terrible seeing him suffer week after week. But they believed I'd done it, all right.'

'Did that have anything to do with you moving to America?'

'Everything. Life became impossible in England. Devon agreed to share my exile, and we've been wanderers ever since.' His voice broke on the last words.

Emily looked appealingly at Luke. Was it really necessary to press Hilary any further at this moment?

But Luke shook his head. Emily knew one of the less attractive aspects of police work was the need to press one's advantage. You had to get people while they were vulnerable – it was the only way to be sure of getting to the truth.

'You said you wanted to strangle Cruella back then,' Luke said. 'How about now? How'd you feel when you met her here at Christmas?'

Hilary's sardonic smile reappeared. 'You may find this hard to believe, Lieutenant. But when I saw her in the flesh – which I never had before, she worked all her havoc remotely – all I could feel was pity. After all she put me through, I ended up with Devon, whom I might never have looked at twice if I hadn't been so troubled. I have love, a home and friends in this charming town, and work that is rewarding, both mone-tarily and personally. What did she have? The scorn and hatred of everyone who knew her.'

His face cleared as he looked from Luke to Emily. 'Honestly, I almost wanted to thank her. Not quite, of course. But kill her? No. She wasn't worth the trouble or the risk. A murderer has to believe himself invulnerable, don't you think? Thanks to Cruella, I could never labor under that delusion again.'

Luke drove Hilary back to his shop. He knew it was foolish to take a suspect's words at face value, but part of him wanted to believe what Hilary had said. He'd put Cruella's persecution behind him a long time ago; seeing her had only brought closure to a painful episode in his life. But despite that, Hilary had motive and opportunity, and Emily had told him ahead of time Cruella would be there. How he could have gotten his hands on cyanide – if it was cyanide – in remote Stony Beach in the middle of a hard freeze at Christmastime was another question. He pretty much would've had to have the poison on hand already, and that didn't seem likely.

Or did it? Hilary spent a good part of every year in the UK. Could be cyanide was easier to come by there. Not that he would have hoarded it on the off chance of running into Cruella, but he might have bought it for some other reason. Didn't people sometimes use it for rats? Then when Emily told him about Cruella visiting, he might have made a snap decision to get rid of her and dug it out.

Of course, Hilary would never have taken the risk of poisoning Emily, so if it was him, the poison would have to have been in the glass. If only labs could get results instantaneously like on TV. He needed those results.

After Luke left, Emily and Marguerite were alone in the library with the cats when the doorbell rang. A minute later Katie ushered Wanda Wilkins into the room. Emily could not conceal the start it gave her. What on earth was that woman doing here? She hadn't seemed like the type who, given the proverbial inch of welcome, would take a mile, especially in a house that had just seen a murder.

'I'm on my way to Seaside,' Wanda said, 'since the roads are passable. But I thought I ought to stop by and check with that handsome sheriff to be sure it's OK for me to leave town.'

'Oh!' Emily didn't know quite how to respond. 'I'm afraid Luke's not here right now. I think he only meant you shouldn't leave the area. Driving to Seaside and back should be fine. But I suggest you call him at the office to be sure.'

She wrote the number down on a piece of notepaper, feeling certain there must be something behind Wanda's visit other than a desire to cooperate with the law. Maybe Wanda wanted to make a play for Luke. She had turned on the flirt with him from time to time on Christmas Day. That would be a nuisance for Luke but hardly a worry to Emily. She couldn't imagine any woman he would find less appealing. Except perhaps Cruella.

Wanda took the number but did not make the call right away. 'Thanks. Wouldn't want the sheriff to think I was sneaking around behind his back. It's so important to be earnest, don't you think?'

Still befuddled, Emily simply nodded and turned toward the door, but Wanda said, 'Don't bother. I'll see myself out.' She went out the hall door and shut it behind her.

Emily was too flustered to object. At this point she would hardly care if Wanda did help herself to one of the expensive ornaments in the hall.

Then it hit her what Wanda had said. 'It's so important to be earnest.' Was that a deliberate reference to the Oscar Wilde play that had inspired her father's name? Wanda hardly seemed like the literary type, but if it wasn't a reference, it was an odd thing to say. Most people would use a word like 'transparent' or 'aboveboard' in such a context rather than 'earnest'. Oh well. The phrase was only a drop in the dubious bucket of Wanda's peculiar behavior.

Emily walked unsteadily over to the bar shelf and poured herself a glass of sherry from a newly opened bottle. She didn't care that it was barely lunchtime. She needed a drink.

After lunch, the atmosphere in the house seemed to undergo a subtle shift, as if the removal of Cruella's body had sent the message that although her murder remained unsolved, the angel of death had moved on and was no longer hovering over Windy Corner. Instead of the guests seeking solitude, they appeared to find safety in numbers. Marguerite, who had evaporated when Wanda came in, returned with her laptop, and Ian, Olivia, and Oscar soon followed. To no one's disappointment, however, Dustin kept to his room.

Emily, not to be outdone, determined to make another attempt at her own writing project. This time the cats left her alone, preferring to pester Marguerite, and she was at least able to get her notes into some sort of order – enough to realize where the gaps were which she would need time in the Reed library to fill. But also enough to realize she was closer than she had thought, not only to having enough material to begin writing, but also to having something to say about Dostoevsky that was worth saying and had not been said before. The exhilaration of discovery leapt up within her. Oh, she had missed this. Detective work was similarly gratifying, but also messy and morally murky at times. Scholarship provided a thrill uncorrupted by considerations of real life.

As she shuffled her notecards and papers at the table, she glanced over to where Oscar sat on the window seat and Marguerite in an easy chair. They were both engaged in works of literary scholarship, as she was, but instead of being surrounded by the chaotic litter of dead trees, they needed only their laptops. They could keep all their research files in perfect order, invulnerable to feline attack or coffee stains. They could type for hours without writer's cramp and make corrections with a few keystrokes at any stage in the process. Perhaps there was something to be said for this technology business after all.

She'd always believed a computer would be incongruous in Aunt Beatrice's stately old library, but Olivia's laptop was thin and sleek, its housing a lovely burnished gold color – so futuristic it paradoxically blended in with its antique surroundings. Perhaps it might be time for Emily to think about joining the modern world.

But for now she would immerse herself in nineteenth-century Russia. Could Dostoevsky have penetrated so deeply into the mysteries of the human soul if he'd been tapping plastic keys instead of dipping his quill into ink? She seriously doubted it.

After a couple of hours with Fyodor Mikhailovich, Emily's brain was spinning; she was no longer accustomed to such concentrated work. She went back upstairs to continue looking through Aunt Beatrice's boxes of papers and memorabilia. That odd remark of Wanda's still nagged at her.

She'd finished with the box of photo albums, so she opened the next box. This one was full of personal correspondence – files upon files of it. Had Beatrice kept every letter she ever received? And carbons of many of her responses as well. All the letters were neatly sorted by sender, recipient, and date.

Emily skimmed over the files labeled with names she didn't recognize. But the family ones she lingered over. Here were all her own letters, spanning forty-five years – from the time

she could write until a few months before Aunt Beatrice's
death. She realized with compunction the file was not extremely
fat, for all that. Her letters had been dutiful and few. She'd
been fond of Aunt Beatrice and appreciated all her aunt had
done for her – including putting her through college, minus
the little Emily could earn on her own – but the businesslike
old woman had never inspired the kind of heart-to-heart confidence Emily might have placed in her mother, had her mother
lived.

Geoff's file was even thinner; he had written to thank
Beatrice for Christmas gifts, and occasionally from college to
plead for a little extra spending money, but that was about all.
Her mother, Eleanor, had written often, though. Emily opened
this file with eager interest.

Eleanor had never been one to complain, especially to her
husband's aunt – although Emily knew Beatrice had no illu-
sions about her nephew's weaknesses nor made any excuses
for them. Instead, Eleanor wrote of the small, happy moments
of family life, moments she was always able to find or create
despite the overall bleakness of their lives. Yet their poverty
and rootlessness were evident between the lines, and many of
Eleanor's letters included a word of thanks for some little gift
or consideration shown to the children or herself. Never cash,
lest Ernest get his hands on it and waste it, but practical gifts
that ensured Geoff and Emily were properly clothed and
equipped for school and could put on a brave face before the
world.

Letters from Ernest himself were few and far between until
after Eleanor died. Then the begging began, subtle at first but
escalating in urgency and tone until the letters sounded more
demanding than pleading. Beatrice's responses, copies of all
of which she kept, were always firm: she would provide for
the children directly, but she would in no way risk abetting
her nephew's vices and irresponsibility with gifts of cash.
More than once she offered to have Geoff and Emily come to
live with her permanently, but Ernest always refused. Emily
suspected he'd feared that would deprive him of any small
hold he had on Beatrice.

The self-portrait of her father contained in these letters was even less flattering than Emily's memories. But she reminded herself this was only one side of him, and the worst side at that. When he was happy and sober, he could be charming, witty, literate, playful, even loving. But those sober and happy times came with increasing rarity after her mother died.

A few years into the begging period came a letter that baffled Emily.

Dear Aunt Beatrice,

Thank you for the shoes and school supplies for Geoff and Emily, and for paying for their hot lunches for the year. These things do make our lives much easier, especially the lunches, as it's hard on Emily having to pack them every day. She's a sweet girl and tries so hard to take her mother's place, but it's a lot to ask of a youngster.

I have incurred another obligation just lately – quite a legitimate and pressing one, I assure you, though I'm not in a position to say exactly what it is. I wonder if you could possibly see your way clear to giving – or even lending – me a few hundred dollars in cash – perhaps as much as a thousand. It would make the world of difference, and I promise you it would not be an unworthy use of your money; I know you're always so scrupulous about such things. If you would be so good as to let me know before the month is out, I would be most appreciative.

Your loving nephew,
Ernest

And Beatrice's response:

My dear Ernest,

You should know by now that I cannot possibly agree to send you cash directly. If this obligation is indeed as legitimate and pressing as you claim, you will have to explain it and provide me with sufficient evidence of its legitimacy. Once satisfied on that point, I would need a reliable third party through whom the funds could be channeled to their intended purpose. I will on no account

give money directly to you. As for a loan, you insult my
intelligence by suggesting it. You might as well offer to
sell me the Brooklyn Bridge.

Your loving aunt – who was not, however, born
yesterday,
Beatrice

Emily smiled in spite of herself at this wholly characteristic
reply. But she couldn't help wondering what the extraordinary
obligation could have been. Usually Ernest's attempts to
wangle cash were much more moderate. Could he have
invented the obligation, reasoning that a substantial request
would seem more credible as a one-time affair? Shooting the
moon, as it were.

She flipped more quickly through the remaining letters until
she came to a file that said simply, *Contents deposited with*
MacDougal and Simpson for safekeeping. The original typed
label on the file had been inked out with a black marker, but
the top of a single ascender showed over the marker at the
beginning of the word. Assuming that letter was a capital, it
could only be an 'I', 'J', or 'L'. None of those letters applied to
anyone in the family.

Emily frowned in concentration as she picked up the phone
to call Jamie. Why had he never delivered this file to her as
a part of her aunt's estate? He'd passed on all the documents
relating to Beatrice's various properties and business dealings, but no personal letters at all.

Jamie answered on the second ring. 'Jamie? Emily. I've
been going through some of Beatrice's old papers, and there's
a file here that says its contents were deposited with your firm.
It's in a box of personal correspondence, so I assume this file
would have contained personal letters as well.'

'Really? That's odd. I was sure I'd given you everything.
Do you have any idea what the date would be? Or what it's
about?'

'Not really. The files are in alphabetical order, then the
contents of each are arranged by date. The label is blacked
out, but it may have started with an I, J, or L. The folder itself
is pretty yellowed, so I'd guess it's on the older side.'

'If it was older than 2010, it could conceivably have been left behind at my dad's old office. I'll check with him and get back to you.'

'Thanks.' Emily put down the phone with a growing presentiment. *By the pricking of my thumbs, something wicked this way comes.* Beatrice would not have deposited that folder with her lawyer for nothing.

TWENTY

At teatime, all the guests in the library cleared their computers away and tucked in with gusto. Brainwork might seem sedentary, but Emily knew from experience it could be quite as draining as physical labor. And the most welcome antidotes to that exhaustion were sugar and caffeine, which Katie provided in good supply.

Emily poured the tea, adding sugar, milk, or lemon according to everyone's preferences, which she'd memorized by this time. She didn't bother offering the honey around, since she already knew no one else would take it. But she put a little extra in her own cup, feeling the need for fortification. After one sip, though, she made a face and put the cup down. Apparently, with this honey, a little extra was too much.

Oscar sat next to her on the loveseat and sighed with contentment as he licked pastry crumbs from his fingers. 'I'm going to miss this when I go back to Reed. Not the murder, of course, but the food, the room with a view, the bathtub. All this comfort is spoiling me for real life.'

'Are you really as poor as all that?' Emily asked. She herself had made a comfortable living as a tenured professor. She knew the junior profs made less, of course, but Oscar talked as if he were a veritable pauper.

He gave a short, wry laugh that was almost a snort. 'I'm an adjunct prof. Do you know how adjunct profs get paid?'

She had to admit she'd never really thought about it.

'By the hour. Of actual classtime. Not a penny for all the hours that go into prep, grading, meeting with students, faculty meetings. Actual classtime adds up to about ten hours a week. The rest of it is another fifty.'

Emily was dumbfounded. She wouldn't have believed her own college could treat anyone that way.

'You've seen my car,' Oscar went on. 'I buy all my clothes, all my everything, at thrift stores. My "room" is literally a closet, barely big enough for a bed – forget about a desk. I live off ramen and peanut butter. I'd scrounge in the cafeteria if I could get away with it, but that's frowned on for staff. We're supposed to be more dignified.'

Emily was well acquainted with scroungers – students who would stand by the racks where diners left their trays after eating and pick up any leftover food. She herself might have been in such a position as an undergrad if not for Aunt Beatrice; as it was, she would often take a little more than she wanted going through the cafeteria line just so she could pass it on. She hated to think of Oscar being poor enough to consider scrounging an attractive option.

She still had some influence in the literature department. Perhaps a word or two in a well-chosen ear could help Oscar to a more stable position for next year. She'd have to confer with Marguerite and brainstorm what might be done.

Luke had been working in his office all afternoon, running a virtual fine-tooth comb through the backgrounds of Ian, Olivia, Dustin, and Hilary with no particularly interesting results. As he was about to head back to Windy Corner with a couple of hours to spare before dinner, he got a call from Jordan. 'Got it cracked for you,' he said.

'I'll be right down. Can you hang around in case I need more help?'

'I guess. As long as I can get home for dinner.'

'Put me through to the lab, would you?'

Caitlyn confirmed she had the lab results ready and the ME had finished the autopsy. He'd be able to get all the info at once.

Luke made the best time he safely could and found Jordan poking around Cruella's laptop and shaking his head.

'Nasty piece of work is right. By the way, what you said about her being a blackmailer was the key.'

'How do you mean?'

'Password's "Amberiotis". Character in a Christie novel. Blackmailer who gets himself killed.'

'Well, now, isn't that interesting?' Luke mused. 'Wonder if she somehow knew how she was going to end up.'

'Dangerous occupation, blackmail,' Jordan replied. 'Practically have to have a death wish. Or else think you're immortal.'

'I'd guess the latter in her case.' He clapped Jordan on the back. 'Thanks for your help. You can go back to your leftovers now.'

Luke grabbed the laptop and headed over to the morgue. He could examine the computer at his leisure, but Caitlyn and the ME would want to get home.

'Whatcha got for me?' he asked as he walked in, holding a peppermint in his mouth to mask the ambient smell. A body, presumably Cruella's, lay on the metal autopsy table, covered by a sheet.

George Tomlinson, the medical examiner, looked up from his computer, where he was presumably writing up his official report.

'Cyanide,' he said. 'Half-hour or so before death. Alcohol present. Can't be sure if they were ingested together.'

'What I figured.' Luke found himself adopting Tomlinson's laconic style in his presence. 'Thanks.' He crossed the hall to the lab.

Caitlyn greeted him with a smile. 'This is a nice one. No gray areas. We found cyanide in the little vial and in the glass. Plus a considerable quantity dissolved in the amaretto remaining in the bottle.'

Luke whistled. So that meant the poison had been added to the amaretto bottle, not the glass. And almost certainly – considering where the poison container had been found – that had been done while the bottle was still in the library, rather than during the blackout, after Katie had carried the tray into the parlor. The table in the parlor had been nowhere near the windows on that side of the house, and to cross the room in the dark would have meant risking noise and detection.

No one – except Cruella herself – could have known before the bottle was removed from the library that she would be the first one to drink the amaretto. So the poison had to have been intended for Emily.

Luke thought he had dealt emotionally with this possibility, but now that it hit him as a definite fact, he felt a chill that began with his fingers and toes and ran all the way back to his heart. What had before been just a job – catching a murderer simply to serve the impersonal interests of justice – now became a personal mission to protect the woman he loved. He took a moment to consider the case as it stood. Given this development, none of his prime suspects had a motive. Ian, Olivia, and Dustin had only just met Emily at the time of the murder, whereas Hilary had known her for several months but had no reason to bear her any animosity. Back to square freaking one.

'Lieutenant?' Caitlyn's voice broke into his reverie. 'Are we done here?'

He shook himself back into the here and now. 'Oh, yeah, sorry. Fingerprint reports done, do you know?'

'Jamal left them for you. Right here.' She handed him a folder.

'Thanks. You can go home now. Really appreciate you coming in over the holidays.'

'Sure thing.' She collected her belongings and walked out. Luke was left staring at the contents of the folder, his mind's eye full of a different sight altogether.

Ignore motive for a minute, he told himself. If he could figure out when the poison was added to the bottle, he might be able to narrow down who could have done it. He'd been going on the assumption that it was done shortly before Katie took the bottle into the parlor – while Devon's team was waiting for the second charade. If that were the case, it would have to have been someone on that team; anyone else would have been noticed and remarked upon. Except Katie or Jamie, but he was ruling them out a priori.

But it didn't have to have been done then. If it was meant for Emily, the cyanide could have been dumped in during the wait for the first scene, or even earlier. One person could have slipped into the library during the carol singing, or in the transition between sherry and dinner, or between dinner and carols. Heck, the room had been crowded enough during the sherry party – somebody could have slipped over to the bar shelf unnoticed then. Not Dustin, because Luke had kept an eye on him personally, but anyone else might have managed it if they were quick enough.

He turned his attention to the fingerprint report in his hand and skimmed it. None of the items had yielded any fingerprints that had no business to be there. Marguerite's, Emily's, Katie's, and Cruella's on the amaretto; Katie's and Cruella's on the glass; and none at all on the amber vial. The killer had been smart enough and cautious enough to wear gloves.

That did mean the job was not likely to have been done while the room was full. Pulling on a pair of gloves would add time and attract attention. For that matter, what had happened to the gloves? Only normal outdoor gloves had been found in the house, on the guests, or among their things. No gloves in the bushes outside.

Luke had an excellent visual memory, which had served him well in this job. He thought back to what various members of the party had been wearing. Who could have had a bulky pair of outdoor gloves in their pockets?

Dustin had been wearing a T-shirt and jeans that he bulged out of; no room for gloves there. Olivia's burgundy velvet dress was elegant and sleek, close-fitting without being tight; he doubted it even had any pockets. Oscar wore a tweed jacket over his dress shirt and slacks – possible he could have had gloves in a coat pocket, but Luke thought they would have made a bulge. Ian was wearing a tailor-made suit whose smooth pockets could never have held anything thicker than a hand-kerchief. Of course, now that Luke thought about it, a dexterous person could have managed the job with a handkerchief instead of gloves, and Ian's long, slender hands looked like they'd be up to the challenge. Oscar with his nervous jitters and Dustin in his alcoholic haze seemed less likely.

He had to consider the local folks, now that he knew Emily was the target. Devon and Hilary had both worn sleek suits similar to Ian's. Marguerite's black dress was as form-fitting as Olivia's. Veronica's vintage blouse and skirt were looser; if she had pockets, a pair of gloves might have fit in them unobserved. But why on earth would Veronica want to harm Emily?

Then there was Wanda. That sleazy slip of a dress she'd had on couldn't conceal a hairpin, but she could have slipped on her fur jacket at some point – he remembered seeing it lying around the library instead of hung up with the others in the hall. And she'd probably brought a purse as well.

In point of fact, gloves or no gloves, almost any of them could have found an opportunity. He wasn't going to solve anything that way. It had to come down to motive. But who would want to hurt Emily?

He went through the people again in his mind, as if he hadn't done so a hundred times already. The guests in the house: Dustin had a grudge against the world, but he could have nothing personal against Emily. Ian and Olivia seemed genuinely fond of her. And, he had to admit, so did Oscar – in a totally innocent way.

Marguerite and the local people had all been Emily's friends for months, if not years. If any of them had any kind of hidden, crazy spite against her, they could have acted on it at any time.

That left Wanda. She did seem vaguely hostile to Emily. But what could she possibly have against her strong enough to make her want to kill?

This line of thinking was getting him nowhere. He took the reports and Cruella's laptop to an empty desk, logged into the laptop, and began systematically exploring Cruella's files and accounts.

He found plenty to back up what he already knew about her persecution of Ian and Olivia and her attempt to blackmail Dustin. All irrelevant if she wasn't the real target. But in addition to all that, he found a file that puzzled him. It was named *Lansing*, and the creation date was December twenty-third – the day after Cruella arrived at Windy Corner.

She must have used her phone to look Oscar up on the internet, then recorded her findings here. The file contained all sorts of biographical details about Lansing – date and place of birth, education, employment history. None of that was anything to get excited about, much less blackmail somebody for. Cruella must have been scraping the bottom of the barrel if she thought Lansing was a promising subject for her little sideline.

Then one seemingly innocent detail caught Luke's eye: Mother's name, Wanda Lansing. Wanda wasn't all that common a name.

Cruella didn't seem to have followed up on that bit of information. But then, she wouldn't have had any time or reason to. She was busy with the group from the time she met Wanda Wilkins up until the moment she drank the poison that caused her death.

Luke pushed the laptop aside and pulled the departmental computer toward him. He searched the police files for Wanda Lansing.

No criminal record to speak of. Few traffic tickets, cited for being uninsured in a minor car accident. One drunk and disorderly. He checked her biographical details. Born September fifteenth, 1951. Gave birth to one child, Oscar Lansing, in 1976; no father listed. Married – there it was – George Wilkins, 1998 to 2005, when he died.

He couldn't believe in that much coincidence where a bunch of less-than-common names were involved. Wanda Wilkins must be Oscar Lansing's mother. And Cruella had been about an inch from finding that out.

But why the hell were they trying to keep the connection secret? Oscar was staying at Windy Corner. So what if his mother wanted to rent a cottage from Emily at the same time?

Oscar might well be ashamed of having his mother follow him around like that, like he was a baby. But that was no reason to think she'd go along with keeping their relationship dark. Wanda Wilkins didn't strike Luke as any kind of pushover. Between the two of them, he was pretty sure who'd be wearing the trousers. Or the skin-tight jeans, in this case.

OK, so Oscar was illegitimate. That might have been a little scandalous back in 1976, but it was no big deal now. Nor was there any reason they couldn't simply have pretended she and his father had been married – casual acquaintances don't generally make a habit of investigating people's backgrounds. Unless they're Cruella Crime, of course.

There had to be more to this than met the eye. Luke leaned back in the chair and locked his hands behind his neck, going over in his mind everything that had happened since Oscar and Wanda arrived in Stony Beach.

Then he sat up suddenly. He'd put his finger on it himself a week ago: Oscar was fortune-hunting, and his mama had put him up to it. Wanda seemed like the designing kind of woman who would engineer a marriage between her son and a wealthy woman, hoping not only to set him up for life but also to profit from it herself. She'd made no secret she was sick of teaching and envied Emily her easy life. That had to be it.

Luke didn't look forward to communicating all this to Emily. She'd pooh-poohed the idea of Oscar being after her all along, and he doubted this new information would be enough to convince her.

Before he left for Windy Corner, he remembered he'd meant to check on Dustin-as-Billy-Williams as well. He plugged the name into the database and found nothing suspicious in connection with Cruella, but he did find one interesting fact that was too coincidental not to be significant: Billy Williams had spent one year as a student at Reed College and flunked out. Academic year 2005–06. Emily was teaching there then. He found a picture of Dustin at about that age and printed it. He'd have to check whether the picture and the name Billy Williams together would jog anything in Emily's memory.

After tea, the other guests trailed back to their rooms, and Emily was left alone in the library with Marguerite, who sat on the hearth playing with the cats. Emily sat next to her, and Levin broke away from accepting Marguerite's worship to claim his proper due from Emily. After greeting her with a kitty kiss, he settled down to be petted.

'I wanted to talk to you, Margot. I feel like we ought to do something for Oscar.'

Marguerite's delicately penciled brows went up. 'For Oscar? What sort of thing?'

'Help him to a better job. Do you realize he's living in a closet on ramen and peanut butter?'

Marguerite shrugged. 'It is the lot of the adjunct professor. Just it is not, kind it is not, but it is the way things are.'

'Granted, we probably can't change the system, but if I leave, that will create a hole in the department. Not that they'd put Oscar in my place, since he's new, but everybody should move up one, right? So he could potentially get an assistant professorship on the tenure track.'

'But what about Lillian? She is taking your classes. Surely she is the logical choice.'

'She never planned to stay more than a year. Peter has a job somewhere else for next fall.'

Marguerite stroked Kitty's ears with a thoughtful air. 'Then perhaps this shift will happen on its own. With no help from you or me.'

'Perhaps. But I'd like to weight the balance. Maybe if I talked to Richard?' Richard McClintock was the head of Lit & Lang.

'*Tu plaisantes, n'est-ce pas?* Do you know how Richard speaks of you these days?'

Emily grimaced. She had indeed encountered Richard's sarcastic bitterness toward her on a visit to campus a couple of months before. He appeared to take her sudden acquisition of wealth as a personal affront.

'Good point. But he likes you, right? Maybe you could speak to him.'

Marguerite shuddered luxuriously. '*Oui*, he "likes" me. As a man likes a juicy steak he wishes to devour. However, for your sake, *mon amie*, I will see what I can do. Oscar is a good teacher as well as a sweet man. He deserves to sleep in a real bedroom and eat meat once in a while.'

'Thanks, Margot.' Emily removed one hand from petting Levin to squeeze her friend's arm.

Marguerite gave her a sly look from the corner of her eye. 'But I have one condition.'

'Condition?'

'That you get off the fence, as you say in this country, about Luke.'

'Margot, that's not fair. One has nothing to do with the other.'

She shrugged. 'And what is that to me? There is no law that a condition must be related to the request.'

'No, but . . . I'm just not ready. I don't want to do anything rash.'

'Rash? How would it be rash? In my not-so-humble opinion,

chérie, you should have accepted Luke six months ago. To have a man like that devoted to you – this does not happen every day. After all, you have waited thirty-five years to be together – why wait a moment longer?'

'That's what Luke thinks. But to me it's more like we've waited thirty-five years, so why *not* wait a little longer? We were too hasty when we were kids, and it ended badly. This time I want to be very sure. We may not be compatible on every level. The passion is there, but we're complete opposites in so many ways. I don't want to risk it not working out.'

'You have it back to front, *mon amie*. First you get married, then you work it out. There is no other way.' Marguerite spoke with all the complacency of the never-married. 'Marriage changes everything in ways you cannot predict. It is impossible to be prepared.'

On some level Emily knew that despite her lack of experience with marriage, Marguerite was right. But they had a murder to solve before she would have time to herself to confront that question.

TWENTY-ONE

Luke arrived as the gong sounded for dinner. 'Emily, I've got to talk to you. Right now.'

'Katie just rang the gong. Can't it wait till after dinner?'

Luke's brows drew down into that look that meant he wasn't going to budge. She pulled out her secret weapon. 'If we don't go in, the others will know something's up. You don't want to give anything away, do you?'

His mouth twisted. 'Shoot, I guess you're right. But the minute dinner's over, we need to go upstairs where nobody can hear.'

'OK.' She led the way into the dining room.

The meal was civil but hardly relaxed. Luke's impatience was obvious and made the others nervous – except for Marguerite, whose nerves were proof against almost any disturbance. Oscar in particular could hardly keep his hands steady enough to eat his soup. Dinner was finished in record time. Emily made some lame excuse not to join the others in the library.

In her private sitting room, she turned to Luke with hands on hips. 'All right now, what on earth is so all-fired urgent that you had to spoil a perfectly good dinner?'

'Oscar Lansing is Wanda Wilkins' son.'

Emily stared at Luke as if he'd claimed the Mojave Desert had given birth to the British Isles. That horrible woman related to her newly discovered kindred spirit? 'Impossible.'

'It's true. There's absolutely no doubt about it.' He spelled out for her the information trail he'd followed.

'But . . . Cruella could have made a mistake. That could be some other Oscar Lansing.'

'Everything matches up. The age is right, the education, the job history – you're not gonna try and tell me there's more than one Oscar Lansing teaching at Reed right now?'

'Well, no, but – Then *you* could have made a mistake. It could be some other Wanda Wilkins.'

'Emily, none of those names is all that common. Wanda, Oscar, Lansing, Wilkins – they're not rare, but they're not exactly John Smith. What are the odds more than one Wanda Lansing had a son named Oscar and later married a Wilkins? It won't wash. His age is right, too. It all adds up.'

Emily paced in a circle and came around to face Luke again. 'OK, then, so what? Why should I care? I'm not proud of my father. So Oscar has a mother he can't be proud of. That doesn't change the fact that he's a really nice guy with whom I have an unbelievable amount in common.' She added quickly, 'Speaking strictly platonically, of course.'

But Luke's expression didn't so much as whisper jealousy; it shouted exasperation and disappointment. 'The "so what" is, why have they been trying to hide it?'

She fell back a pace. That was an excellent question. Oscar might be ashamed of Wanda, but she would have no reason to be ashamed of him – or to go along with his wanting to disown her. Emily felt behind her for a chair and sat down. Her head was spinning.

'You obviously have a theory about that. You might as well spit it out.'

Luke sat opposite her and took her hand. 'Em, I know you don't want to hear this, but it's my duty to say it. The only reason I can think of for them to hide it is because they're fortune-hunting.' At that word Emily snatched her hand away.

He huffed but went on. 'Wanda's decided Oscar should try to marry you for your money. She doesn't want to jinx the deal by letting you know what kind of a mother-in-law you'd be getting, but she's too invested in the project – and has too little confidence in Oscar – to stay on the sidelines and let him get on with it.'

Emily turned sideways and buried her face in the chair. Kitty, who had followed them upstairs, sensed her distress and leapt into her lap, nuzzling her nose against Emily's cheek. Emily hugged her fiercely. At least her cats would never let her down.

Though in this case, she couldn't be sure who had let her down – Oscar, Luke, or both.

She turned back to face Luke, who had risen and was pacing the cramped space. 'I just can't buy it. Oscar has never said or done the slightest thing to hint he has that kind of intentions toward me. He's only ever been simply friendly.'

'Maybe he hasn't fully bought into the program. Maybe she's still trying to talk him around.'

Emily thought back to that inexplicable visit Wanda had paid her last week, and her whispering to Oscar as she left. She couldn't deny it fit. And for all she knew, Wanda could have had a secret conference with Oscar during her other bewildering call that very morning – she hadn't seen Wanda out, after all.

But Emily would never believe Oscar had any intention of falling in with his mother's scheme. Even if he was living off ramen and peanut butter.

'So what are you thinking this has to do with the murder?'

Luke stopped his pacing and stared at her. 'Well, nothing, actually. At least I don't see how.'

'I guess Cruella could have told her she'd found the connection and Wanda didn't want her to spread it around.'

'Yeah, about that.' Luke rubbed the back of his neck, which usually meant he had to say something he knew she wouldn't want to hear. 'I got the lab results too. The poison was in the amaretto bottle.'

Emily didn't need the significance of that spelled out for her. A chill ran down her neck. 'So it was meant for me.'

Luke nodded, his eyes dark. 'And Wanda wouldn't want to kill the goose she was hoping would lay the golden eggs.' He stuck his hands in his pockets and his eyebrows went up. He pulled his left hand out holding a folded piece of paper.

'Oh yeah, I forgot about this. I found out something kind of interesting about our friend Dustin. Aka Billy Williams. He spent a year at Reed about a decade ago.' He unfolded the paper and handed it to her. 'This face ring any bells?'

The picture showed a young man a good thirty pounds lighter than Dustin, notably thinner in the face, with shorter hair and no scruffy whiskers but with the same truculent expression. 'Billy Williams . . . I think I do remember him. He was in my Hum One Ten section. If I have the right person, I think I failed him. He never turned in a single paper.'

Luke frowned, pouching his lips. 'Seem to you like the kind of guy who would hold a grudge?'

'I wouldn't be a bit surprised.'

'Me neither. I wonder . . . could being flunked out of Reed make him mad enough to want to—'

'Murder me? Heavens, I hope not. That would be pretty extreme. And he hasn't seemed to single me out for any special animosity – he's equally rude and nasty to everyone.'

'True. Still, I'm going to talk to him about it. It's all we've got at this point. Otherwise, we're back to square one. Again.'

Emily went down to the library with Luke but excused herself early. She was feeling unusually tired, and she was in too much emotional turmoil to enjoy the others' company. She said goodnight to everyone, then Oscar reminded her she'd promised him an Ambien.

It was a struggle to look at him, treat him the same way as before she knew his parentage. Or half of it. 'Oh, of course. Come up with me, won't you?'

Levin and Kitty seemed to think this invitation was intended for them. They didn't normally sleep with her, but tonight she would be glad of their company.

Oscar waited in her sitting room while she fetched the bottle from the bathroom. She handed it to him, then turned to pour herself a glass of water. The glass needed rinsing, so it took a couple of minutes. When she turned back, he held the bottle out to her.

'Thanks. I'm looking forward to a good night's sleep.'

'Me too.'

Oscar went downstairs, and Emily swallowed her own little pink pill with half the glass of water. She completed her night-time ritual and got into bed, but despite the Ambien and the coziness of her furry companions, she lay awake for some time. Her dinner – delicious though it was, especially the chocolate mousse for dessert – didn't seem to be settling well. Her thoughts wandered chaotically from the murder to the revelation about

Oscar to the state of her stomach. But before long her stomach demanded her full attention. She barely made it to the bathroom in time.

Once she finished vomiting – for the time being – she felt too weak to cross the sitting room to her bedroom. Her limbs seemed weighted and stiff. She slumped on the floor, feeling as if she might never move again. Her eyes and mouth watered uncontrollably, and her consciousness ebbed and flowed – but mostly ebbed.

When it flowed again, the thought crossed her mind that she had never felt this terrible merely from eating something that disagreed with her. The word 'poison' hovered in her weakened mind. She needed help – fast.

All the others were still downstairs. She dragged herself to the intercom, pushed all the buttons at once, and said with all the volume she could muster – which came out barely above a whisper – 'Help!'

Then her consciousness ebbed and did not return.

Luke heard Emily's whispered plea from the library, where he happened to be standing near the intercom; otherwise it would have been lost in the general conversation. Immediately he kicked himself for leaving her alone, now that he knew for sure she was in danger. He should have gone up with her – but he'd wanted to listen to the others in case anyone dropped any sort of clue.

He raced up the stairs two at a time and burst into her apartment, calling, 'Emily?' No response – except from the cats, who were yowling like the world's end. He checked the bedroom first, then the sitting room, and finally found her slumped on the bathroom floor. Dear God, why hadn't he thought of this? The killer had poisoned once – why wouldn't he or she try it again?

He knelt next to Emily and felt for her pulse, sagging in relief when it fluttered beneath his fingers. Slow, though, and weak. The smell of vomit was strong in the air. He had to get her to a doctor right away.

While his heart panicked, his brain went into crisis mode. He pulled out his cell phone and called an ambulance, then

Sam Griffiths. Toss-up which would get here sooner. In the meantime, he carried Emily into the sitting room and laid her on the loveseat, on her side in case she vomited again. After calling Pete and Heather to bring in the crime scene team – he was betting on attempted murder here, praying for all he was worth it wouldn't turn into more than that – he returned to the bathroom to see if any clue jumped out at him.

The only thing out of place was the bottle of Ambien, which Emily had left on the sink. Luke picked it up with a handkerchief and dropped it into his pocket. That would be the first thing to analyze. It was possible the medicine was fine and she'd simply had a bad reaction to it, but he knew she'd taken it before with no ill effects. More likely it had been tampered with, though how and when, he had no idea.

He thought back over the day. He'd been here for all the main meals – all except tea – and he hadn't seen Emily eat or drink anything the others hadn't taken as well. The Ambien was his best bet.

He used the intercom to warn Katie of the coming invasion of personnel. After what seemed a lifetime but was really about ten minutes, everyone arrived – Sam Griffiths first, ambulance hot on her tail, and Pete and Heather bringing up the rear. Emily's little sitting room was crowded to bursting point.

Luke told them the little he knew. Sam examined Emily, then said, 'No sign of corrosive. Best bet gastric lavage. Do that in the ambulance. Get her out of here.'

Luke gave some quick instructions to Pete and Heather, then followed the gurney down the stairs. He wasn't about to let Emily out of his sight until he knew she would live. If she didn't, nothing else would matter.

Luke spent the night at the hospital, alternately pacing the waiting room and collapsing exhausted in a lumpy vinyl chair, while a team of doctors and nurses worked frantically to save Emily's life. He wasn't a churchgoing man, but through the small hours he prayed from the depths of his soul that Emily would live.

Let her live, God, and I swear I don't care if she never marries me. I don't care how many brainy fortune hunters she gets a

crush on. I don't care where she wants to live or what she wants
to do with the rest of her life. Just – let – her – live.

By four a.m., his nerves were taut as a violin string; he
swore one more minute of waiting would make them snap.
Then Sam stumbled into the waiting area and slumped down
beside him.

'She's safe,' Sam grunted. 'Keep her a couple days, but
she'll do.'

Luke started to his feet. 'Can I see her?'

Sam raised one eyebrow at him. 'She's asleep. Sedated. Go
hold her hand if you want.'

He was halfway out the door before she finished talking.
At Emily's bedside, he collapsed into a chair and reached for
her hand, then raised his eyes to her face. It was pale, almost
as white as the pillowcase beneath her head; her auburn hair
flamed out between them like the dividing line between life
and death. A line she had come so perilously close to crossing.

He stroked her cheek, relieved to find it warm as normal
beneath his hand. 'You gave me quite a scare there, girl,' he
said softly. 'Please don't ever do that again.'

Her lashes fluttered as if in response. He leaned over and
kissed her forehead. 'I'm gonna find out who did this to you
and how. We'll get the bugger this time, Em. He'll have gotten
careless the second time around – they always do. We'll get
him, and you'll be home and safe for Twelfth Night, just like
you planned.'

Reluctantly he left her and went back out to Sam, who was
still slumped in the waiting room chair. 'Any idea what caused
this?' he asked her.

She jolted awake. 'Huh? Oh, what she took? Hard to say
at this point. Have to get stuff analyzed. Million things cause
vomiting. Other symptoms more distinctive – tearing, drooling,
partial paralysis. First guess, some kind of andromedotoxin.'

'What's that in layman's language?'

'Biological poison, found in plants like rhododendrons,
azaleas, mountain laurel. Not hard to extract if you know what
you're doing. Small dose, though. More and we wouldn't have
been able to save her.'

'Couldn't be botulism? That causes paralysis, doesn't it?'

'Yeah, but botulism, you get dry mouth. She was drooling.'
'So we're definitely talking deliberate poisoning – not accidental food poisoning.'
'I'd say so, based on symptoms.' Sam gave a tremendous yawn. 'Gotta get some sleep. Talk to the lab tomorrow.' She glanced at her watch. 'More like later today.' She pushed to her feet and staggered off.

Luke paced a circle around the waiting room. His impulse was to get the Ambien to the lab immediately, make them start working on it that very minute. But the reality was that no one would be there for hours. He might as well get some sleep himself.

It wasn't worth driving home at this point. He went back to Emily's room, checked she was still sleeping peacefully, and made himself as comfortable as possible in her bedside chair. He set his phone alarm for seven-thirty. He'd be at the lab the minute they opened the doors.

TWENTY-TWO

Emily was still sleeping when Luke's alarm went off. He made a few calls – to the main office to request a deputy to guard Emily's door, and to Pete at Windy Corner to make sure nobody entered or left the property without authorization.

He made himself presentable while waiting for the deputy to arrive. In a few minutes he opened the door to a boy who looked about sixteen but was dressed in a deputy's uniform. Luke groaned inwardly, then reminded himself that while the young ones lacked experience, they were usually zealous and eager to please.

'Deputy Mario Gonzalez reporting for duty, sir.' The young man stood at attention, and Luke half-expected him to salute.

Luke stuck out his hand. 'Lieutenant Luke Richards. They tell you what this is about?'

'Not much. All they said was guard duty.'

'Right. This lady here' – he gestured toward Emily in the bed – 'is Emily Cavanaugh. She's been deliberately poisoned. I don't know for sure who did it or how, but there's a good chance the perp will try again. So I need you to make sure nobody gets in here who isn't authorized medical staff or specifically approved by me. Make sure you check their ID – the perp could dress up as an orderly or something. And no outside food or drink from anybody. Got that?'

The young deputy's eyes went wide. 'Yessir.' He looked both intelligent and excited to be entrusted with such responsibility.

Somewhat reassured, Luke took off for the lab. Sam had already sent samples of Emily's blood and the contents of her stomach. He dropped off the Ambien and told Caitlyn to look for a match. 'Doc thought maybe a—' He consulted the card where he'd scribbled down what Sam told him she suspected. 'Andromedotoxin. So look for that first. Fast as you can, please.'

'Sure thing,' Caitlyn said. 'Not much else going on right now anyway.'

'Oh, and if the Ambien turns up clean, any chance you'll be able to tell how the poison was administered?'

'Not likely. I mean, we can tell intravenous versus ingested, but if it was in her food, it'd be hard to tell which food. But we'll give it a shot.'

Luke flashed her his best smile, which occasionally still worked even on young girls. 'Thanks. I owe you one.'

He returned to the hospital to find Deputy Gonzalez still standing at attention outside Emily's door. Luke bit back a smile. 'Anything to report, Deputy?'

'Nothing, sir. One visit from the day nurse. I checked his ID.'

'Good man. You can go take a leak, get coffee or whatever. I'll be here for a little while.' Gonzalez turned to go, and Luke added, 'Oh, and when you get back, it's OK to sit down.' He pointed to the folding chair he'd placed next to the door before he left.

Emily was awake but groggy. 'Hey there, beautiful,' he greeted her, sitting by the bed and taking her hand. 'You gave us quite a scare last night.'

'Sorry,' she mumbled. 'Don't know what happened. Never been sick like that before.'

'You've never been poisoned before. Lab's working on what the poison was. We've got to figure out how it got into you.'

She gave a tiny nod.

'Did you take some of that Ambien last night?'

Another nod. 'Just one.'

'Is that when you started feeling bad?'

'I guess so.' Her speech was slow and a little slurred. 'I was pretty tired before that, though. That's why I went up so early.'

'OK. Now listen, Em, this is important. Did anybody else know you had that Ambien? Was the bottle ever where somebody else could get to it?'

'Oscar knew. I gave him some. Last night.'

Luke's pulse raced. 'Did you see him take it?'

'No. He took the pill back to his room.'

'Was the bottle out of your sight at that point? Even for a second?'

'I handed him the bottle . . . then I poured a glass of water. I had my back to him while I poured the water. Why?'

So Lansing could have removed his own pill, then poured something over the rest of them. Probably wouldn't take more than a few drops, and if it absorbed quickly, Emily might have been too tired to notice. 'And you took your own pill out of the bottle after that?'

'Yes.' Her eyelids drooped.

Luke was grateful she was too out of it to realize the implications of his line of questioning. She wouldn't thank him for suspecting Lansing of being in any way involved.

He had more questions for her, but she was almost asleep. He'd come back later. He kissed her gently and slipped out.

Gonzalez was sitting in the folding chair, sipping a steaming cup of coffee. He moved to stand, but Luke waved him back down. 'Here's my number,' he said, handing the deputy a business card. 'Call me if you have any questions, and let me know when she's fully awake, OK?'

Gonzalez took the card as if it were made of glass. 'Yessir.' He looked up at Luke as if unsure whether to speak further.

'Something on your mind, son?'

'It's just – well, it's none of my business, really. I only wondered if – she's a personal friend of yours.' He nodded toward Emily.

'She's my fiancée,' Luke answered. Emily might not acknowledge that relationship, but he was determined to make it real. 'Guard her with your life.'

Luke stopped by his office to change into his uniform and pick up his gear, then headed back to Windy Corner. He didn't dare wait till he had lab results to begin his investigation.

Breakfast was over. He found Katie washing up in the kitchen and gave her an update. She raised her gloved and dripping hands to heaven.

'Oh, thank God. I've been so worried about her. Do you have any idea what caused it?' She went pale. 'It wasn't anything I cooked, was it?'

'It sure as heck wasn't run-of-the-mill food poisoning. It was deliberate. We don't know yet exactly what or how. So it could have been in her food, but somebody would have had to put it there. Anybody else been into the fridge or pantry lately?'

'Not that I know of. But I'm in and out of here all day. And the last few days have been so chaotic. Somebody could easily have slipped in when I was upstairs or something.'

'Ever see any sign of anything being tampered with? Not quite the way you left it? Even a lid out of place.'

Katie frowned, slowly shaking her head. 'Not that I recall. But honestly, I've been run off my feet lately – there could be an elephant in the pantry, and I might not notice unless he polished off the peanut butter.'

Lizzie whimpered from her play-space under the table. Katie sighed heavily and bent to pick her up.

'It's OK, sweet cheeks,' she cooed, ruffling Lizzie's hair. 'Even Lizzie's worried about Mrs C. Kids are very sensitive to atmosphere.' She rubbed her nose against Lizzie's, then looked back at Luke. 'You know, I think I did notice something – not wrong exactly, but a little off. It's nagging at the back of my mind, but I can't put my finger on it.'

'Right. I'll be here for a while, talking to the others. Let me know if it comes to you.'

The others. That was a euphemism for Dustin and Oscar Lansing. Lansing first, since he definitely had access to the Ambien. Luke headed upstairs.

Marguerite was coming out of her room and caught him on the landing. 'Emily – is she all right? May I go and see her?'

'She'll be all right, but no visitors for now. Not till I have a better idea what happened. I've got a guard on her door.'

'*Mon dieu!* Then it was poison?'

'Yep.'

'And you think the poisoner may try again?'

'Don't see why not. This is the second attempt – the cyanide in the amaretto must have been meant for Emily. If the poisoner didn't stop after one failure, no reason to think they'll stop after two.'

Marguerite raised her hands in bafflement. 'But who would want to kill Emily?'

'I have a glimmer of an idea about that, but I can't discuss it. Meanwhile, probably best to keep to yourself as much as possible.'

'*Oui, je comprends.* I will not get in your way. Find this fiend, Luke. Find him quickly. Emily must be kept safe.' She slipped back into her room, and he heard the bolt slide shut.

Luke turned to Lansing's door and raised his hand to knock, then paused. He could hear voices, or a voice – probably Lansing talking on his cell phone. Luke strained but couldn't catch the words. After a few seconds of silence, he knocked.

Lansing opened the door almost immediately, looking pale and pinched. He raised a hand to smooth back his tousled hair, and the hand was trembling. 'Lieutenant! Any news about Emily?'

'She's going to be all right.'

Luke observed his reaction narrowly. Lansing's face relaxed, and he staggered to the desk chair and fell into it. 'Oh, thank God. Thank God. I was so worried about her.'

'You up to answering a few questions?'

'Questions?' His face took on that pinched look again.

'Looks like you were probably the last person with her before she got sick. Just need to go over what happened.'

Lansing swallowed visibly. 'Right. What do you want to know?'

'Emily said you knew she had a prescription for Ambien. That right?'

'Yes, I overheard her asking you to pick it up for her. I haven't been sleeping well either, so I asked her if I could borrow some.' His mouth curled slightly. 'Well, have some. I wasn't planning to give it back.'

'That was day before yesterday. Did you take any that night?'

'No, that night I forgot about it. By the time I remembered – because I couldn't get to sleep – Emily had gone to bed, and I didn't want to disturb her.'

'But last night you remembered.'

'Yes, I was so exhausted I couldn't forget. I followed her when she went up, and she gave me a pill.'

'She gave you a pill? Or did she hand you the bottle and let you take your own?'

His eyes widened. 'Oh, I guess she handed me the bottle.'

'So what did you do then?'

'I shook out a pill, put the lid back on the bottle and gave it back to her. Then I went to my room, where I had a water glass, to take the pill.'

'You didn't by any chance add anything to the bottle while you had it in your hand?'

Lansing looked genuinely confused. 'Add anything? Why would I do that?'

Luke ignored the question. 'Did you actually swallow your pill?'

'Yes, as soon as I got back here.'

'And you haven't been sick at all?'

'No. I got a good night's sleep and felt much better until I heard about Emily this morning. I even slept through all the excitement last night.'

Luke pouched his lips and rubbed the back of his neck. This line of questioning wasn't panning out the way he'd expected. Of course, he had only Lansing's word, and the man could be lying, but his physical reactions seemed genuine.

Lansing sat up straight in his chair. 'Are you thinking Emily had a bad reaction to the Ambien? She'd taken it before, hadn't she?'

'Yeah. Wasn't that. Not the right symptoms.'

What little color had returned to Lansing's face drained out again. 'Do you mean – you think she was poisoned?'

Luke nailed him with his eyes. 'What do you think?'

'Me?' Lansing's lip trembled. He turned toward the desk and moved some papers around, but his hands shook like aspen leaves in an autumn breeze. He shoved them under his arms. 'How should I know? You're the detective.'

'You don't know of any reason anyone would want to harm Emily?'

'Of course not. I've only known her a week. I can't imagine anyone wanting to harm her, but if there were someone, how would I know?'

His protestations were less convincing than his previous body language had been. Lansing might not be guilty himself, but he knew – or suspected – something. Luke would bet his badge on that.

Luke trudged back down the stairs. The Ambien was looking like a less probable medium for the poison than he'd thought. That left the field wide open for anything Emily had consumed the day before. And Dustin, who occupied the room right next to the kitchen, would have had the easiest opportunity to doctor something she ate.

Luke knocked on Dustin's door and got a slurred 'Whaddya want?' in response. Good grief, the man couldn't be drunk already – it was barely ten o'clock in the morning.

'Sheriff here. Need to talk to you.' No response. 'Now.'

He heard shuffling, then the door opened a crack. Luke pushed it far enough to see into the room, which was littered with clothing and empty bottles and reeked of whiskey. Dustin was slumped on the bed. 'Not here. In the library.'

'Oh, all right, Mr Lawman. If you insist.' He pushed himself up with a visible effort and dragged his feet into the next room, where he immediately flopped in a chair.

Luke took a detour into the dining room and poured a large cup of coffee from the thermos there, leaving it black. He carried the cup into the library and shoved it in front of Dustin. 'Drink. I need you coherent.'

Dustin waved his hand. 'I'm not drunk. Just sick of all this crap. World-weary.' He gave a derisive snort. 'The world-weary anti-hero, that's me.'

Luke's hand with the coffee did not move. 'I don't care if you're drunk or not. You need coffee. Drink it.'

With a theatrical sigh, Dustin took the cup from Luke's hand and downed half of it in one long gulp. Luke supposed it had been sitting long enough it was no longer really hot.

He sat opposite Dustin and leaned toward him. 'You neglected to tell me something. Something that could be pretty important, as it turns out. You knew Emily before.'

Dustin's face scrunched in what looked like genuine confusion. 'Emily? Nah. Don't recognize her. Don't remember the name.'

Luke gritted his teeth. This guy tried his patience more than most. 'Think back to your year at Reed. You had Professor Cavanaugh for Hum One Ten. She flunked you, along with a couple of other profs. You had to leave the school.'

Light visibly dawned. 'Professor *Cavanaugh*? Why didn't you say so? I don't think I ever heard Emily's last name.' His face split in an ugly guffaw. 'Hell, yeah, I remember Professor Cavanaugh. I gave her hell. She thought she could make something of me. "Redeem" me or something. I showed her.'

'And she flunked you. That must have hurt.'

'Nah. I deserved it. And I was only there 'cause my parents made me go. I never wanted to go to Reed. Not my kind of place at all. All those brainy types sweating it out for no good reason. Did my year, flunked out, my parents had no choice but to accept I just wasn't the academic type.'

Luke eyed Dustin narrowly as he calmly finished his coffee. What he was saying had the ring of truth, but Luke wouldn't take it at face value. Dustin had as good an opportunity as anyone to put cyanide in the amaretto at some point between dinner and charades, and until they knew how Emily had been poisoned yesterday, he couldn't be ruled out for that either. Luke was keeping this poor excuse for a human being on his suspect list for now.

If the poison Emily consumed had been in anything she ate, the person who'd know best about that would be Katie. He headed back toward the kitchen, but Katie met him in the hall.

'Luke! There you are. I remembered what was off.' She beckoned him back into the kitchen and shut the door. 'Look at this.' She pointed to a small jar sitting on the table.

He bent down and squinted at it. 'Honey?'

Katie nodded. 'Mrs C's been putting honey in her tea the last few weeks. I had a jar of local blackberry honey she especially liked. When I was in the pantry a minute ago, I saw that jar and realized it's not the same one. But I think it is the one I used at tea yesterday. I remember thinking something was odd about it, but I was in a hurry so I went ahead and put it on the tray.' She paled. 'So maybe it was my fault after all.'

Luke scrutinized the bottle. The label, which looked home-made, said *Oregon Coast Blackberry Honey*. 'You sure it's different? It says it's local blackberry honey.'

'Yes, the label's the same – that's why it didn't strike me at first. But this jar is fuller than the one I had. The old one was practically empty. Over Christmas I'd been worrying it wouldn't last till the weather cleared and I could get out to get some more.'

Luke straightened, frowning. 'You sure you have no idea who might have been in here?'

Katie shook her head. 'I've been over and over the last day and a half – it had to be after tea the day before yesterday, because I know I had the old jar then. But I can't think of anything. I never saw anyone in here except Mrs C herself. She'd hardly poison her own honey.'

'No. Was she the only person who ever used it?'

'Yes. The others took sugar or nothing.'

Luke heaved a sigh. 'All right. I'll get this to the lab and see what they can figure out.' He took out a glove and an evidence bag, picked up the jar by the lid, and dropped it into the bag. 'Probably won't be any fingerprints – except yours, of course – but we can always hope.'

Before leaving, he made the rounds of the guests to ask if any of them had been in the kitchen or the pantry at any time in the last thirty-six hours. They all denied it and seemed sincerely baffled by the question.

Luke took the honey to the lab, where Caitlyn met him with a smile. 'We've confirmed andromedotoxin in the patient's blood,' she said. 'Still have to test the Ambien.'

He handed her the bag with the honey jar. 'Do this first. Ambien's looking less likely.'

Caitlyn raised an eyebrow. 'Honey, eh? Now that is interesting.'

'How come?'

'Andromedotoxin comes from certain flowering plants – rhododendrons, azaleas, that sort of thing. And honey made by bees that feed on those flowers is as poisonous as the plants themselves.'

Luke started. 'You don't say. So the honey itself could be the culprit. As opposed to somebody adding something to it.'

'Sure could. If this is it, your victim had a lucky escape – wouldn't take more than a teaspoon to kill.'

'What about the taste? Would that give it away?'

'It would taste bitter. Or so I'm told.' Caitlyn removed the jar from the bag with gloved hands. 'I'll get right on this. Let you know in a couple of hours.'

TWENTY-THREE

Emily dozed fitfully through the morning, awakening every time a nurse came in to check her monitors or fuss with her IV. One would think, if rest were the best healer, a hospital would let a patient actually rest instead of disturbing her every ten minutes. But no.

She felt weak and sleepy, but otherwise well enough – the nausea and the horrible creeping paralysis in her limbs were gone. Thank God. According to Sam, she'd had a lucky escape. If she'd consumed more poison, or if medical help had been delayed . . . Emily shuddered. No, she wouldn't think about that.

In her intervals of wakefulness, she struggled to remember something, anything, about the previous day that might point toward how she'd been poisoned – and by whom. Luke seemed to think it was the Ambien, but that was silly; no one would have had the opportunity to tamper with it, and surely she'd have noticed if there'd been anything different about those familiar little pink pills.

She thought over everything she'd eaten and drunk the previous day, and even tried to make a list, though her writing was still shaky. Breakfast – she'd helped herself from the common dishes on the sideboard, so if any of those foods had been poisoned, other people would have been affected as well. Mid-morning pastry – no one could have predicted which one she'd take. Lunch – soup and salad from common bowls, bread from a common loaf. Theoretically, someone could have added something to her plate – as they could have at breakfast, for that matter – but her neighbors had been Marguerite and Olivia at lunch, Luke and Ian at breakfast. None of those people could have reason to harm her. And those meals seemed too distant from the onset of symptoms, anyway.

Tea. That might be getting into a reasonable time frame – roughly six hours before she began to feel ill. She'd eaten pastries and sandwiches from the common tray, drunk tea from the common pot.

But only one sip of tea. She remembered now – the honey tasted bitter, so she'd set the rest aside undrunk.

No one else used honey. And anyone in the house could have noticed that.

She was reaching for the phone to call Luke when the door opened and he stepped in.

'Hey, beautiful. You're looking almost human.'

She made a face at him. 'Charmer. Well, I feel almost human, so there.'

He bent over her and kissed her forehead. His voice came out in a hoarse whisper. 'I thought I'd lost you there for a while.'

She pulled his head down and kissed him properly. 'You can't get rid of me that easily. We Worthings are tough.'

'That you are.'

'I was about to call you. I think it might have been the honey.'

Luke's eyebrows shot up. 'Oh, you got there too, huh? Katie realized the jar was fuller than she'd left it when she used it yesterday for tea. I took the jar to the lab, and they told me it could easily have contained the stuff that got to you. They're testing it now.' He told her what Caitlyn had said about andromedotoxin and honey.

'So someone got into the pantry and switched the jars? Or added honey to the old jar, I guess, but that would take longer, be messy. Wouldn't be hard to find another of the same kind of jar – they sell it at that roadside stand in Garibaldi.'

'One thing I wondered – Caitlyn said a teaspoon would've killed you. Did you use only a tiny bit?'

'*Au contraire*, as Marguerite would say, I put in more than usual. But the tea tasted bad, so I only drank one sip.'

Luke blew out a long breath. 'Thank God for that.' He leaned forward and gripped her hand – the one without the IV. 'Em, if I'd lost you – God, I can't even think about it. I'm tempted to make them keep you in here till I've got this killer safely behind bars.'

'Oh, please, Luke, not that. I can't even sleep in this place. It's like a mall on Black Friday in here.'

'I can't let you go back to Windy Corner. That honey had to have been switched by someone staying in the house. My money's on Dustin, but whoever it is, they might easily try again.'

Emily could not believe any of her guests – even Dustin – could want her dead. 'Actually, that's not quite true. Wanda could have done it when she came over yesterday morning.'

'Yesterday morning? You never said. What for?'

'For no good reason, apparently. She said she wanted to check with you if it was OK for her to go to Seaside. You weren't there, so I gave her your number, and she left the room. I didn't see her out, so who knows what she got up to before she left the house?'

He frowned. 'Gotta admit she does seem kinda like the poisoning type. Poison*ous*, at any rate. But why would she want to hurt you? She's expecting you to provide for her comfortable old age.'

'I don't know why. But she had the opportunity. And I don't see how Dustin could have gotten hold of that honey. He hasn't left the house since he arrived, so he'd have to have known ahead of time I'd be using that particular type. No one knew that except Katie. Not even Marguerite.'

'Yeah, but we don't know for sure the honey was substituted. Dustin could have added poison to the jar after he found out you used it and nobody else did. After bungling it with Cruella he would have wanted to be sure it got to you.'

'I suppose.' Given her intense dislike of Dustin, Emily wasn't sure why she should be reluctant to consider him as a murderer now. Perhaps she didn't want to believe in his motive, as it would, so to speak, poison her memories of her teaching time at Reed.

Luke clapped his hands to his thighs. 'No rest for the wicked. I'm going to go back and search Dustin's belongings again. Think I'll check on Wanda's supposed mother in Seaside too. And I better apply for a search warrant for her place in Corvallis.'

'Corvallis?' Emily's heart sank. 'I don't like the idea of you being that far away.'

He leaned over and gave her a quick kiss. 'It's only a couple of hours. I'll wait till tomorrow to go over there so I'll be sure to have daylight. You'll be fine. Gonzalez out there is the soul of vigilance, let me tell you.'

He stepped to the door, opened it, and said, 'Deputy, come in here a sec, would you?'

A dark-haired young man who looked as if he'd dressed up in his daddy's uniform stepped tentatively into the room.

'Emily Cavanaugh, I'd like you to meet Deputy Mario Gonzalez. He's guarding your door with his life, aren't you, Deputy?'

The young man stood at attention, his right hand jerking a bit as if he'd just stopped himself from saluting. 'Yessir. Absolutely, sir.'

Luke thumped him on the back. 'All right, Deputy, back to your post.' He turned to Emily. 'And Pete's on duty at Windy Corner, so nothing's going to happen while I'm gone. I promise.'

'You shouldn't make promises that involve other people. You have no control over the outcome.'

'No, but if anybody threatened you, I'd sense it from miles away and be back here in a flash. I've got superpowers like that.' He grinned at her.

The twinkle in his eye dissipated her fears. 'All right, Superman. But come back as soon as you can.'

The next day, Luke told Emily he'd found out from his granny that Wanda's mother in Seaside Rest, or at least her visit to her, was a fabrication; no visitor of Wanda's description had been seen there. 'So her showing up at your place was completely pointless, unless she came for one of two things: either to conspire with Oscar or to plant that honey in your pantry.'

Both were uncomfortable thoughts for Emily. But now that she'd recovered from being poisoned, she felt the worst possible news would be that Oscar had any kind of nefarious intentions toward her. Wanda as a poisoner was more believable than Oscar as a fortune hunter – though her motive was still obscure.

Luke took off for Corvallis, and Emily was left alone in the hospital – alone, that is, except for Deputy Gonzalez at the door and the constant parade of medical personnel checking on this and that. By this time Emily felt fine, more or less, and was impatient to be home; but Luke and Sam agreed that stay she must, so stay she did.

Thus when the parade of unknown nurses and orderlies was interrupted by a familiar freckled face peeking past the strong restraining arm of Deputy Gonzalez, Emily was overjoyed. 'Jamie! Come in!'

'You know this man, ma'am?' Gonzalez asked with a frown.

'He's my lawyer. I promise he's not a threat. Please, let him in.'

The deputy reluctantly lowered his arm and stood back. Shooting him a nervous smile, Jamie came in, briefcase under his arm.

'I found those files you were asking about,' he said, pulling a fat sheaf of paper out of the case. 'The "L" was for Lansing.'

TWENTY-FOUR

The following afternoon, Emily lounged in her own chair in her library, her feet up on an ottoman, a cashmere-blend afghan of her own making tucked up around her by a loving Katie, a glass of sherry in her hand, and Levin in her lap. But despite all these creature comforts, her soul was in turmoil. Murder investigation aside, the revelation contained in the files Jamie had found had turned her world upside down, and she'd had little time to process it. Now here she was, surrounded by all the surviving guests from her Christmas party, anticipating what promised to be one of the trickiest, tensest scenes of her life.

On his return from Corvallis the previous evening, she and Luke had traded the information they'd each acquired during his absence. They'd agreed on two things: they had a clear suspect, and their evidence against that suspect was all circumstantial, not enough to be sure of a conviction. Then Emily had an idea: they would stage a mass confrontation scene, straight out of a Christie novel. With any luck, they could trick the murderer into confessing. It always worked for Poirot.

She surveyed the room. Luke's deputy Heather lurked in a dark corner with a recorder, her eyes sparkling with excitement. Emily's local friends exhibited varying degrees of curiosity, from placid Veronica to controlled Hilary to wired Devon, who was practically bouncing in his seat with excitement. He'd whispered to her when he came in, 'This is it, isn't it – the confrontation scene? Who'll be Poirot, you or Luke?'

She'd smiled without answering. Continuing her survey, she noted that Marguerite and Jamie were alert and engaged; Katie gripped Jamie's hand, looking as if she'd far rather be in her apartment, where her sister Erin was currently getting Lizzie ready for bed. Katie always hated to admit that any human being could harbor enough evil to murder – even though she'd been witness to and victim of plenty of evil in her young life.

The writer guests huddled together with their backs to the fire, Ian and Olivia on the loveseat and the two young men on straight chairs. Ian and Olivia hid their nervousness under polite chat with Oscar, but the white knuckles of their linked hands gave it away. Dustin sat silent and sullen, checking his watch. He could not be more anxious to leave Windy Corner than Emily was to have him gone.

Oscar was jumpier than Emily had ever seen him. He gave disjointed, irrelevant answers to Ian's innocuous questions, and he adjusted his tie so many times Emily feared he would strangle himself.

Looking at him was too painful given what she now knew. She fixed her eyes on a small table in the center of the room on which stood a carved wooden box. Only she and Luke knew what it contained. Several people looked at it curiously, but no glance lingered.

The last person to arrive was Wanda Wilkins. Pete had been dispatched to collect her and instructed not to take no for an answer.

Wanda sauntered in, dressed in a strip of leather – too short and tight to be properly called a skirt – over fishnet stockings and her usual high boots. She slipped off her shaggy fake-fur coat to reveal a plunging halter top that bared far more of her sagging, leathery chest, back, and midriff than any sane person would ever care to show or see. Emily's guess was that she had coaxed Pete into allowing her time to change. Not even Wanda would parade around her cottage in the dead of winter in such a getup with no one to witness it.

Apparently her outfit gave her confidence, perhaps even a feeling of power; she took the one remaining seat in the room, a straight-backed wooden chair, with an air of one who expects nothing to happen that she won't be able to handle with one red-taloned hand tied behind her back. When her eyes fell on the box on the table, her confident air shimmered momentarily, like a hot country road, but then settled back into place. Pete unobtrusively took up his station a couple of feet behind her chair.

Luke and Emily had agreed that he would play Poirot and lead the conversation, with her as – despite the literary non sequitur – Miss Marple, rather than the bumbling Hastings, acting as his foil. At least Emily vaguely resembled Miss Marple, or would in another decade or two; but the very thought of the tall, casually masculine, quintessentially American Luke playing the part of the dapper, fastidious little Belgian with his 'little gray cells' and his precious moustaches threatened to destroy her composure before they even got started.

When Wanda was settled, Luke waited a minute to let the atmosphere simmer, then stood and said, 'I guess you're all wondering why I called you here.'

A polite titter ran around the room.

'I want to go over the events of the last few days with everybody here together. Now, as you all know, Cruella Crime died of cyanide poisoning here on Christmas night. We've found some evidence of how that was done, but nothing conclusive about who did it. In terms of opportunity, it could have been any one of you.'

Part of Emily's job was to notice people's reactions as Luke spoke. At this point she saw curiosity on most faces, with a tinge of relief on some. But Wanda's mouth twisted in a complacent smirk.

Luke continued, 'Naturally, we looked first at the people who obviously had something against the victim – Dustin, Ian, and Olivia.' He turned to face the three of them, and Emily noted the heightened tension in their posture. Dustin scowled furiously, while Ian and Olivia sat alert as cats poised to flee.

'Ian, you showed the most overt hostility to Cruella, and it didn't take long to find out why. You were married to her briefly a number of years ago.'

'For my sins,' Ian muttered, and Olivia covered his hand with her free one.

'Not only did you have a messy divorce, but she blamed Olivia for your breakup.' Ian frowned and opened his mouth, but Luke held up a palm. 'I'm going to have to ask you all not to talk unless I specifically ask you a question. Now, you two both claim that accusation was false, and whether it was or not doesn't enter into this investigation. The point is, Cruella persecuted both of you professionally and caused considerable damage to your careers. Either one of you separately, or both of you together, would have had a plenty good motive of revenge for doing her in.'

The two clung to each other, pale and wide-eyed. 'The only problem with that theory was you had no way of knowing she was going to show up here. The digital trail you both left suggested you did everything you could to keep away from Cruella and forget she even existed. Whereas the way this murder was done, it was pretty certain it had to have been planned in advance. The murderer had no way of obtaining the cyanide after he or she got here, since you were all iced in. So I tentatively ruled the two of you out.'

Ian and Olivia sagged against the back of the loveseat and exchanged a look full of something that might have been hope. Emily fervently prayed some good would come out of all this in the form of a new start for that long-suffering couple.

'Next up was Dustin,' Luke went on, shifting to face him. 'It turned out Cruella had been blackmailing you.' When Dustin looked fit to explode, Luke held up a palm again. 'No need to go into why except to say your career was on the line. The point is, you had one heck of a strong motive for getting rid of her. And in your case, the difficulty about the planning ahead didn't apply. You'd told the whole world via Facebook that you were heading down here for the holidays. You knew Cruella was watching you online – you could easily have done that on purpose to lure her to follow you.'

'Lure her!' Dustin spluttered. 'You're out of your freaking head!'

Luke continued as if he hadn't spoken. 'And poison, being a coward's weapon, seemed like the way you'd go. However, I couldn't find any evidence of you procuring poison. And we soon found out we had another suspect whose motive for killing Cruella was almost as strong as yours.'

He turned to Hilary. 'Years ago, one of Cruella's books more or less ruined your life – tacitly accused you of murder and drove you out of England.'

Devon spun in his seat to face his partner. 'Hilary! You never told me they'd found out about that.'

'Hush, Dev. I didn't want to worry you. There was nothing in it.'

'We questioned you, but we had the same problem with you as with Ian and Olivia. You didn't know till the day before that Cruella was here, and the freeze was on by then. Unless you keep potassium cyanide lying around the house – which is possible, but only barely – you'd have had no chance to obtain it.'

Hilary whispered to Devon, 'You see?'

Devon subsided into his seat.

'That pretty much exhausted the obvious suspects in Cruella's case,' Luke went on. 'But we did also have to consider the possibility that the poison was actually meant for Emily. The amaretto did belong to her, after all. That would let Ian, Olivia, and Hilary out altogether – none of them had any reason to harm Emily. But it did make us take another look at you, Dustin.' Luke whirled to face him again.

'Turns out you were a student of Emily's years ago, and she gave you one of the failing grades that got you kicked out of Reed. Some people might call that a motive for revenge. And in this case, you knew you'd be spending the week with Emily and could easily have brought the poison with you.'

'But—' Dustin spluttered. 'I told you! I don't care about flunking out. I was grateful to those profs for giving me a way out of a place I never wanted to be.'

'You did say that, yes. People *say* all sorts of things.' Luke gave him a hard stare worthy of Paddington Bear before moving on.

'But we hadn't yet ruled out the idea that Cruella was in fact the intended victim. And in poking around on Cruella's computer, I came across another possibility for her murderer. Or you might say two.'

He turned to Oscar, who was sitting next to Ian and Olivia, across the room from Wanda. 'I found an innocent little file with some information about Oscar Lansing. Including the fact that Wanda Wilkins' – he stepped back to have them both in his sights – 'just happens to be your mom.'

A subdued uproar shook the room. Clearly everyone found this news as incredible as Emily herself had at first. Devon leaned over and stage-whispered to her, 'The unacknowledged child trope! I *knew* this was a Christie novel!'

Oscar's already pale face turned pasty white. His eyes darted toward Wanda. 'I didn't say a word – honestly I didn't.' His tone was that of a small boy attempting to evade a spanking – or worse.

Wanda simply smiled. 'No big deal, sweetie. After all, our relationship is hardly a motive for murder.'

'That was my first thought,' Luke said. 'Even though Oscar was born out of wedlock, these days that's nothing to write home about. If Cruella tried to blackmail the pair of you with that, you would've laughed in her face.' Oscar relaxed slightly, and Wanda's smirk intensified.

'But then I started to wonder: if it was no big deal, why were you keeping it secret in the first place? What did the two of you have to gain from that – or to lose if the secret came out?'

He let that question hang in the air for half a minute. Oscar merely looked baffled, but Wanda's smirk became fixed and brittle.

'First I thought maybe you were after Emily's fortune. Oscar and Emily hit it off right from the start – what if Wanda had the bright idea of marrying her son off to an heiress in order to set him and herself up for life?'

Wanda's sagging flesh jiggled with silent laughter, while Oscar became indignant. 'I would never do such a thing! I mean, not deceitfully. Not that I'm not terribly fond of you, Emily, but – well, we're friends, aren't we? Anyway, I knew you and Luke were an item from the first day we met.'

Emily spoke for the first time since Luke had begun. 'I never believed it of you for a moment.' She gave Oscar a reassuring smile, and he leaned back in his chair.

'Emily pretty much convinced me of that, too. But the clincher came from a different quarter.' Luke turned his attention away from Oscar and Wanda and made a slow circuit of the room, coming to rest by the bar shelf. 'We discovered a couple of things that made us start to look at the murder in a different light. For one thing, the lab results showed the cyanide had been added to the amaretto bottle, not the glass. The amaretto that was meant for Emily alone.'

He let that sink in for a moment as shocked faces turned toward Emily. 'We also found the vial that had contained the poison right outside this window.' He gestured behind him. 'So it was pretty clear the cyanide had been added earlier in the evening, before anybody knew Cruella was going to drink it at all. That meant Emily had to be the intended victim.'

He strode back to the middle of the room. 'Now, that made nonsense of the Wanda-and-Oscar-as-fortune-hunters theory. If they were going to kill Emily to get her money, they'd have to do it *after* Oscar and Emily were married, not before. But we didn't let go of that theory, since it was the only one we had.

'But there was another wrinkle we didn't take into account. Someone who hoped to inherit as a spouse would have to wait till after the wedding to kill the bride. But someone who thought he had a chance of inheriting as next of kin could kill at any time – and he'd have a much better chance if he did it *before* the heiress married someone else.'

'Next of kin?' Oscar spluttered. 'Who are you talking about now? Mother and I aren't related to Emily.'

Emily gazed at him with deep compassion and regret. If she'd had her way, she would have broken the information from the old files to him gently, and in private. But Luke had insisted that for the confrontation to work, Oscar had to be openly shocked by the revelation of his paternity.

'We found out who your father is, Oscar,' she said softly.

'My father?' He looked from her to Wanda, who made a failed attempt to look nonchalant. Her façade of control was crumbling like old plaster. 'What do you mean?'

Luke turned to the box and took out a sheaf of documents – copies of the contents of the folder Jamie had found. 'According to these papers, your father was Ernest Worthing.'

Though she already knew it, those words turned a knife in Emily's heart. But Oscar looked merely baffled.

'Ernest Worthing? But that's a character from a play. *The Importance of Being Earnest*, by – Oscar Wilde.' His voice faded out on the final words. '*Oscar* Wilde. I see.'

'Ernest Worthing was my father,' Emily said. 'Worthing is my maiden name.' She gave a pale smile. 'So it's a good thing you weren't trying to marry me – because I'm your half-sister.'

Oscar stared at her open-mouthed, then blinked and turned to Wanda. 'Mother? Is this true?'

She didn't speak, but the pain and anger in her eyes belied the wooden smirk still pasted on her mouth.

Luke took back the reins of the conversation. 'So you see, Oscar, your mother had a pretty good motive for wanting Emily out of the way – getting you, and consequently herself, provided for, for life. Plus, as a chemistry teacher, she would've had no problem getting hold of potassium cyanide.'

He turned to face Wanda. 'I had a very interesting day yesterday. I went down to Corvallis. Had a look at your high school chemistry lab. Colleague of yours obligingly showed me around. Turns out you've got quite a little stash of chemicals out in that storage shed. Including a nice big jar of potassium cyanide – with signs of being recently disturbed.'

Wanda's eyes darted from Luke to Oscar to Emily, but she didn't speak.

'And in case the cyanide didn't work – which, of course, it didn't – you had your ace in the hole.'

He set down the papers and removed a small jar from the box. 'As you all know, Emily got very sick on Wednesday night. What you may not all know is that she was poisoned. Between Katie and Dr Griffiths and the lab, we managed to track down what did it.' He showed the jar around the room. 'A nice, innocuous-looking jar of honey.' He turned the label to face him and read, 'Oregon Coast Blackberry Honey. Tasty and wholesome.'

He nailed Wanda with his eyes. 'Only it isn't really, is it? This honey came from a hive in your yard in Corvallis. A hive – as I discovered when I visited there yesterday – that had recently been raided for honey. And a yard in which the only flowering plants are rhododendrons. And here's a little-known fact – little known, that is, unless you happen to be a chemistry teacher – honey made by bees that feed on rhododendrons is poisonous. Poisonous enough for a tiny taste of it to send Emily to the hospital.'

Wanda's façade crumbled to dust, revealing her true face

– the face of a cornered beast, fangs bared in fury. She sprang forward before Pete could stop her, grabbed the honey jar from Luke's hand, and lobbed it with unbelievable force through the open window and out into the yard.

'You'll never pin this on me!' she shrieked. 'You can go begging for your precious proof now!'

Pete caught up with her and pulled her arms behind her back, holding her securely as she writhed and kicked. Luke skewered her with his eyes. 'Oh, did I say it was *that* jar of honey? Just a little ruse on my part. The real jar is safe in the evidence room. Along with your beekeeper's outfit, a piece of the honeycomb from your yard, and the jar of potassium cyanide from the storage room at your school.'

Emily was astonished to see Wanda actually foaming at the mouth. She turned toward Emily, and involuntarily Emily cowered in her chair, although Pete's hold on Wanda was firm.

'*You!*' Wanda spat. 'You were all Ernest would ever talk about. His precious, perfect Emily, the image of her sainted mother. He would have married me if it hadn't been for you, making him feel guilty every time he looked at you. My Oscar would have had a decent life, and when that old battleaxe Beatrice died, all this would have come to him. It's his birthright, and you stole it, you bitch. You deserve to die. I should have slit your throat – no chance of failure that way. Covered your precious library in your polluted Worthing blood.'

Emily didn't know whether to be more shocked by Wanda's venom or by the revelation that her father had cared for her, Emily, so deeply – he certainly never showed it to her face. But she kept her voice as level as she could.

'I stole nothing, Wanda. You have to remember, I had no idea Oscar existed until a month ago, and none whatsoever that he was my half-brother until yesterday. If you had only told me, I would have been happy to share. All Beatrice's wealth is much more than I need or even feel comfortable possessing. I've already given a lot of it away.'

She turned to Oscar, who was curled up in a ball as far from his mother as he could get. 'I'm still happy to share with *you*, Oscar. None of this is your fault, I know.'

Oscar shook his head, rocking himself like a baby. It would

take time for him to recover enough from the revelation of his mother's true nature to be able to absorb anything positive that might come of knowing he was a Worthing after all.

Luke nodded to Pete, and he dragged the gibbering woman into the hall, where Heather was waiting to help him take her away. Once the front door had closed behind them and the sound of the departing engine wafted through the broken window, Luke turned to the others in the room.

'I'm sorry we had to put you through all that, folks. Fact is, though we have a lot of evidence against Wanda, it's all circumstantial. I couldn't be sure a jury would convict her without a confession. And this seemed like the best way to get one.' He nodded from Emily to Oscar. 'Better see what you can do with him. Poor guy. He's gained a sister and a dead father, but lost the only family he ever knew he had.'

TWENTY-FIVE

Emily helped Oscar to his room and did her best to soothe him, but he was so far beyond comfort that in the end all she could do was to call Sam Griffiths and have her bring a sedative to settle him for the night, since Emily's bottle of Ambien was still at the lab. 'He'll be better in the morning,' Sam predicted.

Emily closed Oscar's bedroom door behind her and sank down with her back against it, staring without seeing at the closed door of the Austen room across the hall. Would either she or Oscar ever find their way past the circumstances of this revelation to enjoy their newfound relationship?

Once again she replayed yesterday's conversation with Jamie in her mind. Could it really be only yesterday? She was living in a whole new world now – one that included a half-brother.

'The "L" was for Lansing,' Jamie had said.

'Lansing? Are you sure?'

'Says so right here.' He handed her the folder. *Lansing* was typed quite clearly on the label.

Emily held the folder unopened for a moment, a strange premonition staying her hand. The original folder back at the house had seemed too old for its contents to relate to Oscar directly; they must somehow relate to Wanda. What sort of dealings could Wanda possibly have had with Beatrice? And why?

Only one way to answer that question. She forced herself to open the folder and take out the first document.

It was a letter from Wanda Lansing to Beatrice Runcible, dated January 1977.

> *Dear Mrs Runcible,*
> *It may interest you to hear you have a great-nephew you probably didn't know about.*

That first sentence chilled Emily's blood. The whole story suddenly unfolded before her like an ancient map. *Here there be dragons.* She steeled herself and read on.

> *Your nephew Ernest Worthing taught with me at North Medford High in 1975–76, and we got to be good friends. He got me pregnant that winter and promised to marry me when the school year was out. But after our son was born in August, Ernest took a job in another city and deserted his son and me. He didn't leave a forwarding address or a single penny for our support. Since then he's managed to become invisible, at least to me; though I bet you know where he is, since he depends on you to clothe his precious kids.*

Emily's hands shook, rattling the paper she held. She'd known her father was undisciplined and irresponsible, and to hear that he'd had an affair after her mother's death was no great surprise. But to father a child and then desert it – that was beyond the pale. His not wanting to marry Wanda she could easily understand, and she could even be grateful for it on her own account – to think of Wanda as a stepmother! – but he should have made some provision for his son.

The letter went on.

> *I went back to teaching last fall, after a few weeks off, but I'm telling you, raising a baby and paying for full-time child care on a teacher's salary is no picnic. Ernest was always talking about how well off you are and how you provide for his other kids, Jeff and Emily.*

She couldn't even spell Geoff's name properly. Well, to be fair, she'd probably never seen it written, only heard it from Ernest's lips.

> *So I'm sure you'll want to contribute something to the support of Ernest's third child as well. His name is Oscar Lansing, though I'd be happy to have it changed to Worthing if you want. I'm sending a photo that will show*

you not only what a bright and adorable child he is but also how much he looks like his father. If you feel the need for additional proof of paternity in the form of a blood test, say the word and I'll get it.

It was starting to sink in now: Oscar was not only Wanda's son, but her own father's as well. Emily's half-brother.

By this time her hands were shaking so violently she could hardly read the remaining words. She took a deep breath and made an effort to steady them.

I'm not asking anything for myself; I'm sure you won't think I have any claim on you. I ask only that a child of Worthing blood not be left to grow up dirt-poor. I'm sure your family pride wouldn't want that any more than I do.

    Sincerely,
    Wanda Lansing

Emily laid the letter back in the folder as gently as if it were made of gold foil. Then she pulled her hands away and wrapped herself in her arms, feeling a sudden chill.

Jamie looked on with growing concern in his eyes. 'Emily? Anything you want to tell me? You look like you've seen a ghost.'

'I think I sort of have,' she replied. 'My father's ghost. Looking like someone I don't even recognize.' Seeing Jamie's look of utter confusion, she handed him the letter. 'Here. Read for yourself.'

He skimmed it quickly, then cleared his throat twice. 'That's . . . that's quite surprising,' he said with proper lawyerly understatement. 'I take it you had no clue about this before?'

'None whatsoever. That is, about Oscar being my father's son. Luke and I had already figured out Wanda was his mother.'

'He doesn't seem much like her, does he? Is he at all like your dad?'

The question startled Emily. At first thought Oscar and her father seemed to have nothing in common. But after all, both were lovers of literature. And everything she and Oscar shared had to come from somewhere. Perhaps on some level Oscar resembled what her father might have been without the booze.

She called both their faces to mind, searching for some physical resemblance. The coloring was right, at least; Oscar's skin was as fair as Ernest's, and the red in his beard suggested his hair might also have been red at one time. The height and build were similar, too. And when she first met Oscar, she'd had the feeling there was something familiar about him. Now she realized what it was – his eyes. Oscar's eyes slanted upward at the outer corners, giving him a bit of an elfin look. Her father's eyes had been exactly the same.

And his name. Now that odd comment of Wanda's made sense: 'It's so important to be earnest.' She was certainly alluding to the play – the play that had given Ernest Worthing his name, and the author of which had supplied the name she gave her son. Wanda had been dropping Emily a hint, if only she'd had the presence of mind to pick it up.

Jamie's voice startled her out of her reverie. 'What else is in there?'

'Oh. Of course. Let's see.' She flipped through several documents, including a copy of Oscar's birth certificate and an affidavit stating that his blood type was the rare AB negative, the same as Ernest's. Then came a letter from Beatrice to Wanda.

Miss Lansing,

I accept that your son is indeed my nephew's progeny. However, it is not my habit to endorse or subsidize immorality, whether on the part of my blood relations or of those with whom they choose to consort. Therefore, I cannot see my way clear to providing any sort of regular support for your son. You made your bed, as they say – rather literally in this case – and now you must lie in it. As you are employed, it seems unlikely you and your son will actually starve.

What I can do is to supply you with my nephew Ernest's current address (see below). He certainly ought to take responsibility for his own actions, and I shall write to him myself urging him to do so.

With this letter I regard all correspondence between us as at an end. Should you persist in pestering me, any communication will be forwarded to my attorney unopened.
Sincerely,
Beatrice Worthing Runcible

Jamie giggled. 'Mrs Runcible certainly knew how to put people in their place.'

'Yes, but that wasn't the end of it. My father died in 1980 – leaving nothing but debts, of course – and at that point Beatrice created a trust fund for Oscar. She deposited enough over the years to put him through state university. The documents show that money was disbursed directly to the school.'

Emily looked up at Jamie. 'Is it possible Oscar got all the way through college not knowing who his benefactor was? Or why she paid his way?'

'She could have had the university disguise the money as an anonymous scholarship. I'd imagine Oscar had the grades to make that plausible.'

'I suppose. Yes, that's the only reasonable explanation.'

Jamie had departed, leaving Emily to process this incredible news as best she could. But she had felt too exhausted at that moment to do anything other than sleep. Only slightly more exhausted than she felt right now.

But she still had duties to perform before she could rest. She knew the group in the library would be buzzing with questions and speculations. She went back down to help Luke answer them all.

Devon jumped her the minute she entered the room. 'Darling, that was absolutely classic Christie! How thrilling! That other murder we had at Halloween was rather a nuisance, but this one – what fun!' He registered the expression on Emily's face and sobered immediately. 'Except, I mean, for the part about you being the target. I hope that whole poison thing wasn't too horrible for you.'

'It was the sickest I've ever been in my life,' she said dryly. 'But it was over quickly, and no permanent harm done.'

'Well, thank heavens for that!' he said brightly. 'And the world won't be any worse off for the loss of Cruella Crime. Surely you agree with me there.'

'*I* certainly do,' Ian put in. He and Olivia had approached as Devon was talking. 'In fact, it's hard to believe her death was unintended when there were so many people who wanted her dead.'

'She certainly made a lot of people's lives miserable,' Emily replied, weighing her words. 'But she was still a human being created in the image of God. I can never rejoice over anyone's life being cut off before he or she had a chance to repent.'

Ian snorted. 'Cruella was beyond repentance, I assure you.'

But Olivia, clinging to his arm, shook her head. 'No, Ian, I think Emily's right. It may be possible for a person to be beyond repentance, but I don't think it's ever up to another human being to say so. That's between her and her Maker.'

Emily said a silent prayer for Cruella's soul, chiding herself for not having done so earlier. 'I hope, though, that you two will not allow the circumstances of her death to prevent you from taking full advantage of her absence.'

Ian and Olivia exchanged a smile that blocked out the entire world around them. 'Absolutely not,' Ian said. 'In fact, we've decided to get married.'

Emily clapped her hands together. 'Oh, that's wonderful! I do hope you'll invite me.'

'We'll do better than that,' said Olivia. 'We wanted to ask you if we could have the wedding here. We don't want a lot of fuss, and neither of us has any family to invite. You and Luke could be our witnesses, if you would.'

'I'd be honored. On both counts. When were you thinking?'

'Well . . .' Olivia blushed. 'Since we don't want a lot of fuss, and we've waited so long, we were thinking pretty much right away. As soon as we can get a license, that is.'

'Twelfth Night.' Emily spoke with decision. 'I was planning a party then anyway – we can make it a wedding reception instead.' Luke passed nearby, and she grabbed his arm and pulled him over. 'Luke, Ian and Olivia want to get married. Here. As soon as possible. Can they get a license by the fifth of January?'

'I don't see why not,' he said and pumped Ian's hand. 'Congratulations. Glad to see some good come out of all this.'

'Thank you,' said Ian. 'And we'd like you and Emily to be our witnesses.'

Luke smiled at Emily. 'How could I refuse?'

Emily read in Luke's eyes that he saw them witnessing another couple's wedding as one step away from having one of their own. Well, she'd deal with those consequences when they arose.

'I think this calls for champagne,' she said. 'Are you ready to announce it to everyone?'

Ian hesitated. 'You don't think Dustin will take it as an invitation, do you? We'd love to have everyone else attend, but I don't think I can afford enough liquor to keep him happy.'

'Don't you worry about that,' Luke said. 'I happen to know he's antsy to be gone. Fact, I wouldn't be surprised if he took off the minute I hand him back his car keys – which I will do right now. Before he has a chance to fill up on champagne.'

Luke suited the action to the word, and Dustin did indeed stalk out of the room immediately. Five minutes later they heard him clattering his bags down the hall and out the front door.

Emily whispered in Katie's ear, and her face brightened. 'I'm on it.' She flew toward the kitchen, grabbing Jamie on the way.

As they waited, Olivia said shyly to Emily, 'Ian has started writing again.'

Emily turned wide-eyed to Ian, who blushed and smiled. 'But that's marvelous! Perhaps Windy Corner does have some creative magic after all. I was beginning to think it was only conducive to murder.'

'It's a bit early to conclude the muse is back to stay,' said Ian, 'but it feels good to put words on paper again. And I do have Windy Corner – and Olivia – to thank for that.' He beamed at his fiancée.

Katie appeared in the doorway, and Ian put on his best public-speaking voice. 'Friends, may I have your attention, please?'

The buzz of conversation stilled as all eyes turned toward him.

'It is my very great pleasure to announce that this lovely lady' – he encircled Olivia in his arm – 'has agreed to become my wife.' After the first murmur of congratulations died down, he went on, 'We're going to be married here at Windy Corner on the fifth of January, and you are all invited.'

Katie and Jamie entered with trays of brimming champagne flutes, which they passed around. Luke lifted his flute high. 'To the happy couple!'

Glasses clinked, and bubbles slid down joyful throats. Emily felt suddenly overwhelmed and groped behind her for a chair. From being hospitalized for poisoning, to discovering her long-lost half-brother, to witnessing the moral disintegration of a murderer, to celebrating her friends' engagement was quite a journey for just a few days.

Marguerite crossed the room to sit beside her. 'You look done in, *ma petite*,' she said. 'All this is too much for a convalescent. Let me help you up to bed.'

Emily nodded faintly. 'Thanks, Margot. I think I'll sleep like the de— like a baby tonight.'

The next morning, Katie had a pow wow with Olivia about the wedding arrangements, but Emily's first priority was Oscar. She volunteered to take up his breakfast tray in order to have an excuse to talk with him.

He sat up in bed when she came in, groggy but calm. At the sight of the tray, which Katie had made festive with a sprig of holly tucked into the red napkin, he brightened.

'How are you this morning?' Emily asked, pulling the desk chair up next to the bed.

'I think I'll live,' he said. He added cream and sugar to his coffee, took a sip, and sighed in satisfaction. He shot her a sidelong glance and added in a tentative voice, 'Sis.'

Emily's feelings had settled overnight, and she was able now to separate her bitterness over her father's actions and her horror at what Wanda had done from the simple, unexpectedly joyous fact that this young man she was already so fond of was actually her next of kin.

She beamed at him and squeezed his free hand. 'Oscar, I'm so terribly sorry about your mother and everything that's happened, but I am more thrilled than I can say to have you for a brother. I've been orphaned for decades, and completely without family since Aunt Beatrice died. It feels like Christmas ten thousand times over to suddenly have a brother – and one that I like as much as I like you. Love, in fact, now that I know.'

He smiled back. 'I feel the same. I just wish . . .' He paused, not meeting her eyes.

'Wish what?'

'I wish our father had been – well, someone to be proud of. On some level. Of course, knowing he'd abandoned us, I didn't expect much, but – well, you know how kids will fantasize. I used to imagine he had some terribly important and glamorous job that meant he couldn't be with us. A spy or something. Or that he had died some heroic death and Mother didn't want to grieve me by telling me. Though knowing I had a dead father would have been better than knowing nothing at all.'

Emily's heart constricted. 'I'm sorry about that too. Father did have some good qualities – he was brilliant, funny, charming when he wanted to be. It was mostly the alcohol that made him what he was in the end. But I have to admit that even without the drinking I don't think he would ever have been the most reliable of men.'

'I wonder what they saw in each other,' Oscar mused. 'My parents, I mean. Gosh, I've never been able to use that phrase before – *my parents*.'

'I imagine your mother was attractive back then. Father could never resist a pretty face, and very few women could resist his charm. It needn't have gone any deeper than that.'

'I suppose.' He took a bite of omelet. 'I do remember Mother being pretty when I was young. I guess all boys think their mothers are beautiful, though. Like we think our fathers are heroes – despite all evidence to the contrary.'

His eyes grew misty, and Emily squeezed his hand again. 'Whatever their failings, you seem to have gotten the best of both of them.' That was the tactful thing to say, though she couldn't offhand see anything Oscar had inherited from his mother. He had something of their father's looks, his literary talent, and a shadow of his charm, but Oscar's gentle and honorable character seemed a complete fluke in terms of the family history. It must be a throwback to their grandparents.

'What will happen to Mother?' he asked in a tiny voice.

Emily spoke as gently as she could. 'I can't say for certain, of course, but it does seem likely she'll be convicted of first-degree murder for Cruella and attempted murder for me. Though she may be ruled of unsound mind, given her final outburst.'

Oscar's tears flowed freely now. 'I think – it's possible – she may have murdered before.' He rattled his coffee cup into its saucer. 'I've lived with this suspicion for years. When my stepfather died – well, it was kind of fishy. And she'd been talking about getting rid of him for quite a while. I thought she meant she'd divorce him, but when he died so suddenly – I couldn't help but wonder if she'd poisoned him. She knows a lot about poisons – she could have done it so no one would know.'

'Did she know you suspected her?'

'I never said anything. To her or to anyone. But that's why I got so freaked out when Cruella was poisoned. I'd seen Mother lurking around the bar shelf. But I had no idea why she'd want to kill either Cruella or you.'

He looked sideways at her for the first time in this confession. 'So now you know the worst of me. I covered for my murdering mother.'

Emily put aside her own feelings toward Wanda and tried to see her through her son's eyes. 'If that's the worst of you, I won't worry. Of course you felt you had to protect your mother. Legally you were in the wrong, but morally I don't think many people would fault you for that. Especially since you only suspected – you didn't really *know*.'

'No. But if I'd spoken – maybe I could have stopped her second attempt on you.'

'Don't you worry about that. It came to nothing – well, not much, anyway.' She shuddered. 'Thank God that honey had such a bitter taste. That's what saved me, really. I guess Wanda couldn't have known that – she'd never have dared to test the stuff. So in a sense she foiled her own plan.'

Oscar nodded. 'Listen, Emily, about that plan – you do believe I knew nothing about it? Would never have cooperated if I'd known?'

'Of course I believe that. No one who knows you at all would ever suspect you of such a thing.'

'Luke did.'

'Well, yes, but it's his job to suspect everybody. And he was jealous, too. He thought I was getting a little too fond of you.'

Oscar's eyes widened. 'Oh! goodness!' He hesitated, then added, 'And were you?'

'Not the way he thought. It's funny, but I think something in me always knew we were related. My fondness for you felt – well, familial, right from the start.'

She beamed at him. 'Oscar, I have to say it again – I am thrilled to pieces to have you for a brother. And I really do want to share the inheritance with you. In fact, I insist.'

He recoiled. 'Oh, no. I could never accept any financial help from you. Not after all that's happened. It would feel – well, like I was profiting from my mother's crime.'

'Nonsense. All she did was create a situation where the relationship could come into the open – something she could easily have done years ago without killing anyone or plotting to get my fortune. Please, Oscar. I really want to share.'

He shook his head with more firmness than she'd ever seen in him. 'No. Not one penny. And that is my final word.'

Not one penny, eh? Well, then, she'd have to find a way to give him something that wasn't cash.

TWENTY-SIX

Emily made her way slowly downstairs, having arranged with Oscar to show him the old photographs of the family once he was up and dressed. In the meantime, she had a plot to hatch.

As she passed the window on the landing, her eye fell on Oscar's ancient, beat-up Honda sitting in front of the carriage house. He'd said when he first arrived that the car's heater didn't work. That was it – she'd buy him a new car. Have it delivered here and his old one taken away. That way he wouldn't be able to refuse.

She found Luke alone in the dining room, finishing his breakfast. 'Luke, do you know a reputable car dealer? Someone who'll be working the next couple of days?'

He almost choked on his coffee. 'Car dealer? What for? You're not thinking of trading in your Cruiser, are you?'

'Heavens, no. I want to buy a car for Oscar. On the sly. He refuses to accept a penny from me, so that's the only way I can think of to share with him. Once he sees I'm serious, maybe he'll let me do more.'

'I do know somebody, as it happens. Cousin of mine has the Toyota dealership in Tillamook. I wouldn't say he's completely reputable, but he wouldn't dare cheat *me*.'

'That's perfect! A Prius would be just the thing. Save him money on gas as well. And I can cover the insurance.'

He cocked his head at her. 'You're really getting into this half-brother thing, aren't you?'

She pulled out the chair next to him and took his hand. 'Oh, Luke, don't you see? I finally have a family again! You've always had relatives enough and to spare – you can afford to dislike half of them. But I've never had more than a handful, and for some time now I've had none at all. I feel like I've found my place in the world again. I have roots. I belong.'

She gazed around the room at the carved wood paneling,

the fine china displayed in the built-in hutch, the embroidered linens and sterling silver on the table. 'All this was just *stuff* before – beautiful stuff, but stuff. Now that I have someone to share it with, it's a legacy.'

Luke stared at his plate and mumbled, 'You could share it with me.'

'Oh, Luke – I didn't mean – that isn't the same, don't you see? I mean, now I have someone to pass it down to. A Worthing. Someone who's blood. And with that awful mother of his out of the way, maybe Oscar will marry, have children – carry on the line.'

'I thought you were leaving the house to Katie.'

'I was, when I thought that was the only way she'd be sure of a place to live when I die. But she has Jamie now. I think they'd rather build their own home together than be burdened with this dinosaur. I'll leave them enough money to be sure they can do that comfortably.'

Luke cleared his throat. 'So – does that mean you feel less responsible for this place? Less tied to it, I mean?'

She stared at him, baffled.

'What I'm trying to say is, could you consider moving in with me? After we're married, of course.'

'Oh!' Her stomach dropped to the floor. 'Oh, dear. That's a whole other question.' She stared past him out the window, her face working as a witch's brew of emotions roiled inside her.

He reached across and took her hand. 'Look, Em, I'm really sorry about that whole being-jealous-of-Oscar thing. I don't know what came over me. Well, I do, kind of – I've always felt like I'm not quite good enough for you, and seeing the way you sort of blossomed around a brainy guy brought all that to a head.'

'Oh, but Luke, don't you see? Now that I have Oscar for a brother, I can share my love of literature with him. I don't need that kind of thing from you. That isn't the issue for me, really. Never has been.'

He cleared his throat, not looking at her. 'And wanting you to prove your love by saying yes. That wasn't right either. I wasn't thinking clearly at that point. I'm sorry.'

She covered his hand with her own. 'Thank you for saying that. I was afraid I was being unreasonable, but I couldn't change the way it made me feel.'

He was quiet for a minute, then spoke in a small voice. 'I do still want to marry you, though. And I'm having a hard time understanding why you won't commit.'

She sighed. 'To tell you the absolute truth, I'm having a hard time understanding that myself. I need some time to think about it. Time without a murder investigation going on. Time without a bunch of people in the house, for that matter. Some nice, quiet time to myself.'

'Can't argue with that. Murder and marriage don't mix.' He gave a wry smile and raised his coffee cup toward her. 'Here's hoping we get a nice long break from murder. Preferably forever.'

Having noted Oscar's preference for earth tones (which matched her own), Emily chose a fun orange Prius C for him, agreeing with Luke's cousin that Oscar could exchange the color if he didn't care for it. She paid for the car on the spot and arranged for an insurance policy with her own carrier as soon as she got home. Then she took Oscar for a walk on the beach – the weather being balmier than it had been since he arrived – while an employee of the dealership delivered the Prius, parked it in the carriage house, and drove Oscar's Honda away. They'd take care of the title transfer later.

The next morning, she wrapped the key to the Prius in a small box and placed it next to Oscar's breakfast plate. When he sat down and noticed it, she said, 'I know it isn't your birthday, but I've missed a whole bunch of them, so this is all your birthday and Christmas presents to date rolled into one.'

Looking mystified, Oscar unwrapped the box and took out the key – not a real key, as the Prius was much too high-tech for that, but the electronic gadget that passed for a key. He stared at her, uncomprehending.

'Come on,' she said and dragged him out to the driveway, where she'd parked the Prius – adorned with a big green bow.

'What do you think? Is the color OK?'

'The *color*?' He gaped at her. 'Emily, this can't be for me? I told you not to give me anything.'

'You said not a penny. You didn't say anything about non-monetary gifts.'

He closed his mouth and walked around the car, stroking its shiny finish. 'I never . . . I mean . . . Me? A brand-new Prius?'

'You. A brand-new Prius. And don't worry about the insurance, I've paid for that. You'll save lots on gas, so you can afford to come visit me whenever you want.'

He turned and gave her an enthusiastic hug. 'Oh, Emily, thank you so much. It goes without saying this is the best present I've ever received. I feel like a real grownup now with an actual fully functional car. What's next? Tenure? An apartment with a real bedroom all to myself? I might even think about getting married!'

'I hope you will,' Emily said, beaming. 'We need to keep the line going. I missed my chance for children, I'm afraid, and so did Geoff. Do you have anyone in mind?'

'Well . . .' Oscar blushed. 'There is this assistant psych prof I'm rather keen on. Lauren Hsu. We've gone out a few times, but I could never let myself get serious – because how could I ever take a woman home to Mother?' His face clouded, then brightened again. 'Now I can bring her home to you. If that's OK, I mean.'

'I'd love to meet her. Bring her down for spring break. If things work out, that is.'

Oscar scooped Emily into a bear hug. 'I have the feeling everything's going to work out from now on.'

Katie and Olivia could handle the wedding preparations far more efficiently on their own, so Emily got out of their way for the next few days and spent some much-needed time by herself. She had promised Luke to think seriously about marriage, and she had no excuse to put it off any longer.

The house was too full of people and bustle, and the weather was holding clear, so she headed up the beach to what she thought of as the Sacred Cove. It was actually a small cave up above the tide line, with an archway one had to stoop to pass through and a flat sandy floor. She and Luke had discovered this cave as teenagers and used it as a trysting place. Those memories hung thick in the air as Emily entered and found a seat on a ledge of rock.

It had been a warm summer – unusually warm for the Oregon coast – that year they met. She'd reported for work at the ice cream stand on the beach that first day, and there he was – tall and lean, with dark hair that waved over his forehead and a laugh that rang for miles. She knew right then it would be the best summer of her life.

And it was. They plunged headlong into love, so fast and so deep they never stopped to question what their future together could be. Whether they could even have one. And because of a run of luck so bad that, in hindsight, Emily could only regard it as providence, it turned out they had no future at all. Until last June.

Somehow their teenage love had been preserved, as if in amber, as if in the cool, secluded atmosphere of this cave where she now sat. After thirty-five years apart it had awakened, and over the seven months since then it had matured into something much more solid and satisfying than they had known in their youth. The adult Luke was a man of character and integrity, a man people looked up to, a man Emily could trust and rely on absolutely – and a man whose kiss could still weaken her slightly arthritic knees. What more could she ask for in a partner for the remaining years of her life?

Her doubts washed away with the receding tide. All the practical considerations, such as where they would live and how she would complete her research, would resolve themselves somehow. Above all else, she would choose love.

Katie – reenergized by the opportunity to do a sort of dry run for her own upcoming wedding – worked her usual magic, and the wedding on January fifth was as elegant as any bride could wish. Olivia looked stunning in an Edwardian lace gown Veronica had produced from her shop and altered to fit, while Ian was handsome and dignified in a rented morning suit. Their happiness shone out to include everyone around them.

They held the ceremony in the parlor at eleven a.m. so the reception could take the form of a wedding breakfast, in which Katie outdid herself. As everyone sipped champagne in the library after the obligatory toasts were finished, Luke pulled Emily aside into the parlor. 'Doesn't this put you in the mood to do it ourselves?' he whispered in her ear, following up with a sly kiss on the spot behind her ear that always drove her mad.

She returned a kiss on his cheek. 'It puts me in the mood to get Katie married off. I think we need to get that out of the way before we contemplate a wedding of our own.'

He sighed. 'I guess that's reasonable. Have they set a date?'

'They're talking about late April.'

'Then we could shoot for June. We could get married on our birthday.' They shared a birthday, June first, though Luke was two years older than Emily.

'What, and have only one gift-giving occasion between one Christmas and the next? Not a chance, buster.'

He laughed. 'I promise I'll give you double presents. What do you say?'

June first was five months away – time enough to complete her Dostoevsky research and work out any other issues. 'In that case, Luke Richards, I accept your proposal. I will marry you on June first – the birthday of our new life together.'

She watched an answering joy suffuse his features. He pulled a small box from his pocket.

Emily gazed at the box, then at Luke in astonishment. 'What – how?'

'Bought it months ago. Just in case you ever got around to saying yes. Open it.'

She pulled back the lid to see a ring with one large pearl flanked by tiny emeralds, all set in burnished gold filigree. 'Oh, Luke, it's perfect!'

'Vintage. I know how much you like old stuff.' He took it out and slid it on to her left ring finger. 'Fits perfect, too.'

She held her hand up to the light. 'How did you know I prefer pearls to diamonds?'

'I didn't. But you're my pearl of great price.'

She beamed at him, speechless.

He pulled her close and gave her a kiss that almost made her want to drag the minister back in to marry them on the spot. Suddenly June seemed awfully far away.

AUTHOR'S NOTE

I have taken some liberties with regard to Reed College, my alma mater. The character Oscar Lansing is supposed to be a grossly underpaid adjunct professor at Reed. In reality, to my knowledge, Reed does not employ adjunct professors and does pay all its instructors a living wage. However, there are certainly many other institutions of higher learning in the US where Oscar's situation is deplorably common.